BOOK ONE

ANDY
SMITHSON

Blast of the Dragon's Fury

L.R.W. LEE

ISBN: 1482312646
ISBN 13: 978-1482312645
Library of Congress Control Number: 2013902058

Table of Contents

The Land of Oomaldee

CHAPTER ONE

The Boy Screws Up

*E*ven before Andy felt the sting of the wizard's curse, he knew he was in trouble.

He woke staring at a dark ceiling with muscular wooden trusses supporting its weight like Atlas holding the world. Sitting up triggered a shrill alarm—screeching like a horde of small monkeys at the zoo. He stuffed a finger in each ear and grimaced. *That noise could wake the dead!*

Shouts raced toward him. He whirled toward the threat. The sudden movement catalyzed an avalanche down a stack of gold discs he'd landed on.

"Whoooooaaahhhh…"

The screeches whizzed closer, and a brown fuzzy blur threw itself onto Andy's chest as he careened downward.

"It's over there!" a voice yelled over the din.

"That blasted boggart!" a second voice sounded.

"Max, open the door! Get it out of here!" a third commanded.

A boggart? Having just finished reading the Harry Potter series, Andy half expected to see Dad standing over him, hands on his hips, shaking his head and frowning like usual.

Andy came to rest behind a short wooden wall. The creature jumped onto his head and yanked at Andy's brown hair as it continued its tirade. He swatted, trying to knock the menace away.

Shouts circled Andy's position and his flailing grew more desperate. Experience had taught him you never want to get found out in situations like this—you're guilty until proven innocent.

He plunged his head into what he now recognized were coins, knocking the pest loose.

"Ouch!" The gold concealed his exclamation.

He surfaced and rubbed his behind, finding a hole in his pajamas. His hand came away with a trace of red. *Mom's gonna kill me!* He ducked down and everything went dark.

"Andy. Get. Up! We need to leave in ten minutes!" Mom's voice echoed down the hall.

Andy wiped sleep from his eyes and shook his head. *I must have been dreaming.* But his left buttock complained as he threw a leg over the edge of the bed, disqualifying his rationalization.

With a reasonable explanation evading his consciousness, he rubbed his backside then stumbled down the hall and into the bathroom. His thoughts continued to whirl as he ran a toothbrush around his mouth.

Bang, bang, bang. Madison pounded on the bathroom door. "Hurry up! You're going to make me late again, little twerp."

I could really mess with her. The thought flirted with Andy's mind, drawing the corners of his foamy mouth upward. *What are little brothers for? What's the world record for the longest time to brush your teeth?*

Bang, bang, bang.

"Don't rush me, I'm flossing."

"Flossing? You don't know the meaning of the word!"

"Now, now. You know the dentist…"

"Open. This. Door. Now!"

Andy spit out the by-product of his brushing and took his time swishing. He wiped his mouth on a towel then turned the door handle as slowly as humanly possible. He was rewarded by the sight of steam spewing from his sister's ears. Madison extended her clutches and sank them into his shoulders. A stiff yank and he stood in the hall. The reverberation of the slamming door caught up with him as he ambled back to his room to dress.

Mom shoved a microwaved breakfast burrito into his hand thirteen minutes later and groaned, "You didn't run a comb through your hair, Andy. No time now. Give Dad a hug goodbye, we need to go."

Mom punched the automatic door opener as they entered the garage. As they climbed into her SUV, neither of them noticed a large golden tapestry land on the driveway, then quickly disappear.

"You need to behave yourself today," Mom began as she backed out the driveway and headed down Elm. "Mrs. Taylor planned to leave you back at school with another class based upon what happened the last time."

"I told you, it was an accident."

Mom frowned before continuing, "There's been a few too many 'accidents' with you on field trips, young man. I convinced her to give you one more chance, but this is it."

Andy nodded slowly. He knew she was justified in saying what she did. He still didn't understand how flames had ignited Mrs. Crabtree's hair as they toured the fire station last year. Nor did he have a reasonable explanation for why Alexis Garnier's backpack ended up in the gorilla exhibit when they visited the zoo. Everyone had pointed to him.

"I wish I could help chaperone, but I've got back-to-back meetings today." Mom and Dad were both CEOs of companies they'd founded and grown.

Andy ate his burrito as he watched limestone houses turn into brick buildings. Mom stopped at a red light fifteen minutes later and Andy's gaze floated over the intersection. A mammoth stone statue, perhaps twenty feet tall, of a medieval knight saluting, stood on the far corner. He and Mom came this way every day and it took a second for Andy's brain to register something was drastically different. As the light turned green, he pivoted. *Hmm…just a metal power pole.* Andy shook his head.

"Something wrong, honey?"

"Uh… no."

First that boggart with the gold, now this?

"You did bring your permission slip, didn't you?" Mom hoped, interrupting his ponderings.

"Hm? Oh, yeah."

Several minutes later she pulled into the drive of a three-story limestone building. BELLROSE JUNIOR ACADEMY announced a stately sign out front.

Mom leaned over and gave Andy a peck on the cheek. "Be. Good."

Andy nodded as he closed the door.

Andy sat in the front seat of the bus, next to Mrs. Taylor, deflecting snide remarks from classmates as they filed on—"Widdle bitty baby. Has to sit next to the teacher." This and similar comments made the muscles in Andy's jaw bulge as he stared out the window waiting for the driver to get the show on the road.

Two long hours later and the bus pulled in to Dinosaur World.

"Stay with me at all times, Andy," Mrs. Taylor warned as they disembarked. Andy rolled his eyes on the inside.

The class toured several rooms containing monster-sized dinosaur skeletons, including a Deinonychus, a vicious raptor-like beast; an Iguanodon, a large veggie-saur; and a Pleurocoelus, a mammoth creature similar in appearance to a brontosaurus. After lunch, the class split into teams to do a dinosaur scavenger hunt—Mrs. Taylor instructed Andy to stay with her.

While the class searched, the teacher led Andy to the dig site where the bones of an Acrocanthosaurus, a super cool carnivore like the T-rex, had been discovered. Archaeologists had excavated the full skeleton, and Dinosaur

World reproduced the bones as they were when discovered. A sign invited guests to dig for fossils but added a caution: Limit one fossil per person.

"Why don't you find a fossil? Looks like tools are over there." Mrs. Taylor pointed.

With nothing better to do, Andy sauntered over and grabbed a hand trowel and gloves.

A row of ten-inch teeth protruding from a jaw that nearly equaled his height enticed Andy, and he headed over to examine more closely. He cleared away the hard-packed soil, freeing the lower jaw, then set to work doing the same for the upper.

Andy had been playing his new video game, Dragon Slayer, all week. *What's the difference between a dinosaur and a dragon?* The seemingly innocent question slithered its way around his brain like a cobra. And true to form, it coiled itself up then rose, expanding its hood. *Other than breathing fire…* The snake struck and the next thing Andy knew the Acrocanthosaurus skeleton rose from its tomb of dirt.

"Ah!" Andy scuttled back.

A rake lay nearby and Andy grabbed the handle, which of course came loose from the head. *Crap!*

The beast of bones stood and shook itself, spraying a shower of dirt. Andy choked and sputtered as the creature bellowed then surveyed its surroundings. He dared not move. *Don't see me. Please don't see me.*

Blinding light from the nearby parking lot caught Andy's attention. Their bus driver had opened the doors, and the glass reflected the sun's brilliance right at the monster. The brute took a step, its massive skeletal foot missing Andy by mere inches. He ducked as the bony tail swished.

The beast let loose a terrifying roar and charged.

It's going after the bus! It'll kill the driver!

Andy raced after it.

Armed with only the rake handle, he didn't really want to attract the thing's attention, but with no other available options, he skidded to a halt as the brute prepared to take a bite out of the bus roof.

"Hey, Mr. T-Rex! Back here!" Andy panted, stabbing at the beast's tail with the handle.

The monster pulled back and turned toward the distraction. Eyeing Andy up and down, it took a step toward him and announced its dissatisfaction.

"Come on, Mr. T-Rex. I'll fight ya!"

The beast advanced another two steps and Andy prepared to engage.

I hope its reactions aren't very fast!

Andy darted below the scrawny forearm, and in a flash jumped and thrust the handle through the monster's armpit, angling it toward the creature's heart, then dashed to safety.

As if in slow motion, the beast of bones looked down to find the weapon protruding from among its parts. A low growl escaped as it toppled earthward and landed in a disheveled heap.

"Yes!" Andy pumped his arm.

"Andrew Smithson! What do you think you're doing? How did you have time—? No, I don't want to know." Mrs. Taylor raised her eyebrows over sequin-studded, cat-eye glasses. (*Who wears those anymore anyway?*) She shook her head as her balled fists found her hips.

How could she not appreciate that I just saved the bus driver, not to mention the bus…?

"You will haul every last one of these back to the dig site. Immediately!"

Andy shouldered the first bone, a femur, and trudged back as his mind whirled, trying desperately to put together the jigsaw puzzle of today's events. By the twentieth trip, the rest of Andy's classmates had finished reboarding the bus and many offered insults out open windows.

Catcalls and hooting greeted Andy when, after ten more trips, he collapsed onto the seat next to Mrs. Taylor. He wiped his brow on his shirtsleeve.

"We are an hour late thanks to you, young man. Rest assured your parents will be notified when we get back to school."

Andy turned toward the window and rolled his eyes.

Andy found himself standing before Headmaster Deitz three hours later.

"That was quite a stunt you pulled, Mr. Smithson," the man observed, trying unsuccessfully to hide his annoyance. "What did you think you were doing?"

Andy opened his mouth to explain but closed it again, realizing anything he said would only get him in more trouble. "I don't know, sir." His eyes dropped to the floor.

The headmaster tried phoning Mom's office, then announced, "Since it appears your mother is in a meeting and unable to be disturbed, let's see what your father thinks about your behavior." He flicked his eyebrows upward to press his point as the last word tumbled out.

The man dialed and Dad's voice emanated from the speakerphone perched on the well-worn desk, a workspace Andy felt sure had witnessed many an unruly child meet a similar fate. Dad listened attentively as the headmaster explained the situation in more detail than Andy hoped.

"Thank you for letting me know, Headmaster. Rest assured, my wife and I will discuss this further with Andy tonight," Dad concluded the conference call ten minutes later.

I'm confident they will, Andy groaned inside. *But what's going on?*

Never happier to be heading home after this disaster of a school day, Andy met Mrs. Appleton, a neighbor from down the street, who drove him, along with her first and third grader toward home. Squished between two booster seats in the back of the SUV, Andy fought to manage his mood while Isabella babbled incessantly, insisting he appreciate the minutest details of her art project. Caden kept pinching Andy's arm and giggling, drawing a growl from his prey.

Andy scrutinized the intersection where his mind had played tricks on him that morning. He shook his head, a plausible explanation for the goings-on still evading discovery.

Mrs. Appleton pulled in the driveway. "You've got your house key?"

Andy scrounged in his backpack and finally located it.

"See you tomorrow!" The neighbor's cheerfulness did nothing to lift his mood.

He slid out of the vehicle and banished the little pests behind the closed door.

Seeing the mailbox he decided, *I better get the mail. I'm in enough trouble already.*

Andy opened the front of the box and reached in as the light in his periphery dimmed, drawing his gaze upward. A man with brilliant blue eyes and wearing coordinating blue robes with a floppy Santa hat came into focus before him. The pair locked eyes.

"Yip!" a duet sounded.

Loud gurgling diverted Andy's attention. Behind the man, laboratory equipment sat haphazardly atop three tables. A copper-colored brew belched vapor from one beaker, making the place smell like rancid dog farts.

"I've got a boy!" the wizardly man exclaimed.

"Good grief! Send him back!" demanded a voice from out of sight. The wizard waved his arms then cast a spell, zapping Andy.

"Ouch!" Seconds later, Andy felt his feet thud into the grass and his knees buckled from impact. The sting pulsed across his face and arms like a bad sunburn.

"What's going *on*?!" Andy clenched his fists and punched the mailbox then winced when it bit back, outraged by the dent he'd left. A line of blood appeared across his knuckles.

Great, one more thing Dad'll freak out about—his precious mailbox. Andy took a deep breath.

Cars passed by on the street and the trees swayed in the gentle autumn breeze. A dog down the way barked. Nosy neighbor across the street peered out her front window, shifted her glasses to halfway down her nose, and raised her eyebrows—a phone grew from her left ear. She turned her back and gestured.

Everything seems normal enough, but I know *I didn't imagine that wizard, or anything else for that matter.*

At a loss for what to do, Andy unlocked the front door, made his way to the kitchen, and threw his backpack on the granite counter before turning his attention to his rumbling stomach. In vain, he foraged for something sweet despite the fact that Mom rarely bought junk food. His scavenging produced nothing he wanted, so he settled for fresh strawberries. He groused to himself as he ate.

"What are you whining about?" Madison broke through his muttering several minutes later.

He had been so deep in bellyaching, he had not heard her arrive home. He jumped, then accused, "Why'd you sneak up on me like that?"

"Why is it my fault you didn't hear me come in?"

In no mood to argue, Andy grabbed the last strawberry and his backpack and headed upstairs, leaving his dirty dish for someone else to deal with. He glanced out the living room window as he passed and noticed dark clouds gathering. *It looks like I feel.*

Not wanting to do homework, he jettisoned his pack on his bed, flipped on his game console, and plopped down in his beanbag chair, controller in hand. Instantly, he morphed into Dragon Slayer, the fearsome, black-clad warrior. He crouched low behind a boulder. Movement and noise emanating from the bushes ahead drew his attention. Through the thick underbrush he could just make out the green scaly outline of the dragon. Barbed spikes protruded from its ugly head. It greedily shredded its most recent kill. *What a pig!* Andy crept forward and raised his bow, ready to take out his frustrations on the beast.

A clap of thunder right outside Andy's window jolted him back to his bedroom. *Missed. Doggone it!*

He paused the game and opened the blinds. The branches of the oak tree beat against the house, driven by the wind. But the light turning off in the attic window caught his attention.

That's weird. Madison's in her bedroom probably checking her homework over for the fifteenth time to make sure it's perfect, and Mom and Dad aren't home yet.

With all the strange happenings of the day, Andy grabbed the flashlight he used to read in bed after he was supposed to be sleeping, then snuck out of his room and down the hall toward the door at the end. Thankfully the hall had plush carpeting that muffled the sound of his footsteps.

"Shhh! Don't let Madison hear you," he cautioned the hinges each time they squeaked. "I don't need you betraying me on top of everything else."

Cold air hit him, making him question whether to go back for his jacket. *Nah…* He turned the flashlight on and started up the unfinished wood stairs. Halfway up, another thunderclap startled him, as if to remind him of Dad's warning that "in no uncertain terms" was Andy to be up in the attic by himself—though Andy never understood why, since Dad hadn't issued that decree for Madison. He persevered and made it to the top step.

He shone his flashlight on his old Nintendo 64 and Game Cube. Both "electronic altars" (*I don't get why they call them that*), as well as the multitude of games belonging to each, remained dust-covered and undisturbed.

Through the window at the far end he noticed the sky had turned a deathly shade of gray and now conspired with flashes of lightning to make boxes of old clothes, a baby crib, Mom's innumerable keepsakes, the rack of Dad's outdated suits, and the rest of the family's treasures come to life—a hunchback here, a zombie there. The creatures rose and staggered toward him. Andy shone the beam at the light switch, squeezed his eyes tight and flipped it on, then ducked, just in case something lunged at him. Nothing did.

Boom! Thunder reverberated above his head as if registering a collective complaint from the dismembered shadows.

Andy stumbled backward, his behind connecting with…he didn't know what. Landing hard, Andy waited, listening for sounds of his sister. But except for the constant howling of the wind and the continued thumping of the oak tree, he heard only the whoosh of pelting rain.

That's new, he thought as he located the obstacle. *A trunk.* He used it to pull himself upright. It was weathered and old, made of oak. It looked like a pirate's chest with a rounded top and leather straps riveted to metal reinforcing bands every few inches. Two of them ended in buckles. Andy loosed the leather straps and then tried the lock that secured the middle. Amazingly, it easily pulled away on its rusted hinge.

After glancing around the attic again, he pushed up on the lid and rested it at an angle, forbidding the maw from gobbling his fingers. A note and one other object rested in the uppermost tray. Andy pulled out the paper and read,

Andy,

What? It's addressed to me? Who'd be sending me a trunk?

I'm sorry you're getting involved in the problem this way, but I felt I had no other option. I was told to find a way to remove the contents of this trunk from the land lest they be found and stir up all manner of unrest among the people. It is pure speculation on my part, but based upon the position I believe is yours, I felt you were the only one who could manage this. Please use the utmost secrecy and tell no one what you have.

The note was not signed.

Andy read it several times. *Where'd this come from? What's it mean by "the problem"…and "the land"? What position is supposed to be mine?* Andy ran a hand through his hair and growled, "Perfect. Just what I need to make this day complete."

He turned his attention to the object. It was a black leather sheath, and even though old and worn, it was still soft and held a shine. *Must be good quality.* At the top was a purple crest bearing three intricately detailed pendants: a spider, a wavy line, and beneath that, a knight on horseback. As Andy ran his finger over the metal pendants, icy tentacles traced the length of his spine. *It's just the cold.* But his gut told him otherwise.

He glanced around again, then heard Mom calling. *She's home.* Andy replaced the shealth, carefully closed the lid, and evaded detection by Madison as he made his way downstairs.

"Dad said he had a conversation with Principal Dietz today," Mom greeted him as he entered the kitchen. The timer on the oven beeped, announcing dinner was ready and delaying the discussion Andy knew was about to happen.

Andy pushed peas around his plate and picked at his fish, waiting for the other shoe to drop. No one said much, and Madison took to ping-ponging looks between her parents. She smirked every time she glanced at Andy. As soon as the dishes had been cleared, Dad's lecture began. "I'm disappointed in you, Andy."

Madison asked to be excused and chuckled under her breath as she left.

"That will do, Maddy," Dad warned.

Andy hurled a sneer at her back before she could escape around the corner.

"It really happened, Mom! You've got to believe me. The dinosaur came to life! It charged the bus. It was gonna kill the driver!"

Mom's frown deepened.

"Nonsense, Andy!" A vein on the side of Dad's neck bulged. "Another of your far-fetched stories. I don't want to hear any more! You're ten years old! You must learn to respect authority and take responsibility for your actions."

And…he's winding up. The sound of a play-by-play announcer echoed in Andy's head, and he settled in for what he knew would be a long "talking to."

The tornado of Dad's correction strengthened and formed a funnel cloud before slowly dissipating and blowing itself out. Andy looked at the clock on the wall. *A new record, only forty-eight minutes tonight. They must have something important to take care of and don't want to waste more time dealing with me.*

Mom and Dad, judge and jury respectively, sentenced Andy to hard labor for crimes against humanity: he was to wash dishes by hand for the next two nights even though they had a perfectly good dishwasher.

Resigned and confused, Andy stood on the step stool before the sink to begin his sentence. He hated having to use the booster. Like so many other things in his life, it made him feel like a little kid. He squirted dishwashing liquid into the rising water, trying to forget the day.

What vicious creatures lurk below these bubble waves? Andy's mind offered a welcome diversion and he grabbed hold, swirling the water and making the plastic bowl boats collide. *Is it a deadly whirlpool, or is that sea serpent back for more?*

"Scrub every dish thoroughly and don't make a mess, Andy. I will inspect when you're done," Mom cautioned as she left.

The sink was just about full of water. Andy reached for the faucet to turn it off. Suddenly, he felt strange, very light and airy. Then everything went dark.

CHAPTER TWO

Curse Day Remembered

A ndy thudded on a cold, hard floor. "Oww," he moaned, absorbing the impact of his crash landing. The pitch darkness amplified the clatter of breaking glass and things falling, and he threw an arm over his head. Something started fizzing and the stench of rancid dog farts assaulted his nose. *Not again!*

"Confound it, Mermin! How'd that boggart manage to extinguish all the candles at once?" The man's voice, more curious than accusing, sounded familiar.

A small, furry body rushed into Andy's thigh and a host of pinpricks stabbed a soapy knuckle. "Ouch! It bit me! Again!"

"Who's there? Mermin?"

Ptooey. Ptooey. Andy felt a mist spray his hand as something spit soap suds then scolded like a small monkey at the zoo, just as it had this morning. He reached for his assailant but it evaded his grasp.

"Candles, Mermin!"

"Yes, Your Majesty. Wight away, sir. I'm twying to find them."

Majesty?

The man must have tripped because something landed with a bang and more glass shattered not far away.

"What can you do about that boggart?"

"I'm not sure. Everything we've twied hasn't worked."

Clearly.

"I'm very sowwy. Between that and the Appeawo Beam acting as if it has a mind of its own today—"

Boggart? Appearo Beam? Am I going to see Wile E. Coyote and the Road Runner next?

"I know I only gwabbed the US Pus box this time."

"You brought that boy earlier. That was unfortunate. I hope he doesn't remember."

Andy wiped the remaining soap bubbles onto his pants and braced for what might happen. Candlelight brought the space into focus: a table lay overturned, and books, papers and broken beakers littered a large, stone-walled room.

A gasp escaped Andy. *I'm back! What is this place?*

The two men's gazes landed on Andy.

That's him!

A silver-bearded man wearing a bright blue satin robe hunched over and peered through the dimness, inspecting Andy. He held a lit candlestick in one hand and cinched up his overflowing robes with the other. The peak of his Santa-like hat drooped and huge stars twinkled gold.

Another man, tall, lean, and dressed in a long-sleeved black T-shirt and faded blue jeans, sprawled across the floor several feet away. He pushed himself up to sitting. "Mermin, I thought you said you'd brought only the Us Pus box?"

The wizard turned his attention to his companion, nearly causing the large pompom on his hat to catch fire. His mouth moved like a fish gasping for air. "Yes…" He scratched his head and pushed his round-framed glasses back up his knotty nose. "There's no way the beam was that wide. I fixed that pwoblem this afternoon. I even tested it."

Andy glanced at his finger. A trickle of blood oozed from a half circle of pin pricks. He covered them with a thumb.

"Then how do you explain him coming back?"

"I don't know, sir. I cannot. But it looks like that boggart bit him."

"Nasty little pest," the black-shirted man groused.

The blue-robed wizard called Mermin took a step forward. "Let me have a look at that."

Andy glanced about the room before consenting.

Mermin reached for Andy's hand, and Andy moved his thumb aside. "Can you bend it?" After flexing it several times, the man knelt and pulled it to within an inch of his nose. Andy felt the man exhale and jerked his hand back. *Gross!*

"Just a nip. No permanent damage."

"What would happen if it was deeper?" Andy asked.

"It would itch madly." The makeshift physician shook his head. "Nothing to fool with."

"It'd drive you crazy, just like the little menace," the companion sulked.

Andy rubbed his thumb over the wound, feeling a phantom itch. His eyes found the mailbox from his front yard behind him, the stones from its limestone base scattered. "My mailbox! You guys stole our mailbox!"

The black-shirted man waved his hands. "Mermin's been having a few difficulties."

The wizard nodded his agreement.

"Forgive me. Where are my manners? Let me introduce myself. I'm King Hercalon V, ruler of the land of Oomaldee. And this is my wizard, Mermin. And you are…?"

"I'm Andy Smithson."

"Good to meet you, Andy son of Smith. To what guild does your father belong?"

"Uh…I'm not sure what you mean."

"Is he a shipbuilder? Yarn weaver? Cobbler?"

"Um, none of the above. My dad owns a company. He's the CEO. My mom does too." The thought of Dad using his hands to build a ship or weave yarn seemed crazy—whenever they needed something fixed, they called a repairman. He could hear Dad exclaiming, "Not a good use of my time to fix things. Do you know how much an hour of my time is worth?"

"A company? I'm afraid I don't know what that is. No matter. So, where are you from?"

"Lakehills, Texas."

The men exchanged furrowed brows. *They've never heard of it?* Andy bit his lip.

"Tell you what, let's explore that later."

"Wait a minute! What do you mean? How'd I get here? How do I get back home?"

The King cleared his throat and glanced at Mermin. "Andy, you may be staying with us for a while."

"What do you mean? You can't abduct me. There are laws against that. I'll…I'll call the cops!"

The King stiffened his posture and any hint of a smile faded. "I've no idea what that means, but let me assure you, we did not abduct you."

"Then send me back. Now!"

"I'm afraid that won't be possible. It seems Mermin did not bring you." The King's voice remained annoyingly calm. "Until we can determine who or what did, we won't know how to send you back."

"Are you kidding? This can't be happening. This can*not* be happening." Andy ran his hands through his hair then exploded, "This whole day has been a nightmare!"

Breath caught in both men's throats.

"I'm sorry to hear that. Mermin and I will work on how to send you home, but I sense you are here for a reason." The King's voice trailed off as he inhaled deeply, scratched the top of his head, then chuckled with an afterthought. "Your situation reminds me of the time young da Vinci dropped in for an unexpected visit. Remember that, Mermin?" Smiles of recognition punctuated both men's faces. "We had no idea where he'd come from. He just showed up."

"I'm glad you think this is funny."

The King held up a hand. "I don't find your situation funny. Experience has taught me that all manner of good can come from the most unexpected events. We will let you know what we determine as soon as we know more."

An uneasy feeling like when he'd navigated the spook house last Halloween gripped Andy's stomach. *What other surprises lurk around the next corner?*

"Why don't you come with me," Mermin suggested.

Andy glanced between the pair but elicited no further response from either. Feeling the sting of defeat, he huffed out a long breath. "Fine."

As the wizard pulled open the heavy wooden door a brown blur brushed the side of Andy's leg as it streaked past, accompanied by raucous high-pitched squeaking.

"Blast it!" the King bellowed.

"I'm on it!" The shout echoed from the hallway, and a boy about Andy's age dashed after the boggart. The boy had bright green hair and wore a royal blue tunic and green leggings.

"Thank you, Alden!" Mermin called after him.

Andy popped his head into the hall and looked both ways but the boy had vanished along with the shrill shrieks.

The wizard shook his head. "Nothing but mischief with that thing."

Andy wrinkled his brow but refrained from comment.

Several steps down the hall Andy asked, "You're Merlin the Magician? We studied you in school last year." *I had no idea the guy was so wacky.*

"You know about Merlin? He was my bwother." Then chuckling he added, "Made quite a name for himself in your world."

"But you said you didn't know anything about Lakehills, Texas!"

Mermin stopped short. "No, His Majesty said we'd explore that later."

Andy furrowed his brow, wanting to demand that the wizard tell him everything he knew about Andy's home, but the man cut him off. "Now, shall we continue?" Mermin directed with an open palm.

Should I trust this guy? Andy studied the mage. *If I have to stay here for a while, best not make him mad.* Andy redirected back to his original line of questioning. "Then are you related to the mermen—like the ones who live underwater?"

"Actually, they are my cousins twice wemoved, on my father's side. I'm afwaid of water myself. You seem to know a lot about my family."

Andy gave a half smile.

"I pwomised Henwy I'd loan him a book."

Andy sighed but traipsed after. The wizard pushed open another heavy wooden door. A sea of books in a multitude of colors and sizes lined the walls from floor to ceiling. Several wooden ladders on wheels scaled the shelves. The room exuded a dank, musty smell.

Whoa, hadn't expected this.

Andy gasped as he spotted a large trunk sitting on the floor near an oversize stone fireplace. It looked identical to the one he had discovered in his attic. The top rested open at an angle and rolled up manuscripts—all standing on end—overflowed its mouth, like a monster needing braces.

"Something wong?"

Remembering the note in the trunk back home had instructed not to tell anyone about it, Andy replied, "Uh, no, just admiring your trunk."

"That is a special twunk. Cwaftsmen from many lands build twunks, but I've never seen twunks as fine as this anywhere except Oomaldee." Mermin moved closer to Andy and whispered, "Don't tell anyone, but the ones made for woyalty have secwet compartments, too. Come in handy for hiding things."

"Really?"

Mermin nodded.

Andy continued inspecting the room. To one side, an oversized oak desk dominated a threadbare red rug under its feet. Its top was completely buried with open books and manuscripts. To the right of the desk stood a tall wooden table submerged under old texts and papers.

Mermin gathered the fabric of his generous robes in one hand and tottered up one of the wood ladders, exposing two scrawny legs. *He's got chicken legs like mine,* Andy smiled, but not for long when the wizard bobbled part way up.

Please don't fall, I don't know emergency first aid!

The man grabbed a book from a shelf and descended, oblivious to the excitement he'd caused his audience.

"Let's intwoduce you to the goldweavers."

"Goldweavers?"

Mermin smiled.

They headed back out the door and soon approached a sign indicating GOLDERY that hung outside a door at the end of the hall.

"A goldewy is where the gold of the kingdom is cwafted," Mermin answered Andy's unspoken question.

They walked through a heavy, metal-reinforced door into a small room with a stone floor. Straw was strewn about. A fiery furnace leaned against the far wall, making the space oppressively hot. An army of water-filled wooden buckets stood at attention to the left. Andy noted that the walls had been charred to the halfway point. Three men wearing brown burlap tunics and bright yellow leggings looked up from their work.

"This is Henwy." Mermin walked over to a man with muscular arms who pumped the bellows, making the furnace angrier still. The wizard handed him the book. "Henwy, this is Andy. He's…visiting."

"Thank you, Mermin," the man acknowledged, patting the wizard on the shoulder and stowing the book away from the fire. "Pleased to meet you, Andy," said Henry, wiping away the sweat freely flowing down his face. He returned to his former position and gave the bellows another pump, which caused sparks to fly. "Keeps me on my toes," he joked, stomping out burning embers as they flew onto the floor.

"And this is Max," Mermin continued, approaching a balding man working at a contraption that reminded Andy of a sewing machine. He kept taking handfuls of straw from a large pile stacked next to him. Each time he pumped a pedal, he fed several pieces of straw into a narrow flame that shot out. With his concentration broken, Max yelped, "Youch! I hate when that happens!" He shook his singed finger, trying to kill the pain.

"Sowwy about that Max. Just wanted Andy, here, to meet our finest gold spinner."

Max smiled. "Good to meet you." He stood, walked over to a bucket of water, and plunged his finger in. "Ahh. That's better."

Andy wiped the sweat cascading down his face on the sleeve of his T-shirt. It was hard to stand such intense heat. He understood why these men were so thin.

"And that's Oscar," Mermin said, nodding to a short man working next to the machine.

Oscar wound the gold thread coming out of the device around a spindle. When a spindle was full, he stacked it neatly with the others in the corner. The towering stack was impressive.

"When there are enough full spindles, they melt down all the gold thwead and form gold coins, which are then stored in the tweasury," Mermin explained.

"This is awesome!"

Max, Oscar, and Henry smiled proudly.

"It takes years of wigowous study to do what they do and make it look so easy."

"Can they show me how to spin gold?"

"We'll see," replied Mermin, stroking his beard. Andy speculated that was code for "no," just like his parents always said when they didn't want to do something.

But Max put up a hand and waved him over. "Not many folks care to learn, but since you're interested, come have a closer look."

Andy's eyes sparkled as he approached the goldweaver's bench.

"Stand right here," Max instructed. "There's lots of really complicated theory behind it, but the short version is this: to convert straw into gold, or anything else for that matter, you must understand the flow of energy within the straw."

"Flow of energy?"

"That's right. The energy is harnessed to break down the straw into a shape that's easier to use."

"I see…" Andy covered.

"From this, then, I can reshape it into what I want."

"Uh-huh."

"This machine harnesses the flow of energy that already exists in the straw. When I add fire and a spritz of water, I can then shape it into gold thread."

"Oscar can you refill the water reservoir for me?" Max requested. His fellow poured clear liquid into a circular opening on the top of the contraption.

"Okay, ready to watch it happen?" the would-be professor asked.

Andy bobbed his head, eyes wide.

The machine whirred to life as the man pumped a pedal beneath. He fed a handful of straw into the flame. "As soon as that mist of water touches it, you'll see it turn into a golden liquid." The instructor pointed. "See that?"

Andy's eyebrows shot up. "Awesome!"

"Now watch what happens. It's not hot, so now I just twist it between my fingers like this and—"

"I wind it onto this spool," Oscar chimed in. A big grin bloomed across his face as he demonstrated.

"That's so cool!"

The goldweavers ricocheted winks. "Glad you like it," Max intoned.

"We need to be on our way," Mermin interrupted.

"By all means. Hey, by the way, Mermin." Max raised a hand. "That boggart got into the treasury this morning and made a horrible mess of things. We haven't begun straightening it up. Not sure if it ate anything or not."

Andy's mouth dropped open. *A boggart in the treasury?*

"I figured the King should know."

Mermin frowned then cleared his throat. "Thank you. I'll pass that on. Do you need help cleaning up?"

"That would be great, thank you. It'll take us at least a month to reorganize everything at this rate."

The wizard nodded. "I'll get back to you with who can assist. Let me know when you want another book."

"Thanks for showing me that!" Andy waved.

"Nice to meet you!" the trio called after him.

Ah, cool air at last! Andy wiped his brow on the sleeve of his T-shirt. "Does that happen often?"

"What? The boggart?"

"Yeah."

"It's a wecent pwoblem—the horseshoe fell and now we can't get it back outside."

Andy cocked his head, but the wizard said no more.

On their way back to Mermin's library, the boy Andy had seen earlier dashed up. Contrasting with the royal-blue livery, the servant's neon-green hair puffed about his head as if he'd stuck his finger in a light socket. The lad cleared his throat and announced, "I was told to tell you dinner is nearly ready and remind you that today is Curse Day."

"Thank you, Alden." The wizard lowered his head and muttered, "As if anyone could forget." Lifting his head he asked, "Did you manage to capture that boggart?"

The boy frowned and kicked an invisible pebble. "No…"

"That's all right. We'll eventually outsmart it. We'll be along shortly. I need to change my wobes."

The servant bowed then turned.

"Did he just say Curse Day?"

Mermin nodded but didn't elaborate. They turned and meandered to the end of the corridor. A set of winding stone stairs led upstairs and downstairs. The wizard headed up.

"My chambers are on the sixth floor."

Scaling one flight of stairs and reaching the landing, they headed down the corridor and stopped next to a black door with a shiny silver crescent moon. Mermin waved his hands.

Is he going to say "abracadabra"?

"Secwet passcode. Can never be too careful." The mage opened the door and they entered a modest-sized room with a large stone fireplace and bed to the left. A dressing area took up the space to the right.

"Please wait here while I change."

Andy looked around the room. Something twinkled and caught his eye. He looked up and saw the black ceiling decorated with thousands of stars. They seemed almost alive. He could make out the Big Dipper and Orion. He couldn't remember any of the other constellations he was supposed to have memorized in science class and regretted it briefly.

He walked over to the large bed to examine the intricate carvings on the headboard: a unicorn stood proudly next to a pegasus. Above them the sun and moon walked hand in hand across the sky. Fairies danced with a troll, all smiling and laughing. There was also the carving of a creature Andy had never seen before. It looked almost like a wolf, but its paws were huge, clown-like, and its snout was pushed in like a pug's.

"That's a herewolf," informed the wizard, stepping out from behind the screen. He had changed into a black robe that looked older and more worn than he did. At one time it had been soft and velvety, but was now threadbare and had a small tear near the bottom of the right sleeve. A royal-blue coat of arms emblazoned the shoulder of the left sleeve. He had discarded his hat and his long silver locks flowed freely, a sharp contrast with the mysteries he seemed to be guarding.

Mermin pushed his glasses back up his nose. "Herewolves are descended fwom werewolves, but they don't change form with the cycles of the moon. They can still be vicious cweatures though. This was carved before the curse…" His voice trailed off.

"Curse?"

"We best get ourselves down to dinner," Mermin instructed, ignoring Andy's question.

The pair headed back down the steps, passing the fifth floor and continuing on down two more winding flights. They emerged into an expansive room the wizard said was the dining hall. Several servants wearing royal-blue livery hurried about finishing last-minute preparations. Plain black banners trimmed with gold hung about the perimeter of the room, hiding ornate tapestries that lined the walls.

A head table at the far end stood perpendicular to three tables that stretched almost the length of the room with benches on either side of them. Above the rightmost table hung a crimson banner with a gold chevron separating a lion at the top from a pair of wings at the bottom. Over the middle table hung an aqua banner with a beaver on the top and a snail on the bottom.

Who'd want to be known as a snail? Andy shook his head.

Above the third table hung a mustard-colored banner. The head of a long-horned bull adorned the top, and a bird nested on the bottom.

Andy's thoughts flashed back to the crest on the sheath in the trunk in his attic, and his eyes grew large. Before this, the only coats of arms he had ever seen were in books. Now, to see so many in use… *What is this place?*

"Something wong?"

"Uh, no…nothing."

Several minutes later, guests began arriving, pulling Mermin to his duties. The wizard hastened toward a doorway at the far left end of the hall and greeted a contingent of about thirty men and women dressed in black robes with an aqua coat of arms on their left sleeves. After exchanging somber nods and hushed tones, they processed toward the middle table. Next came several more men and women also wearing black robes but sporting a mustard-yellow crest on their left sleeves. One more group arrived shortly thereafter bearing a crimson coat of arms on their black robes. They blended into the whirling mass of uniformed humanity. *I'm not dressed for this,* Andy worried, still clad in a T-shirt, jeans, and sneakers.

Andy narrowly avoided being trodden underfoot by a burly man wrestling a bulky cask into place. "Watch yourself, son," the man warned with a heavy hand to Andy's shoulder once he had unburdened himself. A woman with bright purple hair clucked orders to several servants while white-gloved attendants offered drinks to their guests from silver trays.

Several minutes passed before King Hercalon entered the hall. He, too, wore a black robe, but distinguished himself with a royal-blue coat of arms on his left sleeve. Conversation ceased and everyone bowed as he strode to the head table. The King invited everyone to be seated, and Mermin joined him at the head table, sitting to his left. Several uniformed officers seated themselves to his right.

Andy stood watching the scene unfold from a back corner of the hall where he had taken refuge from the bustle of preparations. He scanned the lengths of the three tables but found no gaps among the myriad of servants and guests. *What am I supposed to do? Where should I sit?* The familiar angst of being picked last in gym class stalked his thoughts, and he prayed no one would notice him.

The King scanned the room, his gaze landing on Andy where he cowered. "Andy! Join me." Dread pounced as everyone turned.

I feel like a turtle without a shell. Determined to preserve a shred of his dignity, he hurried to the front, eyes fixed on the floor, wishing he had jet packs on his feet. He ignored the traitorous warmth rising in his cheeks. Hushed whispers dogged each step.

Before he reached safety, the King intoned, "I'd like to introduce you all to Andy, son of Smith, Sea Eee Ohhh. He arrived this afternoon, quite unexpectedly." The monarch paused for emphasis. "Mermin and I were working on our most recent experiment to break the curse when Andy suddenly appeared."

A murmur went up from servants and guests alike. As the king paused and waited for Andy, Mermin shuffled everyone down one seat on his right. Andy splashed down into his chair, never happier to be out of the limelight.

But the King was not done. He raised a hand for silence and continued, "I know what you may be thinking. The same thought occurred to me. Time will tell… Please make Andy feel welcome."

The dining hall erupted in loud applause and Andy wished he could disappear. *What's he talking about? What 'occurred' to him?*

The King called for silence and everyone rose. Andy conformed, not wanting to stand out.

"Today we commemorate Curse Day," the sovereign began. "Over five hundred years ago, the darkest period of our history began. I take full responsibility." The King drew a hand to his chest. "I was young, jealous, and impulsive. My pride was unchecked by the wisdom and humility only age brings. We cannot change the past but must look to the future. I continue to diligently seek for a solution to break the curse, but I am also aware the solution may come from beyond ourselves."

Andy felt the weight of innumerable eyes bounce on him then ricochet back to their sovereign as the King continued, "Know that I will not rest until the curse is broken. As you know, I wish more than anything to see our land restored to its former glory and technological superiority. Please join me in a toast." The ruler raised his goblet and bellowed, "To breaking the curse!"

"To breaking the curse!" The echo rose along with everyone's glasses.

"Please partake of the meal before you, and we will complete our remembrance after," the King invited, then took his seat.

The hum of conversation and clinking dishes overwhelmed the silence. Andy's brain whirred. *Both the King and Mermin have talked about a curse. I don't get it, but everybody else seems to.*

Mermin interrupted Andy's thoughts as he passed him what looked like mashed potatoes, except they were dark purple. Next came what the wizard said was roast duck and wild boar. They smelled okay but were blackened and did not look appetizing. As he scanned the rest of the table, all of the dishes seemed to be black or some dark color. Seeming to read his thoughts, Mermin leaned over and whispered, "Our twaditional Curse Day fare."

"Oh," was all Andy could muster, picking at his food.

A shriek pierced the din, then two more. Protests rose from the middle of the room and everyone gawked as maniacal laughter overwhelmed the hall. The scene looked like an out-of-control popcorn popper. Mashed potatoes leapt from bowls. A platter of wild boar launched, distributing its abundance on guests. Dinner plates flew skyward, then smashed against the stone floor. A bowl of gravy catapulted toward the aqua banner, soiling it before raining on the unfortunate souls beneath.

A bevy of servants converged in a scrum, arms grasping and flailing at the epicenter of the storm, eliciting more high-pitched laughter from the villain whose small, brown-haired body bounced just out of reach.

The path of carnage spread toward the back of the hall, then circled and headed forward. No food was sacred and no one immune. Servants and guests cowered under tables.

The officers at the head table bolted up and surrounded the King, swords drawn, as chaos reigned. At length, the high-pitched shrieks retreated out the doorway through which many of the guests had arrived. Servants and guests peeked out from under tables, wiping rubbish from their clothing and hair. Several slipped on the slick floor.

The King called for order. When quiet resumed, he wiped purple potato from an eyebrow, pulled a hand to his chest, and declared, "My people, I apologize. A boggart has beset the castle for the past moon, since the horseshoe fell from the drawbridge."

Murmurs rose and he raised his arms. "It seems this furry menace has accurately depicted how I view our situation."

A host of nods acknowledged.

"Seeing as our dinner has been concluded prematurely, please join me on the porch to complete our remembrance of Curse Day."

Andy continued wiping food from his hair, T-shirt, and jeans as he meandered along with the crowd out to a porch. It was the first time Andy had been outside since he'd arrived, and the dark night air felt crisp. He took a deep breath and let it out slowly, shaking his head. *What a day.*

A dense fog blanketed the area, restraining the light of the moon to a dim glow and obscuring everything beyond the railing.

"Governors, please join me," requested the King.

Three men squeezed through the maze of the guests.

"Is all in readiness?" the monarch inquired once they had joined him.

"Yes, Majesty," each replied in turn.

Three servants handed a long trumpet to each governor.

"Very well. Then on my count." The King counted down, "Three…two…one. Begin." Each governor raised his trumpet and, one by one, sounded a distinct call.

What Andy heard next more than puzzled him. It sounded like a huge herd of cows mooing. A second later he heard loud popping noises and then— he hated to think it. His mom would tell him to grow up. It smelled like…farts! *Whewww! What a stench! This is crazy!*

Andy couldn't help himself. His imagination started running wild. He pictured the scene. He tried to cover his mouth but a snicker snuck out. Mermin furrowed his brow beside Andy.

"Sorry," he whispered, desperately trying to contain his amusement. Andy finally resorted to pretending to cough in order to squelch his bursts of laughter, but a snort escaped. People around him glanced over and frowned.

It was all so strange. Everyone around him acted like they had expected the smell, casually pulling their sleeves over their noses. Andy covered his nose with his sleeve as best he could. *Oh, this smell is awful!*

Slowly, the dense clouds thinned and then disappeared, leaving a long trail of flickering lights clearly visible. *Okay, this is REALLY weird!*

Mermin moved closer to Andy and explained in a voice muffled from beneath his sleeve, "That's the city of Oops." He pointed downward at flickering crimson lights.

The wizard moved his arm to the right and pointed. "And that's the town of Ooggy." Andy could make out aqua-blue lights off in the distance.

"Over there," he said, pointing further to the right, "is the village of Oohhh." Andy could clearly see bright yellow lights.

A couple minutes later everyone heard a return trumpet blast from each of the communities.

"Please join me in a moment of silence," the King requested.

When the minute had elapsed, the sovereign concluded, "Thank you all for your continued support. We *will* break this curse." Determination laced his words.

At this, the attendees began conversing in hushed tones. Most greeted Andy pleasantly yet solemnly. Once everyone had left, Mermin rejoined Andy.

"We best find you your woom. It's late."

Andy turned to follow the wizard back inside but glanced over his shoulder and saw dense clouds again blotting out the scene. Thankfully, that horrible stench had nearly gone. *How strange...what just happened?*

They retraced steps back up a flight of stairs and turned down the hall to the left. Stopping outside a door, Mermin extended an arm and quipped, "For our unexpected guest." Hinges groaned. "This will be your chambers. You should have everything you need. Sleep well."

A fireplace popped and crackled at one end, casting dim shadows about the space. But with no other light, there was nothing for Andy to do. He removed his shoes and slipped between the abundant covers.

Andy yawned, but his mind refused to quiet. His brain choked and sputtered as it attempted to process the events of this very, very strange day. *How will I ever get back home?*

CHAPTER THREE

The King's Taster

A rooster awakened Andy the following morning. He knuckled sleep from his eyes, trying to orient himself. Foggy sun shone through a window to the left of his bed, struggling to illuminate the large stone-lined chamber. *It wasn't a dream.*

Like most other rooms he had been in the day before, this one was sparsely furnished. His bed stood in the middle of a long wall. At one end a dressing area had been arranged with a mirror, two freestanding closets, and a lumpy, overstuffed chair that looked like someone's attempt to soften the otherwise spartan décor. At the other end stood the large fireplace. The fire had long gone out. The wooden door on the wall opposite his bed displayed the King's blue coat of arms above it.

A soft knock disturbed his study of the space and he slipped from between the warm covers. His bare feet hit the cold stone floor and sent a shiver up his back.

"Please excuse me, sir. I was told to assist you in dressing and to bring you down to breakfast."

It was the boy with neon-green hair he'd seen yesterday.

"Why do you call me sir?" Andy asked, allowing him entrance.

"Because you are a guest of His Majesty."

"Just call me Andy, okay?"

"Oh...okay. If that's what you prefer, sir. Oh, I mean…uh, sure Andy."

They stepped over to the dressing area. To Andy's surprise, a clean pair of blue jeans and a bright blue long-sleeved T-shirt lay neatly folded on the arm of the chair. The T-shirt had the intricate royal crest sewn on the left sleeve. It looked like both had been ironed for no wrinkles dared show themselves. He chuckled. Andy usually wore extremely wrinkled T-shirts because he hated folding and putting away his clean laundry, one of his assigned chores. Mom always complained his clothes made him look like he had slept in a laundry basket.

"His Majesty had the tailor make these for you overnight so you would be most comfortable. The tailor will make you more today. I'll hang them in your closets when they're ready."

"Can the tailor make black T-shirts?" Andy hoped aloud. "Black is my favorite color."

"Black T-shirts are reserved for the King."

Oh well, it was worth asking. Andy only wore black T-shirts at home, preferring that to colors.

"Please follow me," the boy instructed after Andy finished dressing.

"Thanks for helping me. I don't think I could've remembered how to get back to the dining hall."

The boy smiled.

"I can't remember your name," apologized Andy as they exited his chamber and headed toward the stairs.

"My name is Alden."

"That's right! Sorry."

"That's okay. You don't have to remember my name. I'm just a servant."

"But—"

"Good morning, Andy!" boomed a voice, interrupting the conversation as they entered the dining hall. "Did you sleep well?" The King beckoned him over with a wave.

"I'll leave you to it then." The boy bowed then turned.

The hall looked different this morning. The three long tables had been shoved over by the wall and the black banners taken down. The colorful community banners had been moved and now draped the wall—the aqua banner was cleaner than he'd seen it last. Only what had been the head table remained. The King, again dressed in his black T-shirt and faded jeans, sat at one end with Mermin at the side closest to him.

A short, bald servant with a beak-like nose and curiously long arms extending nearly to his ankles tasted the King's breakfast.

"Everything seems to be in order, Your Majesty," the man finally declared. He bowed to the King, but as he turned to leave, he scowled at Andy.

What? I didn't do anything wrong!

Andy took a seat across the table from Mermin. Immediately another servant brought him a bowl of Apple Jaxs, toast, and a tall glass of milk. *How could they know that's my favorite cereal? Where'd they get it from?*

"Yes, I had a feeling you'd like that, Andy," the King intoned, then winked. "Mermin and I were just discussing how to get the Us Pus box working. Perhaps you can give us some insight."

Not used to being asked his opinion, let alone made to feel like he had any expertise to contribute, Andy stammered, "Uh, sure." He bit into his toast. "But what's an Us Pus box?"

"After breakfast, let's all go up to the laboratory. It's up there."

When they'd eaten their fill, the three adjourned. As they walked Andy asked, "Have you figured out how to send me back home yet?"

"Goodness no, not yet. What with the Curse Day Remembrance and everything else going on, we've not had any time to work on it. Don't worry though, that is Mermin's next task. I expect you will be home very shortly."

Somehow I doubt that. Andy bobbed his head, choosing to let it go…for now.

They walked up to the fifth floor and into the laboratory, which had been cleaned up since yesterday. The tables had been righted, the broken beakers cleaned up, and the floor mopped. It smelled like lemon. Against the far wall stood Andy's mailbox with the stones from its base in a loose arrangement.

The King walked over and indicated with a flourish of his arm, "The Us Pus box."

"That's my mailbox. You took it yesterday."

The King cleared his throat. Mermin raised a finger and objected, "We bowwowed it. We just want to see how it works."

"Why do you call it an Us Pus box?"

"Because that's what it says. See here? USPS." The King pointed to the raised letters on the door.

"Umm, USPS stands for United States Postal Service. It's a mailbox."

"Can you show us how it works?" The King looked at Andy with hopeful eyes. "How do you get it to give you those papers?"

"What do you mean?"

"Mermin has been watching several…uh, mailboxes for me."

"Wait, you watch people's mailboxes?"

"Oh yes," the wizard confirmed. "The King has me observe all sorts of things for him. I've observed pawades and carnivals, aiwplanes and cars and people—all sorts of things. Sometimes we bwing a book or something back to study further."

Or send trunks to people's attics perhaps?

"Yes, yes. I like observing people best. I once observed Steve Jobs. Fascinating guy. The King weally liked how he dwessed, so he started dwessing like him, too. He hoped Mr. Job's cweativity might wub off on him. Took some doing to get the clothes just wight." A smile tweaked his lips as he remembered.

"As I was saying," the King asserted, "he tells me papers magically appear in them. Sometimes there are thick picture books and other times there are thin papers inside…what do you call them? Envelopes, is it? Isn't that what you call them, Mermin?" He looked to the wizard who nodded.

"Mermin's theory is that what appears is based upon how happy you are. The happier you are, the more magical papers appear. The less happy you are, the fewer papers you receive. Is that right?"

"Uh, no."

For the next hour, Andy explained what he knew about the postal service and mail carriers. He cleared up the King's misconception that the dogs that chased the mail carriers were sent by their masters to demand more magical mail be left for them.

He also assured the King he would never receive any mail and pointed out tampering with the US Mail was a crime punishable by imprisonment.

"Send it back, Mermin! Send it back!"

The wizard attempted to reverse the settings of the Appearo Beam, but as Andy had expected, his attempts failed. He did manage to suck a duck that had been innocently flying over the castle into the laboratory. It stood there, several feathers short, quacking its disgust until a servant came and chased it around the space, sending papers flying and beakers crashing. The servant finally cornered it and removed it to the kitchen. No sooner had that servant left than a kitchen servant apologetically interrupted, explaining lunch would be delayed because anything in or near the fireplaces had been inexplicably sucked up the chimneys by a great whirlwind.

"Out of curiosity, why were you watching my mailbox?" Andy wondered, bringing the pair's attention back.

"We wanted to see if being on your mail route might bring us magical papers to help us figure out how to break the curse."

"But why *my* mailbox?"

"It just happened to be one of the mailboxes I was observing," replied the wizard.

What a strange 'coincidence.' He observes my mailbox and I end up here.

"Oh well, one less thing to try in breaking the curse," the King reasoned as they headed down for a late lunch. "Mermin, I need you to keep trying to send that mailbox back. I don't want to be imprisoned for taking it."

"Of course, Majesty."

Andy could only shake his head.

The three governors from the surrounding communities had stayed overnight and now joined them for lunch. As with the previous evening, Andy saw their clothes were trimmed in crimson, yellow, and aqua, corresponding to the color of their community. They looked much better without cranberry sauce, squash, and mashed potatoes accenting their attire.

The King informed, "This afternoon, the governors, Mermin, and I will be finishing up plans for the Oomaldee Festival that starts in a few days. After lunch, why don't you explore the castle on your own. Just stay out of the dungeon, it's dangerous."

Wow! He hardly knows me, yet he trusts me to explore on my own? That'd never happen at home. Andy bit his lip. *I'm gonna stay out of trouble...*

"Okay," Andy accepted. A corner of his mouth inched up but didn't linger.

As soon as Andy finished his lunch, he excused himself and set out to discover what secrets he might coax from the castle. He thought about checking out the trunk up in Mermin's library, but the spiral stairs leading down from the dining hall beckoned. He decided to head that way first and investigate the trunk later.

As he descended, the stairs broadened into a grand staircase that ended in a huge foyer across from an ornate door. The space was deserted.

This must be the castle entrance, Andy reasoned, *since all the guests from last night's dinner came from this direction.*

Andy saw doors leading to rooms behind the staircase, but he decided to continue down another set of stairs he spotted behind and to the right. Reaching the next landing, he heard voices echoing down the corridor.

A small servant girl who looked a little younger than he was halted hurried steps and inquired, "Are you lost?"

"No, just exploring."

"Well, I'm Hannah," she replied with a smile. Wisps of blond hair peeked out in several directions from under a blue headscarf. She attempted to straighten her blue dress that was wet in places. "Sorry I'm such a mess. I'm helping do laundry."

As they spoke, another servant paused on his way down the hallway. The tall, thin man wore a royal-blue tunic and bright green leggings, which Andy now recognized as the uniform for the King's staff. The man's face was gaunt and his pepper-gray, patchy whiskers gave him an unkempt look. He bent slightly back, attempting to ballast an oversize bundle of firewood with his chin.

The stack shifted unstably. "You lost?" he grimaced, bobbling his arms, perspiration beading his brow.

"No. I'm exploring the castle on my own since the King and Mermin are busy."

"These are the servants' quarters. Nothing more to see down here other than the dungeons, and they're dangerous, so don't even think about exploring there." The man fought the topmost log with his chin before adding, "Best get yourself back upstairs."

The dungeons, huh? So that's where they are.

"I better get going," Hannah intoned. "See you around."

"Yeah, see ya," replied Andy.

The firewood refused to be controlled and made a bid for freedom, compelling the other servant to quickly excuse himself. Andy watched him wobble down the hallway. When the man vanished from sight, Andy glanced around. The two voices he had heard down the corridor had erupted into a full-blown argument. He closed his eyes and listened, and after a minute satisfied himself no one else was coming. He headed back to the stairs and started down.

Better get a light, he thought, confronted by the darkness. He found a torch in the entry and lit it on an already glowing one, then returned, creeping down the remaining steps. A green mist greeted him along with the stench of rotten eggs that made his stomach flip. He batted the fog then plugged his nose with his free hand. *This is worse than those cow farts.*

Undeterred, he moved the torch forward. In front of him stood a metal door with reinforcing bars running diagonally in both directions across its cold, gray surface and secured by metal rivets. A large dent on the door's lower left looked like whatever was kept in the dungeon had punched it with a massive fist. Above the door hung a wooden sign with words carved in it. Andy stepped closer. The sign read, FEAR YE TO TREAD HERE. Wisps of green vapor seeped from under the barrier. Cold fingers danced down Andy's spine.

Not having enough hands to plug his nose, hold the torch, and open the door, he retreated back to the stairs and up three steps, inhaled deeply, and held his breath. His fingers tingled as he approached the door once more. Gripping the frigid metal of the handle he pressed down. Locked.

Darn. While his thoughts announced disappointment, his insides didn't echo the sentiment. He took another swipe at the rancid green vapor then retreated back up the stairs. As he reached the servants' quarters, Andy heard a soft thrumming emanating from the wall on his right.

That's weird. Machinery? Here? I didn't hear anything before. The protests of creaking wood sounded from the entry hall above. Andy froze. Jubilant voices chased the strange sounds, then evaporated.

He put his ear up to the stone wall as renewed creaking sounds reached him. *Whoosh…whoosh…whoosh…whoosh.* Definitely machinery. He felt along the length of the wall but found no opening. About to give up, he stepped on a stone and his foot sunk down. A six-foot section of the wall inched sideways to the sound of stone scraping stone. Andy winced, praying no one came to investigate.

Whoosh…whoosh…whoosh…whoosh, the rhythm continued, now louder. Andy felt the wall and found the opening led into a second wall.

How do I open it?

A loud thud echoed down the stairs and the whooshing ceased. He searched for several more minutes, turning up exactly nothing. Approaching footsteps made him freeze.

Crap! How am I going to explain?!

A short, plump woman in a royal-blue dress, white apron, lime-green leggings, and bright purple ponytail noticed him standing with a torch in the shadows and said, "I'm Marta and this is the Drawbridge Power Room. It's His Majesty's and Mermin's invention. It used to take six men to raise and lower the drawbridge. Now they use water power. It's quite ingenious if you ask me. I have no idea how it works. I just know everyone was told to stay away from it, for safety reasons. By the way, welcome. Sounds like you have an interesting story to tell."

"Yeah. The King and Mermin are working out how to get me home."

"Well, why don't you come with me. I'm headed up to the kitchen to help prepare dinner. I think there's someone you might like to meet."

Andy exhaled in relief when she turned and started up without comment concerning his handiwork. He slipped on the damp stone floor as he turned to follow.

Hmm, didn't notice that before.

She headed to the left behind the grand staircase and he followed. The smell of baking bread emanated into the curving stone corridor.

Mmm…

As they entered the kitchen a second smell commingled with the first.

"Are they making chocolate chip cookies?" His mouth watered.

Marta grinned. "Your nose is very discerning."

A hive of activity met them. Servants washed and chopped vegetables at sinks along the far wall. Some made sweet desserts at a center island. At another workspace near the fireplace, others prepared freshly butchered chickens and what looked to be the duck that protested in the laboratory earlier. Andy saw Alden peeling potatoes at one of the sinks—he couldn't miss the neon-green hair. Alden waved.

"You know my son?"

Andy laughed. "I figured you had to be related. You're the only ones I've seen with such…such…bright hair."

The woman chuckled. "Alden and I fled from the land of Carta a few years back when King Abaddon attacked. My husband and the rest of my family were killed in the fighting. Most people in Oomaldee don't like foreigners, but King Hercalon is a gracious and generous man and he took us in. We have served in his house since then."

"I'm sorry about your family."

Marta leaned forward and kissed him once on each cheek. "Thank you." She paused, then brightened. "Would you like a chocolate chip cookie? They're the King's favorite. He tells me they might just be your favorite, too. Although I'm not sure if he told me that so I'd bake more for him."

Andy laughed. "Actually, he's right, they are my favorite. Although my mom never makes them because she's really busy…and she thinks they're junk food."

"Junk food?" Marta cocked her head.

"Food that's not good for you."

The woman pushed back a stray purple strand, wrinkled her brow, and opened her mouth to speak, then closed it again.

Yeah, I guess they wouldn't have junk food here.

"I can't wait to learn more about your home." The woman immediately made Andy feel at ease. She was so different from his mom, who always seemed too tired or too busy for him.

Andy wandered over to Alden.

"I've got all those potatoes left to peel—" he pointed to a stack of spuds about a foot tall in the neighboring sink "—but as soon as I'm done, I think my mom will let me play."

"I can help! You'll get done faster."

"Are you sure? This is servant's work, and you're a guest."

"My mom always makes me peel potatoes for Thanksgiving." Andy didn't add that he hated the chore more than just about anything. This was different.

Andy and Alden attacked the pile of spuds. They raced to see who could peel fastest. Peels flew into the sink, around the sink, on the floor, and in their hair and clothes.

"Woohoo!" Andy yelped.

The rest of the servants in the kitchen watched the spectacle unfold. One portly man kept raising his eyebrows and shaking his head. The short, bald man with curiously long arms, whom Andy had seen earlier testing the King's breakfast, scowled. Alden's mom kept looking up and smiling.

When the pile had been decimated, they counted their spoils: 97 potatoes for Alden and 91 for Andy.

"Oh, so close!" shouted Andy.

"Not bad for a new recruit," Marta laughed. "Clean up your mess and then Alden can go."

A few minutes later the boys headed out of the kitchen, their mouths full of cookies.

"The festival starts in a few days. Do you want to come with me to the stables and watch me practice? I'm in the Tower Chase event with my pegasus, Optimistic."

I have no idea what he just said. "A pegasus? Really? That sounds like fun!" Andy covered.

"Let me change into my riding clothes first."

They headed downstairs to the servants' quarters. The floor around the stairs now had standing water, but in their shared excitement they paid no attention as their feet splashed.

Alden led Andy down a lengthy corridor with doors jutting off either side. They stopped at a room at the end and entered. The space was smaller than any Andy had seen thus far. Two beds lined the stone walls on either side of a narrow window—one was neatly made, the other not so much. A small desk rammed against the near wall held a short stack of papers to one side and a candleholder in the middle. A fireplace with a roughly hewn wood mantel squatted opposite. To say the space was cozy would have been an understatement. Cramped was a better description.

Alden headed for the wardrobe and pulled out what he called his equestrian uniform: a royal-blue jacket with tails and green riding breeches that were baggy at the top and tapered to the knee, making it look as if a hamster had burrowed in the top of each leg. Andy suppressed a snicker. *He looks funny.* Alden pulled on his tall black riding boots with a grunt.

"They're a little small. Mom says I need to stop growing; it's costing her too much. Okay, I'm ready."

They headed back upstairs, past the kitchens, and out into dense, sunlit fog. Andy could not see five feet in front of him.

"The fog's really thick!"

"This is normal."

"Normal? How can you see anything?"

"Mermin told me it's been this way ever since the curse."

Andy and Alden felt their way across a cobblestone terrace. Andy could barely make out a stone building they approached. It had two huge wooden doors, the kind you'd see on a barn. Carved in the middle of the right door was a round circle with the head and wings of a pegasus. The left door had fancy letters inscribed into it: "His Majesty's Stables, Center for Advanced Preparation."

"Advanced preparation? Preparation for what?" Andy asked.

"The Cavalry of Oomaldee is stationed here. They keep all of their pegasi in these stables and also use this facility to train."

They train pegasi?

A statue of a knight in full armor greeted them in the immense foyer. The warrior held a lance level, charging into battle on his steed.

"I think that's Sir Lancelot. The King likes that guy a lot," narrated Alden.

They turned left and passed stall after stall filled with amazing creatures. Some stuck curious heads over the half doors as the pair passed. The animals' fur came in a multitude of colors—orange, red, gray, green, purple, and more. Their heads looked just like horses, and they peered at the boys through large brown eyes with long lashes.

"Do you want to pet one?"

"Yeah!" gawked Andy, his eyes growing wide. He reached out his hand to touch one.

"Don't pet these pegasi. They're trained for combat and they'll bite."

Andy quickly withdrew his hand, checking it even though he knew it remained unharmed.

After walking past at least a hundred stalls, Alden finally stopped, opened a door, and stepped in.

"Hey girl." Alden spoke softly and held his hand out, inviting the creature to sniff it.

A second later she gave a low whinnying sound.

"You have to let them accept you before you try to touch them. Here, put your hand in front of her nose."

Andy moved slowly to her head and stuck out a trembling hand. Two blasts of warm air hit his arm seconds later. "She's got whiskers! They tickle."

The pegasus hesitated briefly and finally whinnied.

"She likes you. Now you can pet her."

Andy stepped around and ran his hand down the animal's neck. Her purple fur sparkled as he stroked it. "It's so soft!"

"They say it's the softest fur of any animal. It keeps them light so they can fly."

Andy had not noticed the creature's wings until now, but when Alden mentioned flying, the pegasus ruffled them to say she was ready to exercise. Her wings attached at the top of her back, just behind the withers. Andy's eyes followed the lines of the feathers and saw they extended down even with her belly, ending just before her tail.

Alden grabbed a halter hanging next to the door and, with the help of a step ladder, put it over her head, sticking the bit in her mouth as he did. She started to prance in the confined space, and Andy leapt up the stall wall to avoid being stepped on.

"Sorry, she's excited."

Alden tossed the saddle over her and adjusted it so the pommel was positioned just in front of where her wings started. He fed the strap under her belly and cinched it tight.

"Come on, Optimistic. Let's go for a ride."

Alden led her by the reins and Andy followed. Optimistic dwarfed Alden. Her shoulders towered at least three feet above him.

"I got her from the King's stock when she was first born two years ago. They didn't want her. They were going to kill her because she was a runt."

"She's not a runt anymore!"

"I've been taking care of her, and now we have our first chance to show everyone she's just as good as the other pegasi, maybe better!" Alden's voice rang with determination, as if he had something to prove. Optimistic gave a whinny and tossed her head, echoing the sentiment. Andy chose not to pursue questioning.

The three walked silently out into a sawdust-covered oval ring where several other pegasi trained with their cavalry masters. The men were dressed in work coveralls of royal-blue. At seeing them, the leader nodded in recognition.

"Good luck in the Tower Chase, Alden. The field this year is seasoned and will not be easy to beat."

"Thank you, Major. I'll do my best for the King!"

They reached the other side of the arena and headed out of the building, back into the sunlit fog.

"We need to train out here so we don't get in the way of cavalry exercises."

"But how will you see?"

Alden whistled and immediately several servants appeared, each leading a cow. "I need to train for the Tower Chase. Can you clear the fog, please?"

At this, the servants walked their cows to positions designated by the King's blue coat of arms. Andy lost sight of the ones who headed toward the opposite side of the ring.

Alden handed Andy what looked like nose plugs and showed him how to put them on. "Breathe through your mouth," he instructed. He led Optimistic several steps forward to a mounting platform and hopped on. "Ready!" Alden announced, sounding nasally.

Andy heard mooing just like last night, followed by farting sounds, and then the fog started to thin and lift. *This is too wild!*

After a few minutes, Andy could clearly see a dozen or more poles, ovals, and arrows floating in the sky above. *I wonder how they stay aloft?*

Alden and Optimistic took off, the mare nickering with delight. Alden directed her around floating poles and through ovals—he had to time this perfectly with her rhythmic flapping or they would not fit, at least not together. He raced her vertically up and up and upside down, finally completing a loop only a few feet above the ground. Two obstacles later, Alden landed, beaming.

"Our best run yet! We've got a good chance, I know we do."

Andy watched the pair train for the next two hours, awed by the beauty and grace of the pegasus coupled with Alden's command of the animal. They were one, inseparable, seemingly reading each other's thoughts, dancing together.

When Alden finally finished, boy and beast both dripped with sweat. He hopped off Optimistic and announced to the servants, "I'm done!" He pulled off his nose plugs, and Andy followed his lead.

Whew! That stench is so bad!

"I need to cool her down and brush her. You don't need to stay."

Vigorously waving a hand in front of his face, Andy sputtered, "Hey, thanks for letting me watch you practice. You're really good!"

"Thanks." Alden couldn't suppress a laugh at Andy's hysterics.

"See you later," Andy waved as he headed for clean air.

I'm definitely going to need to ask Alden about that stench, but not right now. Why do they do that?

He walked back across the sawdust-covered arena, past the men training. The Major waved and Andy reciprocated. He had just entered the stable area when he saw a servant who looked similar to the man he'd seen in the kitchen earlier. He was short but with more hair, and just like the other guy his arms extended nearly down to his ankles. His nose was beak-like and bumpy. He watched the cavalry train, but when his bulging, frog-like eyes caught sight of Andy, he frowned and darted into the nearest aisle between the stalls.

That guy's not very friendly.

Andy navigated the cobblestone terrace and reached the back door of the castle. He didn't think anything of the fact that it stood ajar, and shoved it open. Seconds later, a heavy wooden bucket that had been teetering on the top retched its skuzzy contents, drenching Andy as it plummeted.

"Ow! Gross!"

Boisterous laughter ricocheted through the corridor as Andy sputtered and crouched, pulling hands over his head.

The brown furry menace that had assaulted him twice yesterday jumped on his head then bounced to the floor. Andy grabbed after it but narrowly missed. "Argh! Yeah, you better run!" He rubbed the growing bump on his head as he dashed after the villain, which continued its ear-piercing shrieks.

Heads popped out of rooms as he rushed by, cheering him on.

Around a sharp corner, up the grand staircase, and through the double doors of the dining hall he raced. The boggart nearly escaped when it plunged under the long communal dining table, but Andy hurdled the obstacle and continued pursuit up the circular stone stairs, taking them two at a time.

The pest glanced over its shoulder and raised an eyebrow as Andy narrowed the gap, but a stitch in his side aided and abetted the nuisance as he neared the fifth floor. Andy held his side, forcing himself up two more flights. Cresting the landing, a furry behind and two short, scrawny legs struggled to propel the balance of the creature under a hulking metal door.

"Hah! Gotcha!" Andy fell panting before the door and swiped at the palm-size appendages…just as they disappeared under the door. He yanked on the handle but found it locked. "Crap!" His fists pummeled the metal as victory shrieks started on the other side.

Andy collapsed like a lawn chair to the floor and waited for his breathing to slow. Shrieks soon ended, but tinkling metallic sounds flowing under the door quickly replaced them. Andy turned furrowed brows to the carob-colored surface, then stood and examined a sign affixed to it: ADMITTANCE ONLY BY ORDER OF HIS MAJESTY. A gold plaque above the door declared this to be the royal treasury.

Is this where I woke up yesterday? Andy rubbed the bump on his head. *That thing's making a mess of the place again. I better tell the goldweavers.*

Shouting from downstairs interrupted Andy's musings. "The servants' quarters are flooded! Three feet of water! Come quick! Everyone needs to bail!"

CHAPTER FOUR

The Flood

A line of servants stretched out the front door from the entry hall down the stairs to the servants' quarters on the floor below. Buckets floated up and down the stairs in the hands of anxious servants as they attempted to bail water back into a moat surrounding the castle. The King led the charge, barking orders.

Andy spotted a gap between two servants on the steps and hastily joined, grabbing the overflowing bucket thrust at him.

"Uhh," Andy grunted as the sloshing water made him lose his balance. He lurched down a step, nearly trampling the stout servant below.

"Easy laddie," the lady cautioned.

"Sorry."

Andy's hand found purchase on the rough wall and he steadied himself then stepped up.

"You gotta keep up," the man on the step above admonished, empty handed. He waved his fingers, motioning for Andy to pass him the offending bucket posthaste.

Andy groaned, muscling the now half-full bucket up to the man, then ducked as an empty pot passed overhead. He spotted Alden laboring at the bottom of the steps far below, thigh-deep in muddy water.

Not used to physical labor, Andy's arms and back soon ached. *I may be a guest, but I'll show them I can be tough. I'm not stopping until they do.* The regime went on for what seemed like hours. With each bucket he passed, blisters formed then burst, leaving his hands raw and bloodied.

When will this end?

Some while later, Andy moved aside as the King and Mermin made their way down the steps. The sovereign gave Andy a smile as their eyes met.

A few minutes later, the sound of something rough sliding across the stone floor could be heard below, followed by the echo of a heavy door closing.

Uh oh, that sounds familiar, Andy fretted.

Still the bailing continued. Andy's back ached and he thought his arms might fall off. Soaked to the bone, he shivered in his wet clothes.

The King made his way back up the stairs with Mermin in tow. He raised his hands and everyone halted.

Phew! A break.

"This was very serious," began the sovereign. "One of the sections of seals had been slid out of place, allowing water to gush in. If Alden hadn't reported it when he did, the breach could have washed out the bottom floors of the castle, making the entire structure unstable."

Excited murmurs erupted.

"Have any of you seen someone tampering with the seal or know anything about this?" the King questioned.

It was an accident! I didn't know what I was doing. I was just exploring! The last thing I wanted was to hurt anyone. If I tell them I did it, they'll probably all hate me and never want me around. Alden won't be my friend anymore. What would they do to me? No, I'm not saying a word.

The monarch's inquiry met only a chorus of wagging heads and more murmurs. The King and Mermin exchanged glances.

"Are you thinking what I'm thinking?" the sovereign asked his wizard.

"Abaddon."

He nodded. "Let's discuss this later."

The King started barking orders again, and the bucket brigade resumed. They bailed until the floor of the servants' quarters, as well as the steps to the dungeon, had no standing water.

"No telling how much water got in the dungeon," Andy overheard the King say to Mermin. "We'll deal with it later. I don't feel like battling those creatures right now."

"I quite agwee," replied Mermin, wiping his brow.

Creatures? In the dungeon? The image of the distended door flashed across Andy's mind and he swallowed hard.

A hush lingered over dinner. Only a handful of those present attempted conversation, and then only for necessities. Neither Marta nor Alden said a word as exhaustion, coupled with the reality of how close they had come to losing the castle, sunk in.

I did this, Andy chided himself then sighed, drawing a look from his green-haired friend across the table.

Alden turned back to Marta and patted her shoulder as she swiped a hand across her eyes.

Andy wanted to go hide when dinner ended, but Marta halted his retreat. "I think Alden would appreciate a friend right now. Why don't you come with us?"

Andy opened his mouth, then closed it again.

"What is it?" she queried.

Andy hesitated but finally spit out, "I'm sorry for your loss." *I'm such a fraud! And a loser!*

She nodded. "Thank you." Then pulling back her shoulders and taking a steadying breath, she put an arm around her son. "It won't get any easier."

The trio descended the stairs to the servants' quarters.

Wailing and shrieking echoed down the corridor as they reached the moist landing. Mud coated three feet of the wall and revealed the crest of the travesty. Andy peeked in quarters as they passed: a burly man shook his head surveying one room. In another, a dark-haired maiden in a smudged dress quaked as she held her head in her hands. A small child with a dirt-striped face held her mother's hand with wide eyes in a third. No matter how many rooms he surveyed, the result was the same.

"Ha, ha, ha!" cackled a girl's voice. Raucous clapping followed. "You burn inside…buurrn! Ha, ha, ha!"

"Imogenia. Stop!" admonished a man's voice.

What? Who? Andy shook his head then chanced a glance around.

"Something wrong, Andy?" Marta inquired.

"You didn't hear that? Just now?"

"Hear what?"

"Two voices."

Marta looked at Andy and furrowed her brow.

"I didn't hear anything either," Alden said.

"Then what?" Andy squeezed his eyes shut and wagged his head. "I'm imagining things."

Reaching the room at the end of the hallway, Andy held his breath as Marta opened the door to reveal the devastation. "Looks like everything's soaked with that filthy water," she croaked.

Andy nodded as he surveyed the brown-tinged bedding that still dripped. Firewood oozed water from between its stacked lengths. A steady trickle ran from under the doors of the armoire.

Exclamations reached them from down the hallway: "Abaddon's going to pay!" "The King's not going to let this go!"

Marta gasped as she approached the small desk against the near wall and picked up a short stack of papers. "Your artwork, Alden! These are still dry!"

Alden gave a half smile.

"These are what matter most," Marta declared.

Andy bit his tongue and took a small step toward the door, wishing he could be invisible.

"We'll all sleep in the dining hall! Gather your things and join us for an all-servants' slumber party." A forced chuckle followed the announcement as it boomed down the hall. "Might as well make the best of things."

"You and Alden are welcome to stay in my room tonight," Andy offered, glad for the opportunity to tame a smidge of guilt that had morphed into a snapping turtle.

"Thank you, Andy. That's certainly better than sleeping on that hard floor. Head up to bed. Alden and I will join you shortly."

Minutes later, Andy threw open the door to his chambers and slammed it shut behind him as he dove onto the bed, dissolving into sobs. *I'm just a big disappointment like Dad says.*

Several minutes later his body still quaked although his eyes no longer leaked. A shiver rocked his body from filthy clothes that swaddled him in cold dampness. A washbasin of clean water and a soft white towel stood next to his wardrobe. He stripped, washed, and changed into a dry outfit. *I don't deserve this. What I did is unforgivable.* His body betrayed him as it relaxed in the comfort of warmth. He shunned the relief, convinced torment was a more fitting partner.

What am I gonna do?

A quiet knock on the door interrupted his sulk.

"Come on in. Let me get some clean water so you can wash up," Andy offered.

Marta raised an eyebrow and exchanged a glance with Alden.

"No, it's fine. You're tired," Andy insisted.

After washing up, Alden put on a pair of Andy's jeans and a T-shirt. Inspecting himself in the mirror, he lit up and declared, "These are really different!" Marta couldn't help but chuckle.

Marta had found a nightgown that had not been soiled in the top drawer of her armoire. After she washed and changed, they all crawled into Andy's bed—even though three of them shared, there was plenty of room.

Despite being bone-tired, Andy's mind whirred thinking about everything that had happened. He tossed and turned for what seemed like hours as his guilt morphed from a snapping turtle into a rabid dog.

"Annndyyyy," sang a wispy voice, interrupting the canine's incessant barking.

More voices? Am I dreaming? Is it that boggart?

Andy sat up and looked around. He glanced over at the still forms of Alden and Marta as the voice repeated its call: "Annndyyyy."

It sounds like the King. After everything that happened today, I better go see what he wants…right away. Andy slid out of bed, trying his best not to disturb his companions.

After the warmth of the thick covers, the frigid night air caught him off guard. A shiver rocked his body as he pulled on jeans and sandals. He eased the door open as quietly as possible and stepped into the cold corridor.

"Annndyyyy."

"I'm coming," he whispered, trying to reassure the voice.

Even though he tried to tiptoe quietly down the hallway, the scuffling of each footstep reverberated off the hard walls and his eyes darted about. The only light was from the moon attempting to shine through the fog-congested window near the stairs ahead, but the shadows it cast heckled and mocked, and he struggled to quell his rising fear. Glancing over his shoulder every few seconds, Andy scurried up two flights to the sixth floor where he knew the King slept. Even though he had never been invited inside, he remembered Mermin pointing out the door to the King's chambers the night before when he had accompanied the wizard to his quarters.

Andy stopped outside the door. A thin line of light shone beneath it and he exhaled. *Surely it was the King calling me,* he tried to reassure himself. He nodded once then raised his fist.

"Who is it?" came the King's voice.

"It's me, Andy."

The King opened the door. He wore a blue satin robe that extended to his slipper-covered feet. "I'm surprised to see you at this hour. I was about to turn in. I've been thinking about everything that happened today and contemplating what to do about it. King Abaddon must not be allowed to harm us."

As soon as the words crossed the King's lips, the rabid canine morphed into a hyena that began laughing uncontrollably. Desperate to rid himself of increasingly vicious predators, Andy opened his mouth, but words failed him.

"So, what can I do for you, Andy?"

"Well, sir, I came because I heard you call me. What did you need?"

The King smiled. "That's very thoughtful of you, but I did not call you. Perhaps after all of today's excitement you thought you heard something. Go back to bed. Rest will do us both good."

"Oh. I'm sorry to disturb you then. Good night, sir." *That was weird*, he thought as he headed back downstairs.

Andy slipped into bed and minutes later exhaustion mercifully whisked him off to dreamland. But not for long, for just as he dozed off, he heard the same voice: "Annnndyyy."

Surely it's the King this time. Andy wiped his eyes, slowly pulled his jeans and shoes back on, stumbled across the chamber, quietly opened the door, walked up to the sixth floor, and knocked on the door of the King's chambers.

"Who is it?"

"It's Andy again, sir. I heard you call, so I came to see what you needed."

A minute later the King pulled open the squeaky wooden door. His hair peeked out at odd angles like he had been asleep.

"Andy, I did not call you. Please go back to your chambers and get some rest. We both need it." His tone was flat.

"I'm so sorry. I could have sworn—" Andy felt his cheeks warm. He turned and headed back to his room. *What did I hear? I know it sounded like him.*

He slipped back into the warm bed but did not have opportunity to doze off before he again heard the call: "Annndyyy. Annndyyy."

Same sing-songy tone. Same unhurried pace. He doesn't sound upset— that's a relief. It's got to be the King! Andy deduced. *But if I disturb him one more time…* He shuddered. *I'm ignoring it.*

"Annndyyy. Annndyyy," it came again.

I'm crazy. That's all there is to it. Okay, fine. He pulled on his jeans and sandals, crossed the chamber, eased the door open, walked up the stairs, and again knocked on the King's chamber door.

"Who is it?" the King yawned.

"I'm really, really sorry, sir, but I could have sworn I heard you call…"

The King eased the door open fully and Andy breathed a sigh of relief when he saw the man wore a curious grin rather than an angry scowl. He had no doubt the latter would have greeted him had it been either of his parents.

"I can assure you I did not call."

Andy grimaced and swallowed hard. "I'm so sorry for disturbing you, sir."

"It's all right, Andy. I appreciate your diligence in offering help. But I'm wondering about the voice you're hearing."

That makes two of us. Andy shuffled his feet.

"Don't feel bad. Why don't you try this: the next time you hear the voice, ask it what it wants. See what it does. Let me know what happens in the morning."

Feeling like a complete idiot, Andy stammered, "Okay." *He's humoring me.* The sovereign gently closed his door and Andy smacked himself in the forehead with the palm of his hand before turning.

He returned to bed. Marta and Alden still slept, oblivious to all that had just happened. *Stupid, stupid, stupid,* Andy berated himself as he stared at the ceiling. And then he heard it again.

"Annndyyy."

This is crazy. I'm crazy!

"What do you want? Please speak," he whispered.

"About time!" came a voice in his head that sounded strangely like his father. "After your conscience brought me up to speed, I sent it back to the land you came from for a much-needed rest."

What?

"I'm your inneru."

My what?

"Your inneru."

What's that?

"In the land you come from, you call us your conscience. In the land of Oomaldee, we are referred to as innerus. Both consciences and innerus hail from the same species of innerbeings; we've always had a symbiotic relationship with humans. However, consciences have evolved to handle a more sophisticated and refined human. They are not hardy enough to withstand the harsh climate of a place like Oomaldee. Innerus are a much tougher breed. We're more down to earth and won't take your crap; we'll tell you the way things are and not sugarcoat it.

"When someone enters this land, an inneru is assigned to take over the responsibility of keeping their human's thoughts in line. That said, I have to admit, I'm not very happy about being assigned to you. I was enjoying a vacation after spending the last seventy-seven years as another's inneru. You slipped into the land very unexpectedly. Headquarters was short on available staff, so they pulled me off my vacation and here I am.

"As I was saying, I just got through being brought up to speed by your conscience. Not a good report, I must say. Seems as though you regularly ignore it and do what you please. It was worn out and despairing from all you've put it through." As the voice spoke, its tone became stern. "I refuse to be treated that way. I will not be ignored. Is that clear?"

Is that you, Dad?

"While your father is the voice of your conscience, and I also sound like him, I'm not him. When you return to your land, I will turn you back over to my counterpart. Hopefully you will treat it with more respect. In the meantime, we have a few issues to discuss. "

This is too weird. I must be dreaming.

"You're not dreaming. The exercise you just went through with the King was me."

What? You made of fool of me! How could you do that?

"Just showing you my power. I can make your life miserable if you choose to ignore me." It paused briefly, then slowly and sternly added, "I am not your conscience. I am your inneru. And I will not be trifled with."

I don't like you.

"Matters not. You can't get rid of me. Now, it seems we have an urgent matter that needs to be addressed."

Andy panicked. *Does it know about the flood I caused?*

"Come on! I'm in your thoughts. Of course I know about the flood. I also know it was an accident. But you're dying inside because you're afraid of what might happen when you're found out. That is very clear. Your stomach is upset, you've been crying, you're on edge."

Andy exhaled loudly.

"Andy, I know you've only been here a couple days, but do you care about these people?"

I guess so.

"You guess so?"

Okay, yes. I care about them.

"Exactly. That's why this is bothering you so much. Why do you care for them?"

Andy considered and finally replied, *I feel like they understand me. But I screwed up so bad! They'll never forgive me. I've hurt them too much!*

"Is your relationship with these people something you want to grow?"

I guess so.

"Then what do you think you need to do?"

Andy hesitated. *No, I can't. I can't tell anyone. They'll hate me!*
"Suit yourself."
Ugh. I really hate you.
"I'm sorry to hear that, but it's your prerogative. May I remind you I wasn't the one who got you into this predicament?"
Andy's thoughts churned until finally he wondered, *What would I even tell the King and everyone else?*
"You're smart, you figure it out."
A real help you are.

The following morning, Andy woke to a rooster crowing. He was alone in his bed. He stared at the ceiling, his stomach clenching as he tried to figure out what he would tell the King at breakfast. As he rolled over and got out of bed, he nearly stepped on a large stone lying on the floor. It was the color of amethyst, perfectly round and highly polished, the size of a baseball.

Where did this come from? He picked it up and the core began to pulse. He brought it up to examine more closely. As he did, a trumpet blast sounded as if an announcement were about to be made by an important official, much like during the Curse Day remembrance ceremony.

"It was my request that brought you here to the land of Oomaldee," a voice boomed. Andy jumped and nearly dropped the sphere. "I have great plans for you that you know not of, Andrew Ferrin Smithson. From before your birth, I have chosen you."

"What? From before my birth? Chosen *me*? To do what?" interrupted Andy. "What do you know about me or my birth?"

Ignoring Andy's questions, the message continued, "I was there as you emerged into the world and your lungs first drew breath. I was there protecting you when you were two years old and you ran out in the middle of the road. I prevented you from being struck by an oncoming car."

Andy scratched his head. "Wait a minute!" He'd heard the story about nearly getting himself killed when he was little. "How would you know anything about my life? Who are you?"

The stone continued pulsing but the voice stopped for a full minute. Andy shook the sphere and struck it against his palm. At length it continued, "I saw your curiosity and what you could do, for both good and bad. Andy, have you ever wondered why your mind works the way it does? Have you ever wondered why you feel like you never quite fit in?"

"How would you know how I feel?" The instant the words escaped, Andy wished he had not yelled. The message paused once more although the stone continued to pulse for another full minute.

"If you do what I ask, you will become a great leader in this land. Even the King will follow you."

What's it talking about? This is crazy!

"You need not know who I am or even trust me right now, although you will in time." The calm of the voice grated on Andy's nerves. He rubbed the back of his neck. With all the strange things that had happened, he was afraid the prediction might just be wild enough to be true.

The stone continued to pulse. "Tell the King everything you have heard. Leave nothing out."

"But who should I say told me?"

The rock stopped pulsing then vanished as suddenly as it had appeared. Andy stood for several minutes looking at his empty hand, trying to make sense of it all. *Well, at least now I know who brought me here.*

"Hey, let my parents know I'm okay!" he called as an afterthought.

Andy entered the dining hall and saw the King sitting at the head of the long table, wearing his standard black T-shirt and faded blue jeans.

"Good morning!" he boomed, motioning for Andy to join. "Sleep well?" he asked with a sly grin.

"I'm sorry for disturbing you last night, sir." Andy felt his face warm.

"You have nothing to apologize for. Away from home, new surroundings—I'm not surprised you thought you heard something."

Better get this over with before I lose my nerve. He took a deep breath and plunged in, "Sir, I caused the flood yesterday. It was me."

The King stopped chewing mid-bite. His eyes wandered up from his cereal, meeting Andy's. "What do you mean?"

Andy recounted everything. Partway through, he paused and took a deep breath, trying to hold back tears. "I'm sorry! I never meant to hurt anyone. It was an accident."

The King sat quietly for several minutes, considering.

Andy fidgeted as he awaited a response. *Please say something.*

"Interesting," the King at last pronounced.

He's not furious?

"I don't understand how you could have found the emergency switch. It's hidden. Only Mermin and I know where it is." He shook his head, continuing his reverie.

"I don't know, sir."

"I know telling me the truth was not easy, Andy." The sovereign's voice was even. "Your actions created a lot of damage for my servants as well as the castle—it could have collapsed."

Andy nodded and squirmed as the full weight of responsibility pressed hard. But while he staggered under the burden, the pressure crushed the cackling hyenas that had hounded his thoughts, restoring a measure of inner calm.

"Yet, you took responsibility," the King added. He paused, letting the words penetrate before concluding, "I'm proud of you."

Andy eyes met the King's. "Really?" *Maybe there's something to this truth-telling after all.*

The King raised a cautioning hand. "I'm proud of you, not for what you did, but for taking responsibility and telling me the truth even though it wasn't easy. This is a virtue I try to live by. I happen to believe that one's success comes only from responsibility, diligence, and dignity."

Andy exhaled. Never before had he done anything like this—he usually tried to take the easy way out by not coming clean.

"Thank you, sir." Andy took a bite of toast, basking in the overwhelming relief and feeling calm for the first time in several hours. But relief proved fleeting as the realization began to dawn on him that he would need to apologize to everyone he had affected. His stomach lurched.

"You okay, Andy?"

"Yeah, just thinking about how I'm going to tell everyone."

"Telling me took courage, and it shows me you care for us. By the way, why did you tell me?"

Andy shifted uncomfortably. After a moment, he blurted out, "I feel more accepted by you and everyone here than I do at home." His face burned.

"I see. No need to be embarrassed, Andy. I'm sorry that's what you think about your family. But I'm honored you feel this way about us, especially after such a short time."

Andy did not know how to respond, so he sat unmoving feeling the burn spread to his ears.

The sovereign cleared his throat. "I'm glad you told me what happened. I had been considering what actions we would need to take against King

Abaddon, assuming he was responsible. That would have resulted in war and loss of life between our lands."

Andy nodded.

"Had it been him, we would have needed to reestablish our strength lest he try to take further advantage of us. Our enemies must always know we are strong. I'm just glad you told me it was you."

Andy took a deep breath. "Oh, I almost forgot. When I was getting up this morning there was a round, purple stone laying on the floor next to my bed. When I picked it up, it started pulsing. A trumpet blasted and then it spoke."

The King's eyes grew wide. "That's a message sphere. They're not common because they're very expensive to send. How curious that you would be receiving one. You say it started with a trumpet blast?"

"That's right."

"The ones starting with a trumpet blast are from royalty." The King rubbed his chin. "What did it say?"

Andy recounted everything, just as he had been told.

"It didn't say anything about breaking the curse, did it?"

"No."

"Still, your arriving on the anniversary of Curse Day—I have to believe it's more than coincidence." The King shook his head. "All these years of enduring under the curse that I am responsible for, all these years of trying to break it with my own efforts…" His voice trailed off. "Did the message say who sent it? Most times these things tell you the sender just before they disappear."

"No. Who could it be from?"

"What color did you say it was?"

"Purple. Why?"

The sovereign shook his head. "I've no idea, although purple was the color of my father's household." He continued pondering and at last concluded, "No, that's a crazy idea."

"What is, sir?"

"Oh, nothing. It's too wild to even consider. But it's got me even more curious about whether you're here to help break the curse."

"I don't know anything about breaking curses."

"You don't have to. It sounds like whoever sent it will show you how. Please don't tell anyone what you shared with me, not even Mermin."

"I won't, sir. I promise."

"Well, at least we know who brought you. They're the only one who can send you back. And that won't happen until they're good and ready."

Andy sighed heavily. *Why me?*

The King rose and patted Andy's shoulder. "Everything will work out in due time."

What do I have to do before I can go home?

"Now, I must be off to a meeting." He gave Andy a reassuring nod. "I'm confident the servants will forgive. Trust me."

Easy for him to say. Andy's stomach started doing aerobics and he pushed his cereal away. *Maybe I'll start with Marta.*

Andy scooted back his chair, then took a deep breath and let it out slowly. Fear reared up and incited a sword fight with his resolve. Fear jabbed, *I can't do this!* But Resolve parried the blow, *Yes, you can!* The war within intensified. Not to be outdone, Fear thrust and nicked Resolve's leg. *I just need to do this!*

Trying to ignore the battle that raged, he popped his head into the kitchens and spotted Marta. *Just do it. Just do it.* The purple-haired servant smiled broadly the instant she saw him. "I made more chocolate chip cookies for you. They're over there." She pointed.

"Thanks, but I need to tell you something."

"Are you all right?" Worry creased her face.

Andy's eyes bored into the floor as the story tumbled from his lips, bringing activity around them to a halt. At length he ended with, "I'm so sorry. I never meant for any of it to happen!"

Silence screamed as he awaited the scorn and punishment he knew he deserved.

But a minute later, he felt Marta's arms around him. "I know you didn't do this on purpose. No one would. Thank you for telling me. I forgive you."

The other servants, overhearing Andy's confession, joined in more hugs.

The tall, thin servant with scruffy whiskers whom Andy had seen wrestling firewood yesterday introduced himself. "I'm Hans. What you did just now was honorable and we respect you for it. I accept your apology." He reached out and placed a reassuring hand on Andy's shoulder.

Word spread throughout the castle about all Andy had done, both bad and good. To his great relief, no one seemed angry with him, and everyone graciously accepted his apology. When he finished confessing to all the servants, he headed down to their quarters, picked up a bucket and sponge, and pitched in to help get their accommodations back in livable condition. He dragged out soggy mattresses, scrubbed walls, and mopped floors. One servant showed him how to sew new mattress covers. While it proved to be his least favorite task, he stuck to it. And even though the blisters on his hands pained him, he felt redemption every time he bumped a sensitive spot. It took nearly all day, but by the time evening came, all the servants declared satisfaction with the improved condition of their quarters.

I didn't wimp out! He couldn't help but smile.

That night at dinner, as Andy sat with the King enjoying his favorite meal of chicken and dumplings, Mermin rushed in, stumbling on his oversize robe, his hat askew. "I'm sowwy to be late for dinner, Your Majesty!" He stopped and waited for the King to acknowledge him.

The monarch nodded and Mermin pressed on, "I was just leaving to come down for dinner when I thought I heard something in your labowatory. When I investigated, nothing had been disturbed, but I happened to open Andy's mailbox and—" He pulled a golden envelope from inside his robe. "This was in it!"

He handed the envelope to the King.

"To Andy, Son of Smith, Responsible One," the King read the addressee. "Well, you seem to be very popular—first the message sphere and now this. Seeing as it is an offense punishable by imprisonment to tamper with the US Mail, why don't you open it and tell us what it says." The King winked as he passed the envelope.

A smiled broached Andy's lips as he tore it open and pulled out a short note. He intoned:

You have been faithful, now give ear to hear,
Riddle and verse and phrase to make clear.
Rely on wisdom, learned, now dear,
The salvation of Oomaldee draweth near.

In a room full of knowledge, give careful search,
To find a True Guide, the soul of the birch.
One single leaf, two covers conceal,
The keys that bring life, to you reveal.

53

"The salvation of Oomaldee! Do you know what this means?" The King beamed.

CHAPTER FIVE

A Clue!

O ver the next two days, Andy, Mermin, and the King fixated on the note, trying to decipher its meaning. They understood they needed to search someplace that sounded a lot like the Forest of Giants based upon the reference to a leaf. But what was the True Guide? And what did "the soul of a birch" mean?

They explored many fuzzy rabbit trails but found only abandoned burrows that led nowhere.

"We're so close," the King moaned two days later. "If only we could figure out this clue." He brought a fist down hard on the table, making both Andy and the wizard jump. An instant later he raised his hands in surrender. "I'm sorry. Pardon my outburst. I *know* things should be exactly as they are, but even monarchs get impatient from time to time. What could we possibly be overlooking?"

Three days later, over a breakfast of eggs and bacon, the King mulled aloud for the umpteenth time, "'Rely on wisdom, learned, now dear.' That's. What. It. Says."

Andy and Mermin met the King's gaze.

He held up his index finger. "What if—? Andy, we've been thinking about this from your perspective since the note is addressed to you. What if it's speaking to me?"

Mermin raised an eyebrow.

"Hear me out. The letter says 'rely on wisdom, learned, now dear.' Over the years I've had to learn a lot about myself. I'm a much different person, much wiser I would say. While I didn't enjoy the process, I prefer who I have become. So, if we look at this from my perspective, what might it mean?"

He read the lines again:

In a room full of knowledge, give careful search,

To find a True Guide, the soul of the birch.

One single leaf, two covers conceal,

The keys that bring life, to you reveal.

"In a room full of knowledge," began the King. "To me, that's Mermin's library. It's full of books with knowledge spanning many subjects with which we've unsuccessfully tried to break the curse."

"Wait a minute!" Mermin interjected. "I wemember a folk legend about the soul of the birch. I have a book about it upstairs in my libwawy."

The trio quickly devoured what remained of breakfast and charged up to the library. Once there, the wizard led the way to the folklore section. He waved his finger at a shelf up high. "It's up there!"

The mage glided a moveable ladder over and the King surged upward, quickly scaling the ten rungs to his target. "Which book is it?"

"The blue one to the wight of your hand, sir."

The sovereign read the spine: "*Princesses and Frogs: A Beginners Guide.* Are you sure?"

"Twy the one next to it."

"*Training Your Therewolf in Three Easy Steps.* Mermin? "

"Let me have a look, sir."

The wizard cinched up his generous robes and the pair switched places. Andy held his breath, remembering the man's recent wobbly ascent.

"*How Faiwies Found Their Home. A Histowy of Twolls. The Legends and Lore of Methuselah.*"

"What about the gold book next to that?" interjected Andy.

"Gold one? Where?"

"There, to your left."

Mermin looked again and frowned. The King tilted his head.

"I don't see the gold book you're wefewwing to, Andy."

"It's right there, by your left hand. Here, let me get it."

Mermin tottered down and Andy bounded up the ladder. He immediately grabbed the book and held it out for them to see. "See? This book."

The King and Mermin exchanged glances as Andy headed back down, book in hand. He walked over to the big table, cleared some of the clutter, and laid it down.

"Ready? What? What's wrong?"

"Andy, we don't see anything. We can't see your book."

"Really?"

"Really," confirmed the King. "But why don't you open it and tell us what you see."

Andy slowly lifted the cover to reveal white velvet lining the inside. He reached to feel it and the King and Mermin's eyes grew wide.

"Your hand!" the King exclaimed.

Andy jerked it back. "What?"

Seeing his appendage reappear, the pair gasped. "Your hand disappeared for a second," the King explained.

"It did?"

To the pair's bobbing heads Andy exclaimed, "Awesome!" He beamed and proceeded to repeat the trick several more times until Mermin interrupted.

"What else do you see?"

Andy ran his hand across the fabric. It felt soft to the touch. A sweet floral scent escaped, reminding him of his grandma. He remembered snuggling next to her reading books when he was little. He narrated his findings as he migrated through the gold tome. "There's only one page in front. It's blank. And there's a compartment behind that." Andy pulled on the matching white, looped handle to open it. "Cool! There's a gold key." Lifting it out, he showed it to his compatriots.

The sovereign recited, "'One single leaf, two covers conceal, The keys that bring life, to you reveal.' The single leaf, I'll bet that's the blank page. Two covers conceal…one cover is that of the book, the other is—the cover of invisibility. Yes, that's it. That has to be it!" A smile bloomed over the King's face. "The keys that bring life—Andy has one key, but it speaks of more than one. What else is in the book?"

"That's all, sir."

"It can't be. There must be more," insisted the King.

Andy looked back at the book. "Oh, wait! The first page has writing on it now." He read:

"A recipe for disaster,
Of the curse, you are to Master.
Collection of ingredients,
Requires diligence, obedience.

Think not to improvise,
But hold true to each noble prize.

For only with integrity,
Will you achieve for all to see.

Of the first, by you pursue,
Impenetrable covering, hard and true,
Of dragon fierce, from whence it flew,
One portion, red, from you is due."

"Interesting," said the King, rubbing his chin. "Sounds like we are to gather several ingredients in order to break the curse. And no substitutions are allowed. The first is a scale from a red dragon. It says it has to be red, so that means it has to be from an adult male."

"Red d-d-dragon?" Andy stammered.

"They are the warest of dwagon breeds, and only the adult males have wed scales. Like most dwagon species, the females and young are gway to help hide them fwom danger. It is said the wed dwagon is the fiercest of all dwagons, which is why their scales are the most valuable."

The King glanced over at Andy. "What's wrong? You've battled dragons before. I've seen you. You're very good."

"When did I ever battle a dragon?"

"In your house, Andy. You used that box with the strange weapon. I was very impressed."

Andy thought back. "Wait! You saw me playing my Dragon Slayer videogame? How's that possible?" His mouth opened and closed.

The King and Mermin exchanged glances before the former replied, "That would be the work of the Appearo Beam."

That again?

"You're weally good!" interjected Mermin.

"There's a big difference between playing a videogame and real life!"

"It's all battling dwagons. I don't see a diffewence."

"With a videogame, I'm just having fun!"

"Is not the purpose of what you call a 'videogame' to equip you with the skills you will need to survive?" the King clarified. "Your training in tracking and stealth is very rigorous. Andy, you are displaying instincts only the best dragon slayers possess, and at such a young age. It is truly a gift. In fact, I've asked Mermin to see about getting these units for our soldiers."

How can I explain? I was only playing.

The King leaned in as Andy's mind vacillated. *He looks so hopeful. He really believes I can do this. That message sphere did say I was supposed to be a leader here, but get a dragon scale? As in battle a real, live dragon? I don't know...* Andy's palms grew sweaty and he exhaled.

"You could single-handedly change this land's future," the wizard intoned.

Andy's eyes ping-ponged between the two. "All right, I'll get a scale from a red dragon for you," he sighed. *I've no clue how—*

"Excellent! Thank you!" The King patted Andy's shoulder. "Well then, we need to find a red dragon!"

"Mewodach, the dwagon master, will be at the festival. Andy can ask him where the wed dwagons are this time of year."

"An excellent idea, Mermin! Andy, Merodach is a seasoned dragon master. He's worked with these creatures longer than anyone I know. He will definitely know where to find them. But you must ask him carefully, so as not to arouse curiosity or suspicion."

"You'll be there. Can't you ask him?"

"I'm sorry, Andy, but I won't be. Neither Mermin nor I can leave the castle. It's part of the curse."

Andy shot a questioning look and the King raised a hand. "I didn't want to burden you with this, but did you wonder why we are so old when everyone else in the castle is young?"

"Actually, I hadn't thought about it, sir."

"Well, I am 509 years old, and Mermin is 507."

Andy coughed. "Did you say you're 509?"

"That's right. Because I'm responsible for bringing the curse upon Oomaldee, I have unending life. Through no fault of his own, Mermin shares my fate. We are not permitted to leave the castle."

"You can't go anywhere?"

"That's right, Andy. My greatest desire is to restore the land to its former greatness by breaking the curse. After all these years, it seems you have been brought here to accomplish this. I have every confidence you will succeed."

"As do I," Mermin echoed.

"I can't imagine—" Andy pondered aloud. "I mean, what could you possibly have done to cause the curse?"

"I will explain in due time. Our primary concern at the moment is to find a red dragon." The King paused and gently lifted Andy's chin in the palm of his hand and their eyes met. "I *will* tell you…when the time is right."

Andy nodded.

"Why don't you ask Alden to help you. You two seem to have hit it off. I'm sure he will be a great asset to the success of this mission."

Andy gave a weak smile then put the key back in the book and closed the cover. He returned it to a lower shelf in the same bookcase for safekeeping.

How in the world am I going to get a dragon scale?

CHAPTER SIX

Where Be Dragons?

The Festival starts today! The thought woke Andy. He moved to stretch but something prevented him. Opening his eyes, he saw sunshine struggling through the fog-clouded window next to his bed, but there was more…much more.

Andy thrust his shoulder at the sheet that restricted most movement save for his head. The covers constricted, making him wiggle like a worm, and he made no progress. "What's. Going. On?"

He surveyed his predicament. He was wrapped snugly in a cocoon. The corners of his sheet had been secured to one side of the bed and the blankets that kept the cold at bay to the other. "How—?"

He tried moving his shoulders, unsuccessfully.

"How do I get free?"

As his angst intensified, movement near his wardrobe caught his attention. A fuzzy brown pest started laughing raucously then darted into the closet it had thrust open.

"Hey, get back here!" Andy struggled more fervently but his frenzied movement acted like a boa constrictor slowly squeezing its meal.

"Help! Help!"

At his protests, the monkey-screeching grew louder and the thuds, thumps, and shaking of his wardrobe told him he would soon face more dire actions from the little menace.

"When I'm free, I'm gonna get you!" His threat only met with the sounds of fabric ripping.

"Help! Help!"

What seemed like an hour passed, although Andy knew it could not have been more than ten minutes, and he began feeling sympathy for mummies.

"Heeelllpppp!" He extended the length of his cries.

"Hhhheeeelllllppp!" He changed the pitch of his calls.

"HhhHeeEeelllLLLllpppPPP!" He moderated the tempo.

"Hhhh. Eeeee. Llll. Pppp." He added a beat, synchronizing the gremlin's thumps with his pleas.

A knock at last came on his door.

"Come in! Please—"

"Goodness! What happened?" A girl apprentice from the tailor's shop just down the hall popped in and spied Andy's predicament.

"Can you free me?"

"Gracious, let me see what I can do."

The boggart slammed a door to the wardrobe and bolted between the maid's legs, drawing a shriek. The girl drew her hands to her face then fumbled with her white cap while twisting to watch the menace disappear out the door. "I hate those things!"

"Yeah, me too. Now can you…?"

"Oh. Of course. Sorry."

Andy told the girl his story as she untied the sheet and blankets. "Do you have boggart problems often? Mermin didn't seem surprised it was here."

"We do. I think it's the same one. The tricks it plays on everyone are horrible. Why, last month it got into the shop and destroyed much of the fabric, not to mention making a complete mess of the place."

"How do you get rid of them?"

"Usually salt and a horseshoe."

Andy tilted his head.

"There's usually a horseshoe at each entrance to keep it away. It probably managed to loose one of them. We have to chase it out before we can put the horseshoe back up."

Now free, Andy scratched the back of his head. "Where's the salt come in?"

"Oh, salt is the only thing it hates, so we go after it with that and direct it back outside."

"I see." Andy suppressed a laugh, although it took everything he had to keep a serious expression. "Is there nothing that can keep it away permanently?"

The maid shook her head. "Not that I know of."

We'll just see about that. It's done one too many pranks!

"Couldn't get yourself out of bed this morning?" the King grinned at Andy's late arrival in the dining hall.

"Actually, sir, that's more true than you might think." Andy described his ordeal, ending with his vow to rid the castle of the pest once and for all.

"You have my blessing! That thing is nothing but trouble."

Andy had just finished his toast and eggs when the King said, "In addition to your self-declared quest to rid us of the boggart, your mission today is to find Merodach, the dragon master. He's a rather large fellow, balding, with only three fingers on his left hand."

Mermin leaned over and whispered, "Bit of a wun in with a dwagon that helped itself to a couple of his fingers, I hear."

"He usually wears a bright red sash with yellow flames, evidence of his accomplishments," the King continued. "Red dragons migrate throughout the year. You need to find out where they are currently. If there are any in the land, he will know. Whatever you do, don't let on you're finding out for me. By the way, I suggest you wear servant's livery so you blend in. I had the tailor make you a few changes. They should be in your chambers by now."

"What if there aren't any red dragons in the land?"

"We'll worry about that if the time comes. For now, let's find out what he can tell us."

As breakfast ended, the King handed Andy several silver coins. "Nine quirts and a spanning ought to give you enough fun at the festival. It's nine quirts to a spanning," he added with a wink.

"But how much is that?"

"You and Alden are going together, correct?"

"Yes."

"I'm sure he can help you figure that out. Now go have fun!"

Andy jogged up to his chambers and spotted a bright blue tunic and green leggings neatly laid out on his bed. The mess of a wardrobe he'd left earlier had been reorganized and set right. He pulled the tunic over his head and found it went only to the middle of his thigh. *I feel… exposed.* He struggled to pull on the leggings—pull and squat, pull and squat, shimmy and squat, shimmy and squat. *Is this what women go through back home?*

As secure as they would ever be, the leggings itched and felt strange as they hugged his legs. He bent and scratched. *Ugh.* At least the sandals are comfortable. He rooted after an itch hiding at the top of his leggings like a gopher digging its burrow. He added the coins to a leather pouch the tailor had also left for him, then hung the small bag around his neck and tucked it inside his tunic.

Andy made his way down to the kitchens and found Marta.

"My, don't you look handsome!"

"The leggings itch," he complained as he leaned over to ferret out another itch.

"Well, you look fine, Andy!" she reassured. "Alden will be here in a minute. Would you like a chocolate chip cookie while you wait?"

Not wanting to dim her smile, Andy downed a tasty treat. He never got chocolate chip cookies at home. He made three more disappear before Alden arrived.

"You look…different!" Alden snickered as he spotted Andy.

"Thanks," Andy mumbled, fumbling with the bottom hem of the tunic.

"Oh, stop it, Alden. I think he looks handsome. The two of you get along now. Have fun, but be home before dinner." Marta handed Alden a few coins and, after each stuffing three cookies into their mouths, the pair departed.

The Festival of Oomaldee had been designed to give all the regions of the kingdom opportunities to compete for bragging rights in a variety of contests. The venue allowed people to hear the latest bands and, given the King's desire to regain technological superiority, festivalgoers could also see and experience new innovations being developed by citizens, as well as by the King. Festivities spanned two full weeks and marked the highlight of the year for most.

The regions of Oomaldee rotated hosting the event. This year the city of Oops, just outside the castle, played host, so Andy and Alden walked. They struck out from the castle to sunshine and lighter-than-usual fog. They could see several feet in front of them, superior conditions compared to what Andy had experienced over the past several days. But the closeness still made him feel claustrophobic.

The trees had turned brilliant gold and orange and red, and Andy stomped on fallen leaves as they walked, grinning. "We don't have Fall where I'm from."

Alden furrowed his brow.

"In Texas, we get hot summers and freezing winters, but not much in between. Certainly not all these leaves!" Andy launched into a clump of gold and red by the path, then picked up a handful and thrust it at his companion.

"Hey!" Alden swept up a pile of his own and dished them right back.

The scowling faces of a passing family called a stop to the melee several minutes later. The pair brushed leaves from their clothes and hair before continuing on.

They had ventured only a short way when they began seeing banners announcing the festival. Arrows directed people toward the entrance. They reached a clearing where crowds gathered, waiting for the commencement of activities.

Andy and Alden recognized several castle servants milling about and joined them. Hans was there, along with several others Andy had met while helping clean up after the flood. He spotted Hannah not far away and waved. She waved back, blushing. The man with the long arms he had seen tasting the King's food scowled when he saw Andy, jerked his shoulders back and waddled away.

"Not a very friendly sort," commented Andy to Alden. "He always scowls when he sees me."

"Don't worry about him," reassured Alden. "His name is Razen. You'd scowl, too, if your name sounded like a dried fruit." The boys shared a laugh.

"I heard he came a long time ago, after Abaddon attacked the castle and carried away the King's food taster, Eliazer," Alden informed. "Hans says he saw Eliazer fighting, but when the battle ended, they didn't find his body. He figures Abaddon's army captured him. Razen came to the castle after that. He doesn't like new people. It took him over a year to stop scowling every time he sees me."

Hans sauntered over. "Are you ready for the Tower Chase, Alden?"

"I hope so. I'll do my best."

"Attaboy! That's all you can ask of yourself. To not be happy with your best is not dignified."

"Please join me in opening these festivities!" the governor of Oops bellowed, at which a roar went up and everyone poured under the entry banner, separating the boys from Hans and pulling them toward a clearing where rows and rows of brightly colored tents stood in lines like soldiers in formation.

The delicious smell of funnel cakes assaulted Andy's senses. *They have them in Oomaldee! I have to get one!*

"Cartesians aren't welcome here!" A youth much bigger than either of them shouted over the crowd, leering at Alden's neon-green hair. "You heard me, boy! You're not welcome here. Get yourself on home where you belong."

"What's this about?" Andy questioned.

"People from Oomaldee consider those of us from Carta to be foreigners, and they don't like us much."

Andy remembered Marta saying something to that effect as well. "Ignore him. He's just a bully. Come on, let's see what there is to do."

"Hey, get back here! I'm not done with you!" the heckler taunted as they hurried away. "Yeah, run ya little sissies!"

They left the crowd and slowed their pace. Andy glanced up. At the edge of the fog, he could make out the shapes of five or six huge black birds circling above, like vultures hunting for their next meal. The birds appeared larger than any Andy had ever seen—and close.

"What are those things?"

"I overheard His Majesty say King Abaddon has bird spies that circle the skies of Oomaldee."

"They give me the creeps. I feel like they're going to swoop down and grab me for breakfast."

Alden laughed. "I've never heard of that happening. Hey, let's grab something to eat."

"Sounds good to me!"

They gorged themselves at booths selling candy apples, fried butter bits, huge barbecued turkey legs, and fudge of all varieties, including chili flavor, which proved to be Andy's favorite because he loved spicy food. After considerable searching, they sniffed out the tent selling funnel cakes, although they were called fried mesh marvels in Oomaldee—the sugary treats electrified Andy's taste buds.

As they munched cheesy popcorn, Andy saw one of the large black birds land nearby then waddle behind a tent. It stood just shy of his height!

"Come on." Andy motioned for Alden to follow.

They crept around to where they spied the large bird's feet under the open bottom of the tent. Clawed feet transformed into bare human feet.

"Did you see that?" Andy whispered.

The creature rummaged in a sack that had been stashed nearby. A minute later a short, plump man with arms extending nearly to his ankles emerged and blended into the mingling crowd.

"His wings transformed into arms!" Alden mimed the sway of the man's appendages.

"We need to tell the King tonight."

Alden nodded, eyes wide.

"Hey, I promised the King we'd find Merodach, the dragon trainer. He said you could probably help."

"Why do you need to find him?"

CHAPTER SEVEN

The Dragon Trainer

A s they walked, Andy filled Alden in on everything that had happened since he arrived. He left out the part about the message sphere and him being chosen, however, since he wasn't sure what Alden might think.

"So, you're supposed to get the scale of a red dragon?" confirmed Alden in the end.

"Yes, and you're supposed to help me."

Alden stopped. "The King said that? But I don't know anything about dragons. I'm just a servant."

"I don't know why you keep saying 'I'm just a servant.' He thinks a lot of you or he wouldn't have suggested you come with me. By the way, if it makes you feel any better, I don't know anything about dragons either. Not real ones at least." Andy grimaced.

Alden shook his head. "Great. Neither of us knows anything about dragons. We're so going to die!" The drama in his tone made both boys snicker and burst out laughing.

They made their way to the main street of the festival late in the afternoon and refocused on finding the dragon master. "Where should we start?"

"I know the general area Merodach probably is," Alden informed. "It's an open field at the back of the festival grounds where there's plenty of room for dragons to stretch out. I've heard dragon trainers say, 'The more room dragons have, the less fierce they are—the more closed in the surroundings, the more fierce they become.'"

"Lead the way."

The festival grounds were extensive, and it took the boys several minutes to reach the area. As they walked, they could hear bands playing off in the distance. They emerged out into an open grassy field. Several makeshift campsites with one-person pup tents dotted the field like white chicken pox. Dragons were staked between.

"How'd you like to sleep between dragons?" quipped Andy.

"Ah, no thanks."

Ten dragons paced a good distance apart across the immense field, each a different color: yellow, pale orange, dark blue, purple, green, pink, bright orange, brown, crimson, and bright blue. They all sported a multitude of horns.

A metal ring around a hind foot staked each brute in place, but that hardly seemed substantial enough if any one of them got upset. For now the dragons seemed calm. As the boys inched closer, they heard a low rumbling sound.

"What's that noise?" asked Andy.

"It's the dragons growling at each other."

"Sounds like a freight train in the distance."

"Freight train?" asked Alden.

"Don't worry about it. Dragons give me the creeps."

Alden glanced at Andy and shuddered. "Me too."

As they drew near, Andy whispered, "These dragons are huge!"

The area was strangely quiet. Ahead they saw a group of twelve or so gruff, unkempt trainers standing around a campfire and speaking to each other in hushed whispers. Several water-filled buckets stood nearby.

"Let's go see if they know where Merodach is," Andy suggested.

"You sure? These guys have a reputation for being ruthless."

"You have any better ideas?"

"Well, no."

"Then come on, let's go ask them."

Andy headed through a large common cook site and past a smoldering fire. Alden followed. On the way, Andy tripped over the handle of a cast-iron skillet that stuck out into the path. He fell, doing a face-plant in the dirt. The skillet hit a lantern that stood next to it. Glass shattered and something else crashed to the ground, making a huge racket. Two dragons nearby raised their heads and roared at the commotion. The dark blue dragon reared up on its hind legs and sent a blast of fire at the yellow dragon several yards away. The yellow dragon retaliated and met its attacker with a blast of its own. The pup tent that had been between the two dragons caught fire. Several other dragons began tossing their heads and roaring.

The trainers sprang into action. Grabbing buckets full of water and two blankets, they doused the sparring dragons, distracting them, while a trainer climbed onto the back of each. Both dragons shot flames at each other, but the yellow dragon's fire connected with the trainer. A deep-throated scream sounded just before the man on the blue dragon fell off. Another trainer took his place. Two trainers tried throwing blankets over the dragons' heads between blasts of fire and struggled to hold on to the lunging beasts. After several failed attempts, they finally secured the blankets around the dragons' horns and under their chins. Both beasts struggled for several minutes, tossing their heads about wildly and trying to remove the blindfold. At last, they both calmed down. The trainers who had ridden out the storm on their backs dismounted.

"You okay, Ror?" one of them asked the man who had been burned.

"I've had worse," he replied, standing up and walking over to the few remaining water buckets and cleaning his burns. "Get me something to wrap this with."

The rest of the men turned piercing eyes on Andy and Alden, then slowly encircled the boys, who froze in terror.

"What do you think you were doing?" accused the self-appointed leader.

"I'm sorry!" pleaded Andy, afraid he and Alden might not live to see tomorrow.

"Keep your voice down, boy," the man scolded in a gruff whisper. "You nearly created a ruckus with *all* the dragons. Do you have any idea what could have happened?"

"I'm very sorry, sir. I didn't mean—" whispered Andy. "Is there anything I can do to make it up to you?"

"Yeah, you and your green-haired friend can get outta here, and stay out," the trainer hissed in a stern voice.

The other trainers remained stone-faced and glaring. One mumbled, "Stupid kids. They have no clue."

Before retreating, Andy summoned his courage and asked, "We are looking for Merodach. Would you happen to know where we might find him?"

"Merodach? What would two servant boys want with him?"

Without missing a beat, Andy said, "I want to learn how to battle a red dragon, and I was told Merodach could teach me."

The trainer stared at Andy in disbelief and then broke out in controlled bursts of laughter that would have been heard for miles were volume not an issue. Several others fell to the ground, holding their stomachs, aching from fits of laughter.

"That's…the stupidest…thing…I've ever…heard," the trainer managed to spit out.

"You two? Battle a red dragon? Are you out of your minds?" interjected another.

After several minutes, the trainer pulled himself together and said to Andy, "Merodach is over there in his tent, catching up on some sleep." He motioned to an oversized, tattered gray pup tent pitched beside a large oak tree. "By the time you've convinced him to teach you how to battle a red dragon, you'll have already mastered the art." He broke off in heaves of laughter once again. The rest of the trainers followed suit.

The pair headed for the dragon master's tent. The trainer hissed a warning after them, "He don't like Cartesians. Might feed your friend to a dragon just for fun." Muted laughter broke out once more behind them.

Andy looked back at Alden who followed. "Don't mind them."

"Don't worry, I don't."

They reached Merodach's tent and stood outside listening. Heavy breathing mixed with snoring came from within. They sat down in the shade of the oak tree and waited for the man to awaken. They played with the grass under their feet and twigs on the ground nearby, and still the dragon master slept on. They climbed the lower branches of the oak tree and gradually made their way to the topmost where they got a bird's-eye view of the festival as far as the fog would permit them. The sun started going down and their stomachs began growling, but the man slept on.

"Do you think we should come back tomorrow?" asked Alden. "No telling how long he's going to sleep."

"I'm not leaving until I've spoken to Merodach. What we need from him is too important." Andy's stomach dissented, grumbling at the news. *And I can't go home...*

"Well, I'm starving. I'm going to get us something to eat."

Alden shinnied down the tree and left to retrieve dinner. He was back in no time, handing Andy some treats that smelled amazing. Andy's belly intoned a blessing over the Cartesian. The deep-fried turkey drumstick and pork rolls in BBQ sauce tasted even more mouthwatering than they smelled!

At the scent of the delicious fare, Merodach roused, yawned a yawn that sounded exactly like the beast the trainer had mastered, and stuck his head out of the pup tent. "Who's there and what'd you bring me to eat?" he bellowed.

His black curly hair stuck out at odd angles, like a startled cat crowning his head. Clearly he was not friends with a comb, for his bushy beard was full of morsels from past meals. As he crawled out of the tent, his enormous belly brushed the ground, adding yet another layer of dirt to his well-soiled plaid shirt, the buttons of which were stretched to their limits over his generous girth. His left hand was missing two fingers. Merodach liberally scratched his big butt as he stood.

Even though Andy craved the food, he said, "I'm Andy, and this is Alden. Someone told me you know all about red dragons and how to find them. You can have our food if you tell us where they are at this time of year."

Merodach, who towered several feet over them, grinned. "Think you can bargain with me, huh, boy? The last fellow who tried that went missing for quite some time. His body was finally found washed down a river."

Alden glanced quickly at Andy, but Andy ignored him.

"Please, sir, I just need to know where I can find a red dragon."

"Well, why don't you start by minding your manners and giving me that turkey drumstick. That might help my memory."

Andy passed his partially consumed dinner to Merodach who had seated himself on the grass next to the tree trunk. Immediately, the man began greedily devouring the turkey leg, dripping grease down his beard. Between voracious bites, Merodach asked, "What would two servant boys from the King's castle need a red dragon for? Surely the King could get one for you if you asked as nicely as you're asking me," he grinned. "Have you asked the King so nicely for a wittle wed dwagon to play with? You can feed your friend to it. Red dragons love folks from Carta," he chided as he took another oversize bite.

Merodach devoured the turkey legs, fried mesh marvels, candy apple, three donuts, and taffy, all the while grunting and slobbering. When he had finished, he let out a thunderous belch, lay down on the grass, and closed his eyes, ready to doze off again.

"So now that you're full, where are the red dragons?" Andy's patience wore thin, and while he attempted to hide his annoyance, his tone betrayed him.

The dragon master ignored the question.

We're getting nowhere this way. Inspiration struck when Andy noticed a bright red sash with yellow flames hanging in the opening of the pup tent, and he moved quietly toward it.

Andy cleared his throat. "Oh Mr. Merodach—"

The beefy brute opened one eye. Andy picked up the sash and slowly walked toward him. Merodach sat up. The dragon master had brawn, but Andy and Alden both had greater speed and quickness, and the man knew it.

"All right, boy, hand that to me."

"Not until you tell me where I can find a red dragon."

"Boy, I said give it here."

Andy took a step backward. Alden followed.

"I'll give you back your sash when you tell me where I can find a red dragon."

Merodach and Andy glared at each other for a full minute before the dragon master relented. "Fine. You can find red dragons in the Dragon's Lair in Abbadon's land, Hadession."

"Is that where they are right now? Because I know they migrate depending upon the time of year."

"Yes, they are there now. I was there not more than a month ago and saw them. Now give me back my sash."

"How do I know you're telling me the truth?"

"You don't, but I can call the other trainers over there. They'd be happy to help convince you."

Andy caught Alden's eye then turned back to Merodach. "Here's your sash, you overgrown baboon." At this, Andy threw the sash at Merodach and the pair took off running, back toward the main street of the festival.

Andy glanced over his shoulder. Several of the trainers had started after them. "Faster, Alden!"

They lost their pursuers before leaving the festival grounds, but with the sun casting long shadows, they headed for home. After crossing the drawbridge, Alden reminded, "We need to tell the King about that vulture-man."

"Do you know where King Hercalon is?" Andy questioned the first servant he saw.

"Up in the laboratory with Mermin," the little woman replied.

The pair bolted up the stairs and knocked loudly on the door.

"Enter," Mermin invited.

The King and wizard sat on tall stools at a large table and studied a scroll laid out in front of them. They looked up in unison.

"Well, how'd you enjoy the festival today?" A grin spread across the King's face. Mermin pushed his glasses back up his knotty nose.

"It was great!" Andy beamed. "There's so much awesome food!"

A duet of chuckles acknowledged his outburst.

"There certainly is," the sovereign agreed.

"But we also saw something we think you should know about," Andy continued. The boys spilled everything they had seen, finishing with, "So, what are you going to do?"

The King sat quietly rubbing his chin. After a long silence, he finally spoke. "Based upon reports I'm getting from my field troops, I knew King Abaddon was using those birds to spy on us. But I had no idea they could change into men."

"How do you know they're working for Abaddon?" asked Andy.

"King Abaddon is our only enemy. Seems to me, he's the only one who would care to spy on us."

"Oh. But I've seen people who look like that guy here in the castle. Aren't you afraid they're informants?"

"What would you have me do, round them all up because they resemble that man?"

"I don't know exactly, sir." Andy looked to Alden for support, but the Cartesian remained silent.

"I wouldn't want spies reporting everything I'm doing."

"Well, these people have been under my care for quite some time. If they are indeed spying on us, they certainly wouldn't have much of importance to report. No, I don't think we need to do anything just yet, if at all."

Andy raised a finger to object but the King continued, "Let's suppose your theory is correct, that Abaddon is gathering information on us. If we got rid of these servants, our enemy would know immediately that we are on to him. What do you suppose would happen then? Would he just stop spying on us?"

"Probably not. He'd just figure out a different way."

"Exactly. And then we'd need to figure out his new methodology."

The boys nodded.

"By not doing anything, we can control what he learns about us. This is a much stronger position to be in."

Mermin smiled. "I have to agwee, Majesty."

"What will he do if he knows about me?" Andy bit his lip.

"No doubt he already does. We need to be careful not to let him know why you're here, lest he seek to harm you."

"Why would he do that?"

"Andy, do you mind if I tell Alden what you shared with me?"

Andy met the King's eyes. *He's asking my permission? That never happens at home.* "No, not at all, sir."

"Alden, you are sworn to secrecy. You may tell no one."

"I understand, Your Majesty."

"As I alluded to during Curse Day, Andy has been brought here to break the curse." The King proceeded to recount what he, Mermin, and Andy had discovered, both about the clue and the message sphere.

Alden's gaze bounced from his sovereign to Andy. "Really?"

"Really," the king confirmed. "But as I said, you are sworn to secrecy. If you let this slip, you could be putting Andy's life in danger. You see, the curse gives Abaddon superiority over us in many ways. He would not want us to regain our former advantage over him. I believe he would come after Andy if he ever found out."

"I understand, sir. I promise not to say a word."

"Not even to your mother."

Alden nodded.

"Thank you. And now, do you have an update on finding the red dragons? Did you find Merodach?"

CHAPTER EIGHT

Poisoned!

"So, Merodach said the red dragons are currently in the Dragon's Lair in the land of Hadession?" the King summarized after the boys had recounted their adventure. "You did well to get this information. While I'm not sure I agree with your tactics in taking Merodach's sash, that was quick thinking, and you and Alden stayed safe." He paused and locked eyes with both of them. "I think you will do well on this quest." He put a hand on their shoulders and gave a gentle squeeze.

Confidence flowed from the sovereign—Andy's insides tingled as if a freshly shaken can of soda released its bubbles and filled him up.

The King stood and shifted to the other table where a map of Oomaldee was spread. He pointed out where the Dragon's Lair was located to the northeast of the castle in the land of Hadession—where King Abaddon ruled with an iron fist and much cruelty according to most reports.

"We must plan your trip carefully," declared the King, studying the map. "There are many obstacles you must overcome to successfully get there and back. One of my biggest concerns is how you'll get past the great wall that surrounds Oomaldee without being seen, for we must keep this journey secret from all. The last thing I want is for Abaddon to find out we are trespassing into his land."

Mermin, Andy, and Alden all bobbed heads.

"Okay then, Mermin and I will work out the best route while you boys enjoy the festival over these next few days."

Alden's stomach rumbled and he threw a hand over his mouth, eyes wide.

"Sounds like it's time for dinner," Mermin chortled.

"Oh, and Alden," the King added, "I wish you much success in the Tower Chase."

Alden's jaw dropped. "You know about that, sir?"

"Of course," he chuckled. "And from the sounds of things, you're very good."

Alden blushed. "I'll do my best, sir."

Andy reached the door first and as he turned the knob, he heard footsteps scurrying away. He yanked it open and raced out into the corridor. He scanned both directions but saw no one.

"What's wrong?"

"Sir, I heard someone hurry away."

"Was it that confounded boggart?" the King groused.

"I don't think so. The boggart usually makes a lot more noise."

"Let's hope no one was eavesdwopping," Mermin frowned, voicing the concern running through all their minds.

The day finally arrived for Alden's Tower Chase event. Andy got up early, rushed through breakfast, and joined Alden at Optimistic's stall. Alden looked all business in his royal-blue riding coat with the castle crest on his left sleeve. He wore his bright green breeches and had shined his black boots until you could see your reflection in them. His royal-blue helmet lay on top of the hay near the stall door.

"How you feeling?"

"A little nervous."

"You'll do great. I've seen you practice. You're ready."

"I hope so."

Alden saddled Optimistic and led her outside into the bright fog of the stable yard. She could sense Alden's nervousness and danced in antsy anticipation. He mounted her and looked down at Andy.

"I'll do my best. I know it's all I can ask of myself. I can't do any better than that."

Andy shook his head and laughed. "You'll do great! And, for the record, I think you're going to win."

Alden smiled back. "Thanks."

"I'll see you over at the arena."

"Okay girl, let's go!" It took no convincing. Optimistic took to a gallop and launched.

As soon as the fog had hidden the pair, Andy turned and caught sight of a servant with arms that brushed his ankles, standing at a nearby door. Andy had seen the guy once before in the stables, and seeing him again sent a chill down Andy's spine. The little man frowned and then scurried away, just as he'd done the first time. The hair on the back of Andy's neck rose to attention.

Andy walked the now familiar path to the festival by himself, feeling strangely alone despite the crowds surrounding him. Since he had arrived at the castle and met Alden, they had spent a lot of time together. Now, by himself, he missed the familiarity of his friend by his side.

I've never had a friend like Alden. I can be myself and he never laughs at me. And Marta is so different from Mom. Andy roused from his thoughts as the throng pushed him under the festival entry banner.

As he approached the arena, that all-too-familiar stench grew stronger. Andy swatted at the odor, receiving chuckles from spectators behind him. But with nothing else to combat it, Andy smothered his nose in the bend of his elbow. *How can they stand it? I've got to ask Alden!* A uniformed attendant thrust nose plugs into his hand as he mounted the steps leading to the spectator seats. "Thank you!" he intoned in a nasally voice.

An official was announcing the order of events that were to follow as Andy scanned the sea of people. Finally, he spotted Alden atop his purple pegasus near a gate at the end of the arena. Andy waved. Alden shot back a big smile and a thumbs-up. Andy spotted Marta and Hans cheering in the Friends box, but there were no open seats near them.

"Excuse me. Excuse me. Pardon me. Oh. Sorry." Andy crawled over half a row of spectators, avoiding as many toes as possible, and finally nested next to a sandy-haired man whose chants announced his allegiance to one of Alden's competitors.

Andy perused his program. Alden was set to ride third. As the announcer introduced each rider, the crowd erupted in a cheer.

"And now, from His Majesty's castle, riding Optimistic, please welcome Alden," crowed the announcer a few minutes later. Alden trotted to the middle of the ring, respectfully removed his helmet, and bowed to the officials. At the sight of Alden's green hair, silence blanketed the arena. Andy's neighbor muttered, "What an insult. Why are they even letting that kind compete?" A few jeers of "Go home, Cartesian!" punctuated the scene.

Alden scanned the crowd and set his jaw.

For someone who calls himself "just a servant" he sure looks determined to make a name for himself

A minute later, Alden launched Optimistic up, up, up. Around floating poles and through suspended ovals they flew, just as they had done in practice—they were beautiful together, flying in perfect harmony. Alden's ride was going flawlessly.

Then, two rows ahead, the vulture-man from the stables stood. He was holding a narrow tube up to his mouth.

What's he doing?

Alden raced Optimistic over everyone's heads as he drove her vertically up and up and upside down, performing the requisite loop. Just as Alden cleared the stands, the little man lowered the narrow tube and ducked down. An official who had been standing in the center ring in front of Andy collapsed.

What just happened?

As Alden approached the stands again for his next obstacle, the little man popped back up, hurriedly loaded something into the straw, and once more raised it to his mouth.

He's trying to hit Alden with something as he flies over!

Andy launched himself over the intervening two rows of people and tackled the bird-man. He grabbed the straw and wrestled it away.

Immediately, Andy felt something scratch him. "Ouch!" he yelped as pain shot down his left forearm.

Andy reached for his arm and yelled, "He's trying to hurt Alden!" No sooner had the words exploded than he began feeling lightheaded.

"Ha, ha, ha, ha, ha!" Andy overheard a lady laughing uncontrollably. Her outburst sounded evil.

I've heard that voice before! What's going on?

"Imogenia! How could you!" a man's voice challenged.

Then everything went dark.

Andy woke to find himself in bed. His head felt like it might explode, and his stomach wasn't much better. His left arm was wrapped in a cloth bandage and elevated in a sling. Alden and Marta sat nearby. Hans stood at the end of his bed.

"Wh-wh-at hap-p-pened?" Andy rubbed his eyes with his free hand.

"You're awake!" rejoiced Alden. "You've been sleeping for three days."

Andy tried to sit up, but his head screamed when he lifted it off the pillow.

"You gave us quite a scare," intoned Marta, leaning over Andy to kiss his forehead.

"That's for sure," added Hans. "I knew it was a poison dart, but I didn't know which poison. It took all my medical training to finally figure it out."

"The King and Mermin have been by regularly to check on your progress," informed Marta.

"I'll let them know he's awake," Alden interrupted, jogging out door.

Moments later the King and Mermin appeared.

"Well, Andy, that was quite a surprise you gave us," intoned the King. "What happened?"

"Near as we can determine, Alden was doing his run in the Tower Chase when one of the stable servants tried to shoot him with a poison dart from the stands."

"Yes, I remember. The vulture-guy. He was sitting two rows in front of me. He shot once."

"Yes, Andy. The first dart hit an official who was standing in the center ring. Unfortunately, she has yet to regain consciousness."

"Really? That's terrible!"

The King and Mermin nodded.

"The guy tried a second time as Alden was coming around again. I couldn't let him hit Alden or Optimistic, so I tackled him. That's all I remember."

"Yes, Andy. Apparently you disarmed him. Unfortunately, he had another dart in his pocket. As soon as it scratched you, the poison knocked you out. Lucky for Alden, you passed out on top of the man and he could do no more harm. The guards arrested him. He's being held in the dungeons."

"Why would he do such a thing?"

"While he is being questioned extensively, his motives are not yet known. It could be he is prejudiced against Cartesians, as you have witnessed, or it could be—" The King glanced quickly at Marta then back at Andy and Alden.

Andy finished the King's thought—*that Abaddon has somehow learned about our plan to visit the Dragon's Lair and wants to stop us. Was that the guy who was eavesdropping?*

"Whatever his motive, we need to take extra care. Andy, I'm very glad to see you're recovering. You did a brave thing in stopping that threat. I'm proud of you!"

Andy felt his cheeks warm and his stomach did a happy dance. Savoring the praise yet trying to hide his embarrassment, he deflected: "Where did you finish, Alden?"

"Alden took first place in the competition!" Marta beamed and pulled back her shoulders.

"I knew it!" shouted Andy. "Oh ouch!" He reached for his head. "I guess I'd better not yell."

"It was awesome. During the awards ceremony, the crowd was completely quiet. There was no heckling. Some even cheered." A smile perched itself on Alden's face.

"Was that better than the award?" asked Andy.

Alden thought for a minute. "I think they were both great."

"I knew you'd win it. I had no doubt."

"You had more confidence than me—"

"I know I've said it before, Alden, but congratulations again," the King interrupted. "You truly did an outstanding job for yourself as well as the castle."

"Thank you, sir."

"We'll visit you again later, Andy. For now, get some rest." With that, the King and Mermin left.

"Well, I've dinner to help prepare. Alden, stay with Andy in case he needs anything. Andy, get some rest," instructed Marta. She walked over to the bed, kissed Andy on the top of his head one more time and tousled his hair, then headed for the door. *I wish Mom would do that when I'm sick, instead of always being so busy.*

Andy's attention was drawn back as Alden said, "I know this sounds weird, but you saved my life."

"You're my friend. What was I supposed to do?"

"Well…thank you."

"You can save my life the next time." Andy smiled, coaxing Alden's brow upward.

CHAPTER NINE

A Perilous Journey

T hree days later, Andy, Alden, the King, and Mermin met in the laboratory. "Have you discovered that servant's motive yet?" asked Andy.

"So far it remains unclear." The King held up a hand. "Until we know why he tried to poison Alden, we won't know what action to take."

"I think Razen might be a spy," Andy blurted.

"Do you now?" Mermin raised an eyebrow.

Andy exchanged a look with Alden.

"What pwoof do you have?"

"Well, he looks like that guy you're questioning and…well, he always scowls at me."

"Andy, if you're suggesting we arrest people who resemble the perpetrator and scowl at you…" the King cautioned.

"But sir, if that guy tried to hurt Alden because he's helping Abaddon—if the servants who look like that are spies—other people might get hurt before we know."

The King shook his head. "All will be made clear in time, Andy. We will continue to press the servant, and he will come to understand that it is in his best interest to tell us what motivated him. If you ever see the dungeon where he's being kept, you'll understand."

Andy's mind flashed back to the wisps of putrid green vapor seeping from under the dungeon door. He also remembered the raised area that looked like someone or something had punched it from the inside. He let his argument drop for now.

"While you've been recovering, Mermin and I have been planning your route to the Dragon's Lair," said the King, changing the subject.

They all moved over to the table where the map of Oomaldee lay open.

"The day after tomorrow, when the festival is over, I'd like you and Alden to set out to retrieve the red dragon scale," the King began. "If all goes well, it should take you four days to reach the Dragon's Lair. Mermin and I believe the best route for you to take is through the city of Oops to the Goozy Bog, right here." He pointed to a location on the map. "Be careful to stay away from the edges of the bog as there are patches of quicksand."

"You don't want to fall into one of those," Mermin interjected. "You could dwown. Your feet get stuck, and you just keep sinking and sinking. The quicksand eventually covers your head and you dwown. Nothing much you can do once you get stuck in quicksand. Yep, you'd dwown."

Andy and Alden ricocheted looks, eyes wide.

The King cleared his throat. "Thank you for that, Mermin. Now, as I was saying…from the Goozy Bog, follow its edge to the village of Oohhh. The Forest of Giants will be off to your right. Be sure to keep your distance, for it is a dark and dangerous place. Many an unwary traveler who has gotten too close to the forest has turned up missing."

"What happened to them?" Andy couldn't keep the quake out of his voice. Alden glanced between Andy and the King.

"No one knows for sure. Some say there are giant plants that gwab people and cawwy them to their deaths. Other folks say vicious giants eat people," explained Mermin matter-of-factly. "The last person to go into the fowest that I know of was an old cwazy lady, Anta Emm. Don't know what made her do it, but she up and walked into the fowest. Never been seen or heard fwom since."

Andy shifted on his stool.

"You will be safe as long as you follow the edge of the bog," the King reassured. "Once you reach the village of Oohhh, travel northeast until you reach the Great Wall. Take care not to be seen by the soldiers stationed in the Greenleaf watchtower. If they see you, they will stop and question you as to what you are doing in those parts. If you can't provide a satisfactory explanation, they will think you are spies and apprehend you."

Andy looked over at Alden as his mouth dropped open.

"Let's make sure that doesn't happen," the King suggested.

The pair bobbed heads.

"The Forest of Giants goes right up to the Great Wall at the Greenleaf watchtower. So you'll want to cross that section as quickly and quietly as possible. Follow the Great Wall until you come to the Victory watchtower. You'll know it easily because this is where the Slither River, Red River, and Blood River merge."

"Excuse me, sir," interrupted Andy, "but why are the rivers named Red River and Blood River?"

"Many years ago, King Abaddon snuck into the land of Oomaldee on the Slither River under the Victory watchtower. He and his troops laid in wait for our forces who were up in that area on training exercises. They ambushed our troops and over fifteen thousand of our men died. The two rivers ran red with blood. Only when our forces took refuge on nearby Mount Hope were they successful in driving Abaddon back and finally defeating him. He retreated back to the land of Hadession."

"Is it possible that King Abaddon could be in that area again?" asked Alden.

"It's not likely. After that battle, we made many improvements to the watchtower. Chances are slim that he would be able to get back into our land."

"But those vulture-men fly overhead all the time," objected Andy. "What's to keep King Abaddon from flying troops into the area?"

"There's a big difference between flying men and flying artillery. Catapults are heavy, and he would have a hard time getting all that into Oomaldee without being detected."

Andy's mind started racing. "What if he killed the guards in the watchtowers? What if…what if he replaced them with guards of his own, so it looks like your watchmen are protecting the land but really aren't?"

The King took a deep breath. "Boys," he spoke slowly and calmly, looking them in the eyes, "I would never send you this way if I thought you would be harmed. We looked at several possible routes, but in the end chose this one because we feel it is the safest."

Andy and Alden locked eyes.

Safest?

"It's completely understandable that you're a bit concerned, but trust me, I want you two to return safely. After all, what good would it do if you couldn't return with the red dragon scale? That is, after all, the whole point of this mission," said the King, putting a hand on Andy's shoulder.

Andy met the King's eyes.

"Now—" he paused for emphasis "—may I continue?"

Andy nodded.

"I recommend that you cross the Slither River just as it is getting dark to avoid notice by the watchmen. Once you cross the river, follow it upstream until you reach Dragontail Tower, but again, be careful you aren't seen. You should be able to go through the Great Wall by way of the tunnel that the river runs through. We sealed up the main access after that battle, but installed a secret door just to the right after you get in the tunnel. It's similar to the way the door to the drawbridge power room works."

Andy squirmed.

"There's a stone at the base that, when you push it, will open the door for you. Follow that tunnel and it will open up into the foothills of the Zwellow

Mountains. Keep following the Slither River northeast and it will take you to the Dragon's Lair."

"Any questions?" asked Mermin.

I wish I had a GPS.

Neither Andy nor Alden voiced their concerns.

"As I said before, we've chosen this route to minimize risk and maximize the probability of success." The King took a deep breath. "Now, tomorrow is the last day of the festival. Alden, you'll want to participate in the closing ceremony with your first place medal. You two enjoy yourselves, and we'll plan to have you leave in two days."

Enjoy yourselves? Easy for him to say.

In the quiet of his chambers that night, Andy could not stop thinking about the route the King and Mermin had outlined for them. Sleep provided no relief, for he dreamed that a giant from the forest was grabbing him. The brute squeezed Andy's chest until he saw stars. Just as the foe reached to pull his head off, Andy screamed and woke himself up. His sheets were damp.

After catching his breath and glancing about the room, he finally dismissed that nightmare, only to find that he was caught in quicksand. He kept sinking and sinking and sinking, all the while unable to catch his breath. Only his lips remained above the surface, and he gasped for air. Andy jolted awake as his arms thrashed and hit the covers. Sleep took its sweet time finding him after being scared off in such a violent manner.

The morning sun finally took pity on him, sneaking rays through the fog-filled window. He opened one eye then the other.

They were just dreams… Somehow the thought only made his stomach tighten. *What will we find?*

He sat up, yawned, and stretched.

Several hours later, Andy savored a fried mesh marvel while Alden munched on barbecued pork rolls.

"We haven't checked out Technology Frontiers yet. Do you want to?" Andy asked around a mouthful of goodness.

"Yeah, that's always the most awesome part of the festival! Last year I saw a pegasus massager. I'd love to get that. It would save me a lot of time."

A pegasus massager? Not quite what I had in mind.

Technology Frontiers was situated near the back of the festival grounds, next to the field where they had encountered the dragon trainers. The dragon fighting competition had ended and the field was empty.

Andy spotted something red in the path and stopped. "What's the difference between a red dragon and a crimson dragon?"

"Not sure. Why?"

To the left of Andy's foot lay something shiny, red, and curved, about the size of a fist. He bent down and picked it up then turned it over several times. "How do we know it was a crimson dragon and not a red dragon that was here? Have you ever seen a red dragon?"

"Well, no, but why would Merodach tell us where to find the red dragons if there was one here? Why wouldn't he have just pointed it out?"

"You trust Merodach?"

"No, but…"

"Do you really want to go on this trip? If we make it to the Dragon's Lair, we still have to get a scale."

"Yeah, there's that…and the Forest of Giants gives me the creeps." Alden rubbed his sleeves.

"Exactly. So if this is the scale of a red dragon, and if we don't have to make that trip to the Dragon's Lair, battle a dragon, and get back in one piece, wouldn't that be better?"

"Yes!" Alden exhaled loudly. "But how can we tell?"

"Let's take this back and see if the King or Mermin can figure out whether it's from a crimson dragon or a red dragon. What have we got to lose?"

"I sure hope you're right."

Andy put the dragon scale in the pouch that hung around his neck, tucked it back inside his tunic, and gave his friend a reassuring nod.

They walked along the path under a dense mass of knotty oak trees. When they emerged, a huge silver sign proclaimed in bold capital letters TECHNOLOGY FRONTIERS: INVENT YOUR FUTURE. The placard hung from an oversized white tent. Set against the brightness of the fog, it created a distinctly ethereal, almost high-tech feeling that set this area apart.

Cool! This could be amazing!

Andy and Alden walked into the first tent. They found a sewing machine on display. There was also a clothes washing machine with a pair of mechanical hands that picked up the dirty clothes from a laundry basket, scrubbed them against a washboard with soap, and then rinsed them in clean water in an adjoining bucket. Several ladies were excitedly clucking about how much simpler their lives might become once these were available for purchase.

"That's awesome!" Alden oozed.

Andy forced a smile.

The next tent featured booths demonstrating a fog removal spray and a message delivery system that was nothing more than homing pigeons. The one after that housed an automated milking machine. A group of men gathered around and tested it out, making excited gestures and talking loudly.

Alden gestured, picking up the men's excitement.

Andy tried to hide a heavy sigh. *Lack-of-Technology Frontiers is more like it.*

But as the thought slogged around his brain, he noticed a device on the table in front of him. ODOR-BE-GONE indicated the sign to the right.

"Guaranteed to manage the nastiest of smells!" a wiry man dressed in a ragged tunic and threadbare leggings announced from behind the table.

Andy started bouncing from foot to foot. "Alden, I keep forgetting to ask. When I first arrived on Curse Day, I could have sworn I heard cows mooing and then farting as the fog lifted. It happened again when you were practicing with Optimistic in the training center, and again during the competition. It always reeks! Am I crazy, or do cow farts make the fog disappear?"

Alden laughed. "You're not crazy. And yes, cow farts chase the fog away. The only problem is the smell."

"I'll say!"

Alden continued, "I've heard that when the curse first started, farmers found that the pastures where the cows grazed were fog-free. They started using cow farts to clear away the fog when there's an event."

"It's a great idea, but someone needs to invent something to kill the stench. It's awful!"

"And that's exactly what Odor-Be-Gone will do!" the man proclaimed.

Andy picked up the device. It reminded him of eyeglasses, except instead of lenses, a wire holding a small sponge extended from the bridge. You could fill the sponge with whatever scent you liked best—mint, lavender, or lilac. Andy put it on. It pinched the bridge of his nose, but he smiled as the fresh aroma of mint filled his nostrils.

"How much?"

"Two spannings for the device. Four quirts for the scent. We're taking orders."

Just as Andy finished placing an order, a trumpet called everyone to the amphitheater for the closing ceremony.

On the way, Alden pulled out the gold medal from under his tunic. Andy smiled. Alden shot back a grin, his expression reflecting more than just happiness at winning an award.

The arena was packed when they arrived. A dozen stages circled the space, and the bands that had performed throughout the festival came together for one final jam session. People were laughing and having a good time, tapping and jumping to the music. Andy spotted Marta and Hans and waved to get their attention before heading over to join them. On the way, the boys greeted Henry, Max, and Oscar, along with their wives and kids, as well as several other castle servants. It seemed as if everyone had turned out.

After several minutes, the governor of the city of Oops mounted the center stage, quieting the crowd. "I'd like to thank you all for attending the Festival of Oomaldee this year. Your participation, your cheering for the competitors and enjoying the bands—" the crowd interrupted with applause and hoots "—has produced another successful event. I feel privileged to have hosted the festival in our fair city. It will certainly be the highlight of my year!"

The crowd started whistling and hollering once more.

The governor motioned for quiet. "I see it will be a highlight for you as well." He smiled then continued, "On a more serious note, as we draw the festivities to a close, I do want to take a moment to remember Uma Flopol, a competition judge. She was killed after being struck by a poison dart during the Tower Chase judging."

Gasps sprinkled the crowd.

"If not for the quick thinking and courageous actions of Andy, Son of Smith, it is probable that others could have been killed as well. Is Andy, Son of Smith, here? If so, please come up to the platform to be recognized."

Hans shouted, "He's right here!" and motioned wildly at Andy.

No! Andy shook his head emphatically, but several folks standing nearby heard Hans. He surrendered as they began pushing him toward the stage, all the while his face warming. He hesitated and surveyed the crowd when he reached the foot of the steps.

"Way to go, Andy! Way to go!" Chants compelled him upward.

The governor shook Andy's hand vigorously when he at last reached the stage. "That was a heroic thing you did. You ignored your own safety and acted to prevent harm to others. I understand you got hurt and spent three days recovering from your injuries." Andy gave a slow nod as his gaze darted across the crowd.

"On behalf of the Festival Committee and everyone here, thank you."

A volcano of applause and whistling erupted, covering everyone within earshot.

"Is there anything you'd like to say?" the governor shouted above the roar, restoring quiet.

Andy drew a hand to the back of his neck. "I've never done anything like that before. I just saw the guy about to hurt my friend and I tried to stop him."

"A hero, and humble!" the governor praised. "Well done, Andy!" He threw an arm around Andy's shoulders, then became solemn. "Now, I ask everyone to join me in a moment of silence as we remember Uma Flopol."

Everyone grew quiet.

After a minute, the governor intoned, "Thank you. And now, would the medalists in the athletic competitions please join me on stage to be recognized."

Andy tried to step away and dodge the attention, but was stopped short when the magistrate kept his arm firmly in place. "Please stay here. Your actions deserve much recognition."

Only as the hundred or so medalists mounted the stage did the official release Andy. He fidgeted until Alden joined him.

The governor then invited the winners of various other contests—such as the jams and jellies competition, the apple pie eating competition, the turkey calling competition, the kite flying competition, and the goat herding competition—to the adjoining stages.

"Please join me in recognizing all of our winners!" the official invited. The crowd again responded.

"Thank you all for attending. I now declare the Festival of Oomaldee complete for this year!"

At this, the bands all started playing a raucous tune while fireworks erupted from the back of the main stage. Cheers went up and people started dancing and swaying to the music.

Wow! I've never seen people party like this! Andy marveled as he spun around.

Andy and Alden rejoined Marta and Hans amid hugs and more celebration. As they danced out of the amphitheater and all along the way home, folks stopped Andy and shook his hand.

Out of the corner of his eye, Andy noticed Alden glancing over at him. While his friend wasn't exactly frowning, he wasn't smiling like Marta and Hans either.

What's wrong? Why's he looking at me that way?

CHAPTER TEN

Gift in a Gold Box

They arrived back at the castle in time for dinner. After washing up and changing back into his comfortable T-shirt and jeans, Andy joined the King and Mermin in the dining hall. He recounted everything he had seen and enjoyed during the festival. Then, remembering the dragon scale, he pulled it out.

Handing it to the King, Andy said, "Alden and I found this earlier today. Do you know what kind of dragon it's from?"

The King passed it to Mermin to examine. The wizard held it up to the light, turning it over several times. He then put it up to his mouth and rubbed it against his front teeth, much like testing a pearl.

"Andy, why did you bring this back?" the King questioned.

"Well, I doubt whether Merodach would have told us if there was a red dragon at the festival. So I figured if this was the scale of a red dragon, Alden and I wouldn't need to go retrieve one from the Dragon's Lair."

The King chuckled. "I'm not surprised to hear you say that about Merodach. Even though he seems questionable in character, in all my dealings with him he has never once lied to me."

"You've dealt with him before?"

"Yes, a few times."

"And?" Andy probed.

"And…I think Mermin has finished his inspection," the King evaded.

"They only bwing male dragons to compete at the festival. It's the scale of a male cwimson dwagon. No mistaking it. See here, there is a vewy light colored gway stwipe at the bottom of the scale. Cwimson dwagons are gway under all their scales. Male wed dwagons are wed under their scales and don't have this gway stwipe. Some say wed dwagons are angry all the way thwough, which is why they are the fiewcest."

Mermin handed the scale back to Andy. He could just make out a light gray band along the bottom of the scale where it would have been attached to its owner. "You really have to know what to look for, don't you?"

"Mermin has studied dragons for many years. He knows every species," praised the King.

Andy forced a smile as the sovereign glanced his way.

The wizard raised a hand. "Sir, if you will excuse me, I need to attend to the expewiment I have wunning up in the labowatory if it's to be weady for tomowwow."

"By all means."

As soon as the mage had left, the King asked, "Andy, is something bothering you?"

"Well…"

"What is it? Tell me." The King locked eyes with Andy.

"Well, sir—" Andy's gaze moved to the table and he hunched his shoulders. "You see, sir, I've never battled a real dragon, and the Forest of Giants, well…"

"Ah, I see. You're afraid."

The matter-of-fact summary made denial impossible and Andy pulled back.

"Andy, that's to be expected. Under the circumstances, I would be surprised if you weren't. But don't let your fear cripple you. This is not a normal quest you are embarking upon. You have been brought here to break the curse. It's not every day you get a message sphere saying you'll become a leader here. I have every confidence you'll not only get this dragon scale but you'll do far more."

The King brought a hand over and rested it on Andy's shoulder. "Always remember you are here for a very important reason."

Confidence again flowed through the King's hand and Andy met his gaze. *I want to believe him.*

"You'll do well. I believe in you."

Andy gave a slow nod.

"Now, if you'll excuse me, I have a few matters I need to attend to."

Despite the encouragement, Andy's stomach clenched and he exhaled loudly. More mulling did nothing but make his insides churn.

I wonder what Mermin's working on. The rogue thought offered a welcome diversion.

"I believe I have it!" the wizard exclaimed as Andy closed the door to the lab behind him. "All I need to do is a final test outside to make sure it works. I'm going down to the porch to test it."

"Can I come?"

"Please do. If this is as powerful as I think, it could completely change life in Oomaldee."

Mermin threw a towel over the shiny dome that was the size of half a soccer ball and picked it up. As they headed toward the door, Andy noticed that his mailbox still stood sentry, but it was open and a gold envelope stuck out.

"How long has this been here?" Andy asked as he grabbed it.

"It must have just awwived. There was nothing in there earlier."

This gold envelope was also addressed to Andy, but now it said: To Andy, Son of Smith, He Who Shall Overcome His Fear.

Why am I the only one who doesn't believe that?

It contained two letters this time. Andy read the first aloud:

"The guide for true steps,

To make your path straight,

Lies in invention,

Of words that negate,

Fear, that is tempting,

To harm and misstate,

The control that you hold,

Beyond armor plate."

The words did little to reassure him, and Andy rubbed an arm, trying to stuff down his anxiety.

"Sounds like whoever wote this knows you'll do fine on this mission," Mermin affirmed. "What does the second letter say?"

Andy read:

"In your provisions make lie,

The key that is golden.

But take not its cover,

Lest enemies embolden.

The right path you'll follow,

Ne'er alone on your quest,

To bring you a journey,

The end that is blessed."

"Sounds like you need to bwing that gold key you found. How 'bout that, a packing list for your twip!" Mermin chuckled.

Andy gave a weak smile. *But it mentions emboldening enemies. Great, we have enemies before we even start.*

As the pair headed down to the porch, Andy motioned toward the object Mermin carried. "What's it do?"

"It should wemove fog for long distances."

"Really?"

Mermin nodded.

"You mean without cow farts? They smell so bad! What are you calling it?"

"'A New Beginning.'" A corner of Mermin's mouth edged upward as he patted the top of the contraption.

Andy caught the wizard's meaning. *It really will be, won't it?*

They emerged onto the porch into dense fog, more dense than Andy had yet seen. He could barely see the wizard standing three or four feet away. Mermin set down the bundle on the floor and pulled off the towel. Then he tipped it up, inserted a small metal sphere into the bottom, and set it back down. Andy watched and waited for something to happen.

"Give it a minute or two for the weaction to begin."

Andy was just beginning to wonder why the King had such confidence in Mermin's abilities when the wizard began to come more clearly into focus. A moment later Andy saw the porch railing appear.

"Mermin! You've done it!"

A few minutes later, Andy could see the moat that surrounded the castle. And then he could start to see the faint outlines of the closest buildings in the city of Oops.

"This is excellent, Mermin! Until this moment, I didn't realize how gloomy the fog makes me feel. I think I understand why the King wants to break the curse so badly."

"That is a small part of it, Andy," the King interrupted from behind, joining them.

The pair turned to acknowledge him.

"Someone told me you two were out here. The fog has oppressed my people for hundreds of years. Most times we like to think that the harder we work, the further ahead we'll get. Hard work, while required, is no guarantee of success. In this case, my people have labored harder but it has not helped. We have lost our technological advantage. We are behind our neighbors in innovation and are, therefore, vulnerable to their attacks."

The King paused and gave a heavy sigh. "My stupidity has caused irreparable harm to this kingdom. I just hope it doesn't cause our final demise. We must break the curse as soon as possible." He turned and looked directly into Andy's eyes. "You had nothing to do with the curse being cast upon the land, but I'm counting on you to help break it."

"I know you are, sir." Andy swallowed. "I'll do my best."

After lunch the next day, Andy headed up to Mermin's library to retrieve the gold key as instructed by the letter. He knocked, but Mermin was not there, so he walked over to the shelf where he had left the gold book, picked it up, and brought it over to the large table. Clearing away some of Mermin's clutter, he set it down and lifted the cover.

As before, the only page was blank. Opening the compartment behind it, he found the golden key still there. But now a second gold object lay next to it. It looked like the hilt to a sword. Andy picked it up and turned it over. Four carvings had been inlaid around its circumference: one was a bunch of clouds with puffed up cheeks, another was a giant wave, the third was a flaming ball of fire, and the last was a pile of rocks. While the detail was beautiful, Andy had no idea what the symbols might mean. Near the top, two stones were set on either side, one pure white, the other ebony. Andy gripped it and pretended it was a real sword. He assumed the pose of a knight in his video game and slashed down, fighting an invisible dragon. A shiny blade shot from the hilt! Andy nearly dropped it.

Andy brought the blade close and examined the full length. He ran a finger down the edge but jerked back when it drew a bead of red.

"Cool…"

Andy resumed his stance then jabbed and thrusted, jumped and bobbed all around Mermin's library. His opponent was quick, and he had to dodge more than one blast of imaginary fire, but in the end, Andy plunged the sword into the dragon's heart and watched the beast collapse. He danced in victory, whooping and hollering.

"Andy?" the King stuck his head in the door of the library.

"Oh, hi sir."

"May I ask what you're doing?"

"Just fighting a red dragon with my new sword!"

"May I see that?"

The King's eyes grew large and his mouth dropped opened. He gasped.

"What's wrong, sir?"

"Where did you get this?"

"Right here, in the book. I was getting the key to pack it for my trip, and I found the hilt next to it."

The King handed the sword back to Andy and took a knee before him.

"Wait…what are you doing, sir?"

The monarch bowed his head. "I am your humble servant, Andrew, Son of Smith."

"What do you mean? What are you doing? Stop it! Get up!"

The King unfolded himself and slowly stood. "Andy, this sword is named Methuselah. It is the sword that divides good and evil everywhere. That's what the black and white stones on front and back represent. The fact that it's gold is significant, for most believe gold embodies excellence, wisdom, light, and perfection. The carvings—wind, water, fire, and earth—are representations of the foundations of physical and spiritual perfection."

Andy inspected it more closely. *Whoa.* "But who would have put it in this book…that only I can see?"

"Until now I thought Methuselah was only legend. Many stories have been told about the battles it has fought to execute judgment and justice."

Andy stiffened.

"Legend says it appears only when there is a significant showdown about to happen. And it only presents itself to the one who has been judged worthy to wield it in victory. I've never seen or heard of it appearing in my lifetime. For it to show up now, and to you—I don't know what we're up against…" His voice trailed off.

Andy waved his hands, trying to make the King stop. "Please, don't say any more!" He grabbed the gold key, slammed the book shut and reshelved it, then bolted for the door.

Out in the hall, the blade retracted back into the hilt, again making Andy jump. Only quick reflexes prevented it from hitting the floor. He raced to his room, heart galloping.

Andy threw open his door, jettisoned the hilt at the foot of his bed, and crash-landed across the pillows. He panted as he eyed the piece. The afternoon sun shining through the fog-clouded window seemed intent on cheering him, but his mind kept replaying all that the King had shared, like a YouTube video on auto-repeat.

What have I gotten myself into? It sounds like a whole lot more than just retrieving a red dragon scale, as if that's not bad enough.

He wiped his sweaty hands on the covers. *When can I go home? I miss Mom and Dad…and even Madison.*

Andy punched his pillow hard once, and then again and again and again. He stopped only when feathers began flying everywhere. He ruffled his hair as they drifted down, scaring them off. His bed now looked as if a thick layer of snow had fallen.

Why me? There's no way I can do to this!

"You're right, Andy! You can't do this on your own," his inneru interrupted. "You need help."

What? Oh, it's you… As the thought launched, a second amethyst-colored stone landed on his bed, barely missing his head.

"Hey, watch it! You almost hit me!" *Where do these things keep coming from?* As before, it started pulsing and a trumpet blast sounded when he picked it up.

"Methuselah has appeared to you, Andrew Ferrin Smithson. It is the sword of your forefathers by which you will become known. Evil must be extinguished from the land, by your hand."

"My forefathers? What do you mean?" The message paused.

"You have not been told, but your ancestors came from Oomaldee."

What? Really?

"It is not I who gives Methuselah, but One far greater. It is given and taken as the times require," the message continued. "You have been chosen to wield it for such a time as this."

No! You can't be serious! You can't mean me!

"Stop!" his inneru interrupted. "Listen!"

Andy slumped and the message continued, "Take courage. You do not yet see your own abilities because you have never been tested. You have never demonstrated to yourself or anyone else all that you can do. Put your fears aside and trust that you will succeed in the challenges that lie ahead."

"What kind of evil are we talking about?" Andy swallowed.

The sphere gave no reply but disappeared, its message complete. Once again it gave no indication who had sent it.

This evil sounds really bad.

"This is not about you," intoned the voice in his head.

Andy sighed. "How did I get myself into this mess? I didn't ask for this."

"It's about all the people in the land of Oomaldee. It's about the King, Mermin, Alden, Marta, Hans, and everyone else."

"I know…" Andy rubbed his arm.

"You don't usually think about others first."

Andy scowled but had no evidence to counter the accusation.

"Maybe this is your chance to change that."

He exhaled heavily. *I'm not going home anytime soon, am I?*

CHAPTER ELEVEN

Where's Methuselah?

The next morning, Andy packed a backpack with everything he thought he might need: a blanket, rain poncho, two changes of clothes, matches, a compass, the gold key, the sword hilt of Methuselah, and more. He then dressed in his scratchy leggings and tunic. *I still don't understand why I've been chosen, but maybe...* He took a deep breath and let it out slowly. *Maybe I can help. I did almost destroy the castle after all.*

With a nod, Andy exited his room, listing to the left under the weight of his pack. In an alcove to the right of the door, a two-foot tall statue of a victorious knight, its foot pressing down on an enemy's neck, looked up and waved. "Fare thee well, lad!" Andy did a double take. He'd passed this statue many times. It had never moved, let alone spoken. He shook his head. *I must be imagining things.*

Andy leaned down.

"I'm Sir Lancelot," the little man squeaked. To the captive under his foot he warned, "Clarence, stop squirming. Show some dignity, man. I'm trying to have a conversation here." Then, turning his attention back to Andy, he said, "Sorry about that. These barbarians lack manners."

"Oh. Hi. I'm Andy. Nice to meet you. How is it that you can talk to me?"

"You now possess a gold key about you."

"Gold key. Oh...really? The gold key makes you alive?"

"At your service."

"Thank you." *That is totally awesome!* Andy glanced both ways down the hall then leaned back in. "I'm headed on a mission to retrieve the scale of a red dragon. But don't tell anyone."

"On my honor, you have my word." The little man saluted.

"Uh...carry on, Sir Lancelot." Andy returned the gesture as he headed toward the stairs.

"I will, sir!" echoed the knight, clicking his heels together. "Fare thee well!"

As Andy made his way toward breakfast, each statue he passed greeted him. *Wow! This is amazing.*

The King's boisterous laugh met Andy as he entered the dining hall. "Andy, you're only going for eight or nine days. Are you sure you need all that? You're going to have to carry it all."

"I wanted to be prepared," he reasoned, taking his pack off and resting it against a nearby wall.

Andy overheard Mermin whisper to the King, "He may pack lighter for the next twip."

The King chuckled his agreement.

Let's hope there's no "next trip."

Andy did not mention his experience with the castle artwork as he ate breakfast. He finished his cereal, excused himself, and joined Alden in the kitchen. Marta was just putting the last of the food she had prepared for their journey into a large backpack that held Alden's supplies. She looked at Andy and gave a half smile. "I don't know why the King is sending you two on this trip. It could be very dangerous."

"We'll be careful. I promise." Andy gave Marta a big hug and a kiss. *She feels like Mom.* He swallowed a lump in his throat, forced a laugh, and asked, "Can you have some chocolate chip cookies ready for when we get back?"

Marta nodded and ran her hand down his cheek. Then, turning to Alden, she hugged him as if she would never see him again. After giving a heavy sigh, she wiped her eyes.

Alden shouldered his backpack. Despite its weight, he uttered no complaint. Joining the King and Mermin in the dining hall, Andy grabbed his backpack and slung it on, tilting precariously in the process. When he had righted himself with a little help from the wall, he felt the side pocket for the key and the sword hilt. *Good. Right where I packed them.*

The four headed down the grand staircase to the entry. Whooshing, creaking, and groaning met them as a servant heaved the gear to lower the drawbridge.

True to form, the fog occluded the end of the span where it came to rest. Mermin handed Andy "A New Beginning," which he had retrofitted to be worn like a hat. Andy put it on and buckled the chin strap. "It's really light."

In just a few minutes, the fog thinned and then cleared for a good distance.

Alden, who was seeing the invention for the first time, dropped his jaw. "This is awesome!"

"Thank you, Mermin!" Andy grinned.

"My pleasure."

The King placed his hands on Andy's shoulders and looked him in the eye. "It is no accident that Methuselah has appeared. I have great confidence in you."

Alden cocked his head and Andy fidgeted before replying, "Thank you, sir."

The King and Mermin gave Andy and Alden hugs, then the two boys headed across the drawbridge toward the city of Oops.

"What he did he mean by that?" Alden probed as they walked.

"I don't really want to talk about it."

Alden frowned and shook his head.

The two hadn't spent much time together since the end of the festival, what with chores and preparations going on. Now, the silence forced an awkward hush. *Should I ask him about why he seems upset with me?*

The thought vanished as a farmer pushing a large wooden cart full of produce passed by. The burly man sent them a questioning look as he continued on his way. The next pair of men they passed raised their eyebrows at seeing them. Andy overheard one of them comment about the sudden lightness of the fog.

"We're probably quite a sight," laughed Andy, trying to lighten the mood. "Between our overstuffed backpacks, this shiny silver bowl on my head, and—pardon me for saying, Alden—your neon-green hair, we're a piece of work!"

Alden gave a half smile.

A bit farther down the path, they passed a young girl leading a cow by a rope halter. The cow seemed happy enough to follow since she enticed it with an apple. The girl recognized Andy from the festival and congratulated him on his heroic actions. Alden gave Andy a passing frown.

Soon they came upon a gaggle of women carrying baskets of clothes on their heads, all heading to do laundry in the Crystal River that flowed nearby. The ladies were cackling to each other like grackles, but when one spotted the boys, she heaped praise on Andy. The other ladies echoed enthusiastically, to which the corners of Alden's mouth fell.

At one point a herd of goats nearly ran over Andy and Alden. A shepherd boy following behind struggled to manage them. It was clear who was boss, and it wasn't the boy. He kept running back and forth to either side of the herd, yelling and waving his arms, trying to stop the animals from going into the trees that lined the path. The animals ignored him. One goat stopped right next to Alden, stood up on its hind legs, and tried to nibble the food it smelled in the top of his backpack. Alden backed away, and the shepherd boy ran over, apologizing profusely. It registered who he was speaking to seconds later and he gasped. "You saved your friend at the festival!"

Andy nodded.

More apologies followed. But when the goats decided to bolt, the boy excused himself. Andy and Alden felt sorry for him, but they knew there was nothing to do to help the kid.

By lunchtime, the boys had reached the southernmost end of Goozy Bog. They found an old oak tree whose branches shaded more than half the road, removed their packs, and sat down to rest.

"Mermin's invention is working great!" Andy observed. "I've never seen it so clear."

"Yeah," Alden agreed, but said no more.

Andy took off his pack and the fog-clearing cap. "Oh, that's better." He ran his hands through his hair and moved his arms in circles, stretching his sore back muscles. "What did your mom pack us for lunch?"

Alden rummaged in the top of his backpack. After spreading the various parcels on the ground, he announced, "Fried chicken."

Andy bit into the still-warm, savory meat with enthusiasm. After downing four drumsticks and a fresh roll, he wiped his greasy hands on some nearby grass.

"My dad took me camping in the woods one time." *Yeah, the only time, what with Dad always so busy running his company.* Andy didn't mention that, but recounted his memories of the event as Alden finished eating.

Lunch complete, Andy replaced the fog-clearing cap while Alden repacked their provisions. They picked up their backpacks and set off once more.

"My pack feels heavier than it did this morning," commented Andy.

"Yeah, mine too. Maybe we shouldn't have brought so much."

They picked their way down the path that wound around Goozy Bog. Alden knew where most of the patches of quicksand were near the road and did his best to steer them around those, but sometimes the path turned soft as the bog spread its tentacles, seemingly dissatisfied with its current bounds.

While Andy had never experienced quicksand, he vividly remembered his nightmares after hearing Mermin's stories. They rounded a bend, and Andy saw bubbles rising from a particularly muddy part of the bog. "What's that?" He pointed.

"I'm not sure, but I once heard that's where a person got sucked under, only they're still not dead. Those are their air bubbles."

A chill went up Andy's spine. "I thought Mermin said if you get sucked under in quicksand, you die because you can't breathe."

"I don't know, I'm just telling you what some folks say."

"Well, if whoever is in there didn't die, why doesn't someone help them out?"

"Lots of people have tried, but they've never found anyone under there. He must be so far down no one can reach him. He'll stay there forever."

Andy's eyes grew wide and he gulped. *What a horrible way to live…or die…or whatever that person's doing.*

They walked on for a bit and started seeing enormous trees off to their right. The trees were bigger than any Andy had seen, and he'd seen some big ones. He remembered the trip he and his family took to Sequoia National Forest. Now those were huge trees! One of them was so big, you could drive a car through the middle of it. But these trees were at least twice that size! And they grew so thick the boys couldn't see far into the woods, even though it was midday and Mermin's invention cleared away the fog.

"What *is* that?" Andy asked.

"That's the Forest of Giants."

"Those trees are gigantic!"

"Remember what Mermin told us about the guy who got dragged in there and was never heard from again?"

"I remember," shuddered Andy. "There sure is a lot of scary stuff out here. It was bad enough when Mermin was telling us about it, but now that we're here—"

"You just have to know what can hurt you and stay away from it."

"That's easier said than done. I'm glad you're here."

They continued walking on the path. Before long, Andy had the strange feeling they were being watched. He glanced into the forest but thankfully didn't see anything. *I'm just imagining things*, he kept telling himself.

But as they continued, the feeling plagued him. Every time he thought he heard something in the trees, which was often, he glanced over to see…nothing. It was a creepy feeling.

"I feel like we're being watched," Andy confided at last.

"I've had that feeling too. Let's just keep a look out."

The sun began casting late-afternoon shadows across Goozy Bog. After all the walking, the boys grew hungry and chose to stop and rest for a few minutes. Alden located bread and cheese in his pack and handed some to his companion.

Andy sat on the ground as he ate. He leaned against his pack, which cushioned a large boulder by the side of the road. He felt the side pocket for the gold key and the sword hilt. He found the key right away but couldn't locate the hilt. He popped the last bite of snack in his mouth as he turned to more closely examine his pack. Plunging his hand to the bottom of the pocket, he felt around. Nothing. Panic began rising. He hauled the contents out in seconds and took inventory. "What happened to it?"

"What's wrong?"

"I can't find Methuselah! It has to be here. It was there this morning before we left the castle, I felt it!" He pushed back the cap.

After a second search of the contents of his backpack, Andy had to accept that the sword was missing. He thought back to where they had been, trying desperately to determine where he might have lost it.

"Did you have it after we ate lunch?"

"I'm not sure. I don't remember checking my pack for it after lunch. We have to find it!"

Andy and Alden packed up their gear and began retracing their steps. With the sun getting lower in the sky, the Forest of Giants looked more threatening and Goozy Bog more ominous. Running most of the way, heavy packs bouncing, they reached their lunchtime location just as the sun set— Andy knew the orange glow would be gone within minutes.

"You look over there and I'll look over here," Andy instructed.

Several minutes of searching turned up nothing, and Andy's panic grew.

Alden interrupted the search several minutes later. "It's getting dark. You keep looking. I'll find some wood and set up camp."

Andy's thoughts raced. *How could I be so stupid? Stupid, stupid, stupid! It has to be here! It just has to be!*

In no time, Alden had a roaring fire built. Andy continued his search, stumbling in the dark over tree roots and rocks.

"Why don't we pick up the search in the morning?" Alden suggested from his seat on a log next to the fire where he prepared dinner.

"I *have* to find it tonight!"

A long while later Andy stumbled over a rotten log and fell to his knees. As he stood, he thought he saw something shining in the firelight not far away. He crept closer. *Could it be?* He had nearly reached it when he felt his footing slip, and he sunk down to his knees.

"Alden, help! I'm stuck in quicksand!" He struggled to escape, and with every movement the muck pulled him closer to its hungry belly. Just then he heard a woman's voice celebrating his misfortune…

"Wahoo!" she cheered, clapping enthusiastically.

"Imogenia, I can't believe you did this! Stop it! Get him out this minute!" a man's voice chided.

"What? I didn't do anything. He did this to himself. He saved me the trouble. Ha, ha!" the lady cackled. Andy barely noticed in his panic.

Alden reached Andy just as his waist disappeared below the surface. "Don't move! The more you move, the faster you'll sink!"

"What should I do?"

"Try floating on your back. You should stay up long enough for me to find a branch and pull you out."

Andy moved as slowly as possible. He had taken swimming lessons a couple years ago at summer camp, and while he wasn't any good at most of the strokes, he had mastered the back float. But floating in water proved completely different than quicksand. No sooner had he laid back than thick sand started to ooze into his ears and smother his hair. All he could think about were the people who had suffocated. He glanced out of the corner of one eye, trying to locate Alden, but there was only darkness.

"Alden! Don't leave me!"

A minute later, Alden appeared carrying a freshly cut branch about an inch in diameter. "I had to find one that was strong enough to drag you to solid ground. There aren't a lot of smaller trees to choose from around here. And the dark made it take even longer. Okay, I'm going to lay this over your arms. When you feel it, grab hold. I'll pull you out."

Andy did as Alden instructed. As soon as he felt the leaves from the branch touch his chest, he grabbed hold. Moving too quickly, his head went completely under and muck went up his nose. He closed his eyes and gasped for air—the ooze took advantage and filled his mouth. He coughed and sputtered and nearly let go, struggling to stave off his rising panic.

"You're almost there!" Alden encouraged.

After several terrifying minutes, Andy felt Alden's hands grab hold of his tunic and pull him to solid ground. He rolled over, coughing and spitting goop from his mouth, then wiped his eyes. "I thought I was going to be sucked under!"

"I wasn't going to let that happen."

Andy caught his breath and staggered up, heading to rest near the fire. The quicksand had a strange, unpleasant smell, like decaying fish. He stripped and used the soiled clothes to wipe as much as possible out of his hair, off his face, and from between his toes and several other crevices, but his efforts proved only partly effective—the quicksand stuck like superglue. Only the pouch around his neck escaped complete saturation thanks to the protection his tunic afforded. He finally gave up, changing into clean clothes and donating the dirty set to the hungry fire. While he felt a little better, Andy knew it would be morning before he could find someplace to wash.

"So much for retrieving Methuselah tonight," Andy moaned as he ate. "But at least I know where it is."

After they finished dinner, Andy turned to Alden. "Thanks for saving my life. I guess we're even."

"Yeah," Alden replied, half smiling as he stared at the ground.

That sure sounded fake. He ran a hand against the back of his neck before opening his mouth to speak, but Alden cut him off.

"Let's turn in. I'm beat." Without waiting for consensus, the Cartesian grabbed his bedroll and lay down with his back toward Andy and the fire.

Whatever. Andy shook his head, then smoothed out his bedroll and covered up against the chilly night air. His thoughts refused sleep admittance, however, as the terror of nearly being sucked under marauded through his brain. Only his mind turning to the challenges that lay ahead overwhelmed the nightmares making them seem like child's play—the nebulous evil he was to overcome, the Forest of Giants, evading detection at the watchtowers, battling a dragon. His stomach twisted.

Andy's inneru interrupted, "Remember when you used to be afraid of monsters under your bed at night?"

Andy remembered the terror he had felt so often when he was little.

"If you had to get out of bed when your room was dark, you used to stand on your pillow and take a running leap so the monsters couldn't grab your legs and pull you under."

Andy smiled, recalling those times. *How'd you know about that?*

"Remember when you told your sister how scared you were of monsters under your bed?" continued his inneru, ignoring the inquiry. "Ha, ha! She scared you good that night. She hid under there and jumped out when you got up to go pee after the lights were off!"

That wasn't funny. I wet myself!

"Oh, come on. Lighten up. It was too funny!"

Okay, maybe it was a little funny…

"So, when did you finally stop believing there were monsters under your bed?"

I…um…I don't know.

"From what I'm seeing, it looks like you stopped being scared shortly after that talk with your grandfather when you visited him a few summers ago."

Andy's mind recalled the conversation. Grandpa had told him, "Being afraid is normal and keeps you alive many times. However, the minute you realize you're afraid, you have a choice. Either you can allow your fear to control you, or you can choose to control it." Andy swallowed.

Yeah, I remember the night after he told me that. I woke up and had to go pee. I remember, I grabbed my toy sword and hopped off my bed. I stood there and challenged the monsters to come get me if they dared. I wasn't going to wet the bed just because of them! None ever showed themselves. Come to think of it, I didn't worry about monsters after that.

Several minutes later Andy deduced, *If I don't name my fear, I can't fight it. It's just scary…no, terrifying. But if I admit to it—if I name it—I can choose to control it because then I can see how it affects me…*

The image of standing paralyzed in the face of a dragon's blast skittered across Andy's mind. He inhaled sharply.

Okay, I'm afraid I'll freeze when I fight that dragon. He exhaled loudly, willing courage to show itself. *If that happens, at least I've said it. Hopefully that's enough to keep me moving.*

His mind brought forth another fear: *The Forest of Giants scares me. I don't know what's in there.*

The admission didn't banish his fear, but it shrunk it from gorilla-sized to bunny-sized, and he breathed easier until his thoughts dug up his deepest worry: *the evil I'm supposed to fight…* His heart raced.

"Andy!" the voice in his head startled him, and he pivoted his head about the campsite. "One step at a time. With practice you'll get better at managing your fear."

Andy exhaled. *Right.*

It felt strange to admit. Usually he tried to ignore and bury his fear, hoping it would go away lest others think he was weak and pick on him.

Minutes later, Andy escaped to dreamland.

Andy and Alden awoke the next morning to the sound of bleating goats. One long-horned beast had knocked over Alden's backpack. It now gobbled up moonberries from among the spilled contents.

"It's eating our food!" Alden yelled, sitting up.

Andy leapt from his blankets and charged the goat. The creature took one look at Andy's spiky hair and bolted. Not only did Andy have a major case of bed head, but the dried quicksand made it look like he had multiple horns. The "herding challenged" boy they had met yesterday made his way over to them and once more apologized profusely. He also mentioned there was a public well in the village of Oohhh where Andy could wash up.

After the unwelcome visitors had left, Alden inventoried what remained of their provisions. The goat had eaten nearly half of their food. They would need to ration what was left.

Andy headed back over to where he had seen Methuselah in the dark. *Ugh. Stupid. If only I'd waited for daylight.* The hilt rested behind a patch of dense ferns right where he had set his backpack during their lunch stop the day before.

"I had no idea we were so close to quicksand," he mumbled to himself. He walked over and snatched it up, declaring, "Found it!" Unwilling to repeat the problem, Andy dropped both the key and hilt in his pouch and tucked it under his tunic. While the weight of the hilt made the drawstring pull at his neck, it was a trade he happily made.

They packed up their gear and quenched what remained of the fire. With Andy's cleanliness challenges, Alden volunteered to wear "A New Beginning," and after buckling it under his chin, the boys headed toward the village of Oohhh. Andy couldn't wait to wash up. The grime between his toes started chafing, working like sandpaper and making his skin raw. Even after stopping a number of times to brush off what he could, every step became more and more painful. *How much farther?*

While the Forest of Giants still gave Andy the creeps as they passed, the pain in his feet and elsewhere gave him something else to focus on. Hunger stopped them before they could reach relief, however. The boys ate a quick lunch and continued on. Andy fingered his pouch for the gold key and Methuselah as they set out.

After passing the farthest limits of Goozy Bog, they passed only a handful of people before reaching the village of Oohhh around mid-afternoon. The well the shepherd boy mentioned was not hard to find—the large stone structure stood in the middle of the town square. Multiple buckets, each with a long rope, hung from posts around its generous circumference. Several women had gathered to fill water jugs as well as to get their fill of town gossip.

While Andy would normally have been modest, his body was so sore from the chafing sand that he stripped down to the bare essentials in front of everyone, silencing conversation and drawing stares. Alden sat down nearby, removed the fog-clearing cap, and waited. Andy drew water, overhearing mutterings about Cartesians as he started washing.

"Got stuck in quicksand, boy?" one woman remarked. "You're lucky to be alive!" Several others made similar comments and more snide remarks about Cartesians.

Andy ignored them. He hoped Alden turned a deaf ear as well. He doused his face and then his hair—*Ugh, my hair is gross*. It took a long time to get the worst of it out, but finally Andy finger-combed his hair into submission, getting it to lay flat on his head instead of sticking up all over like he'd inserted his finger into a light socket. He grabbed his backpack, headed behind a nearby building, and changed into fresh clothes.

He reemerged to hear a woman commenting to Alden, "Didn't you win the Tower Chase competition at the festival? I recognize your bright green hair."

"Yes, I did," Alden replied, beaming.

"Then your friend must be the one who saved you," continued the woman, pointing at Andy.

"Yes, that was me, ma'am." Andy puffed out his chest.

At this, the woman shouted, "Hey, this kid is the one who saved his friend from the poison dart at the festival!"

A host of villagers immediately surrounded the boys, praising Andy for his heroic actions.

"You must be relieved that your friend saved you," one villager gushed to Alden.

"Yeah…relieved," Alden smiled begrudgingly.

A round, silvery-haired woman stepped forward from the crowd. "I'm Bee, the innkeeper's wife. You must join me and my husband for dinner tonight, to celebrate."

"Thank you, ma'am," replied Andy. "We'd like that."

He glanced over at Alden and saw a frown flit over his face.

"What's the matter?" Andy asked as they followed Bee.

"It's not important." Alden said no more.

Andy shook his head. He wanted to press him, but the moment wasn't right.

Bee hustled them homeward. In fact, she was in such a hurry that for a brief moment the thought "What's the rush?" tickled Andy's mind. He checked the pouch for the key and Methuselah. They were both there, but Methuselah felt warm—warmer than usual at least. *That's weird. No, I'm just imagining things.*

CHAPTER TWELVE

Trapped!

V ILLAGE BED AND BREAKFAST. The crooked sign hung from a peeling white picket fence surrounding the cramped front yard of the inn. Several slats lay on the ground. The grass was overgrown and patchy with weeds and looked like it hadn't been mowed in quite some time. *Dad would have a cow if this was our yard.*

As they followed Bee up two rotting steps onto the porch, Andy noticed the painted siding of the inn was also peeling.

"Looks like they don't get many customers," Alden whispered as they walked in the front door. Alarm bells sounded in Andy's head and he tensed.

A burly man stood in the parlor as they entered. He wore a shirt that hung untucked—it was so stained Andy could hardly make out its plaid pattern. His pants looked like "floods."

"I'm Belzy," the man growled. "What brings you two up to these parts?" The man crossed his arms and narrowed his beady eyes.

"We're on official business for King Hercalon," replied Andy.

"I see." They heard him mutter under his breath, "They get younger and younger." Then he prompted, "Well, come on. I'll show you to your room."

Belzy led them down a narrow hall with yellowed, peeling wallpaper. They passed rooms numbered one, two, and three before stopping outside an unmarked door. He unlocked it and led them in. A small common area had been furnished with a threadbare sofa and chair, and a separate bedroom was just big enough for two lumpy cots, one against each wall. There was no window, and the darkness and warmth combined with the musty smell to make the room feel claustrophobic. Belzy instructed the boys to leave their things in the common room, then led them farther down the hall to the shared guest bathroom.

"Wash up," he huffed. "Dinner will be ready in a few minutes."

Andy and Alden thanked him and headed back toward their room. On the way, they saw a maid wearing a white apron over a canary-yellow dress. A white cap covered her hair, but that's not what made them freeze. The woman was short, with a beak-like nose and long arms that nearly touched the floor. Andy and Alden exchanged glances, trying not to be obvious. The maid looked up as she passed and gave a half smile. They returned plastic smiles.

As soon as they had closed the door to their room, Alden spoke in a hushed tone. "Abaddon's going to know we're here and on a mission for the King!"

"Dinner's ready. Join us in the dining room," Bee called down the hallway.

"We'll have to figure this out after dinner."

They entered a cramped room to find they were the only guests dining with Belzy and Bee tonight. A small table had been set for four. The silverware was tarnished. Bone china plates, which had once been painted with the sun and moon walking hand-in-hand through a meadow, were chipped and missing large parts of the scene.

The maid—her name was Miss Chairee—had prepared dinner. After everyone was seated, she brought out mashed potatoes and turkey, cranberry sauce, green beans, rolls, and all the trimmings—it looked like Thanksgiving dinner! The boys had not eaten since their early lunch and were famished. Everything smelled so good!

Andy took a huge helping of mashed potatoes and turkey and started devouring them. Alden did the same. With each bite, Andy relaxed and even started to feel sleepy from all the activity of the day. He noticed Belzy and Bee share glances periodically. The couple only nibbled at the meal but Andy didn't think much of it. By the end of dinner, both he and Alden were more contented than they had been in a long time.

Bee proved to be quite the conversationalist, for she kept probing the boys on the details of their journey between tales of life in the village.

Andy yawned, triggering Alden to do the same, which only made Andy yawn again. And once they started, it seemed they couldn't stop themselves. Just before they dozed off, Belzy and Bee helped them up from the table and led them to the lumpy cots in their room.

"Sleep well," Belzy said in a sweet tone.

Why's he so nice all of a sudden? flitted through Andy's mind.

Even in his very sleepy state, Andy felt the pouch for Methuselah and the key. They were still there. He vaguely heard the door click shut and the lock turn before he drifted off.

It must have been a few hours later when Andy woke with a start. He thought he'd heard someone screaming at him to wake up. His mind felt fuzzy, beyond normal morning grogginess, but a quick survey of the room revealed nothing unusual. Everything was quiet. With no windows he couldn't tell what time it was. He rolled over.

He'd barely drifted off when he thought he again heard someone pleading for him to wake up. He opened an eye but everything remained still. Andy stretched and yawned.

"Alden."

"Hmmm."

"Wake up."

"Huh? Whhyy?"

"I think we're in trouble."

"What do you mean?"

"I think I heard a voice. It was trying to tell me to wake up."

"Tell it you're tired."

"No. I'm serious. Wake up."

"Fine." Alden roused and began fumbling to find his clothes in the dark.

Andy stood and reached over Alden. He grabbed hold of the doorknob and turned. Locked. He tried again but it didn't budge. "The door won't open." His voice rose as he spoke.

Alden stopped searching and sat up between the cots. "Want me to try?"

"Be my guest."

Alden tried with the same result.

"What should we do?"

Andy slammed a fist against the wood, then another. Alden joined him. "Help! Let us out!" the pair yelled at the top of their lungs. No response.

After waiting several minutes, they pounded and yelled again. Still nothing.

Andy started feeling around the walls and ceiling for an opening. "Help me see if there's any other way out."

Several minutes later Andy concluded, "This room is sealed tight. We're not going anywhere."

"So now what do we do?"

"I don't know."

What seemed like hours later their stomachs started complaining and the stuffiness further intensified their discomfort.

"We have to do something. We can't just sit here," declared Alden. He tried pounding on the door and yelling for help once more, but no help came. "I'm starving."

"Me too, but whining about it isn't going to fix the problem!"

"I'm not whining."

"Yes you are!"

"No I'm not!"

"Yes. You. Are."

Alden gave Andy a shove to press his denial. Andy pushed back. Jostling quickly escalated into punching and an all-out brawl ensued.

"You got us into this mess! You suck up to anyone who congratulates you on saving my life. Bee praised you in front of all those people. Now look where we are!" accused Alden, pushing Andy into the wall.

"What do you mean? I didn't hear you objecting to the dinner invitation," Andy shot back, landing a jab to Alden's chin.

"And you, going on and on about you and your dad doing stuff together. I only wish my dad was still alive." Alden boxed Andy's ear.

"He took me camping. It was only once, okay!" Andy's fist found Alden's shoulder.

"I've watched you! Anyone who praises you—" shouted Alden. His fist found Andy's back.

"What are you talking about?"

"Since the governor brought you up on stage at the festival, you get all puffed up every time people congratulate you!" huffed Alden, landing a blow to Andy's ribs.

"So what! I'm proud of what I did! I saved your life! You should be thankful!" Andy shoved Alden back against the wall. "You're just jealous!"

"I'm not jealous!" Alden cuffed Andy's thigh.

"Yes you are! Why else would you be fighting me?"

"What's it matter? We're never getting out of here!"

Alden hit Andy's chest, catching his fist on Methuselah. "Ouch!" he yelped.

Andy rubbed his chest under the pouch.

"What was that?"

"Methuselah."

Andy stopped scuffling and pulled the hilt out. Immediately the blade extended to its full length, but it did more—it began glowing brightly. Andy could see Alden sitting on the adjacent cot, eyes wide.

"Awesome! I didn't expect that!" Andy exclaimed, examining the blade more closely.

"Can I see it?" Alden's tone came out hushed.

"Sure, if you stop hitting me."

Alden frowned but nodded.

As his friend investigated the blade's light-generating capabilities, Andy remembered the gold key. "Wait a minute. I wonder…" He pulled the key out and scooted down his cot toward the locked door.

"Can you bring the light closer?"

Andy held the key up to the lock.

"It's too big," Alden observed.

"I have a feeling…" Andy pressed the key against the faceplate of the lock and pushed. It gave way and shrank to fit.

Alden's mouth gaped open.

Andy inserted the key as far as it would go.

"Cross your fingers," he instructed Alden.

Not familiar with the idiom, Alden looked puzzled and, still holding Methuselah, extended both index fingers and crossed them.

Andy looked over. "Nevermind. It's just an expression." He slowly turned the key and…*click*!

"It worked?" Alden studied his crossed fingers.

Andy smiled as he removed the key from the lock.

"How?" Alden chirped, studying the tool. "Where'd you get it?"

"Like Methuselah, it just appeared to me."

Alden continued inspecting the key as Andy pondered aloud, "Whoever sent us on this mission knew we'd need it. But how? What's that even mean?"

Alden handed the key back to Andy who returned it to the pouch.

"No idea, but let's get out of here," Alden whispered as he handed Methuselah back, reached for the door handle, and encouraged the protesting hinges to permit them exit.

The common room was gray with dawn's first light, and its coolness refreshed the boys. They crept over to their backpacks, still leaning against the wall where they had left them. Empty. The contents had been taken along with the fog-removing cap. Alden rubbed his empty stomach.

"We'll find food as we walk," Andy whispered.

Alden nodded.

They stepped into the hall and Andy closed the door behind them as quietly as possible. They crept down the corridor. Halfway along, Alden stepped on a loose floorboard. It creaked and Andy shot him a look of alarm.

"Sorry," he mouthed.

Just fifteen feet from their goal. The front door practically screamed of the freedom it would afford. But someone moved about in the kitchen to their right. Andy peered around the corner. The maid was standing at the stove with her back to them. They darted past the hallway, but lumbering footsteps approaching behind them sent bolts of electricity up both their spines. They shared a glance and Andy pointed toward the front door.

They made a run for it. Andy prayed it was not locked. He turned the handle and out they flew across the front porch, down the steps, and past the peeling white picket fence. Belzy started yelling, "Stop thieves! Stop thieves!"

Andy glanced back. The man stood on the front porch waving his fists at them, his arms now grown abnormally long. The maid had joined him and was also yelling. She turned quickly and nearly hit Belzy's now beak-shaped nose with a kitchen spatula.

Reassured that Belzy did not pursue, the pair slowed to a walk, but rest was not to be, for Alden pointed upward and yelled, "Look!"

They no longer had the benefit of Mermin's fog-clearing invention. Through the thick fog they could barely make out the forms of several large black birds circling overhead, and they were getting closer!

Andy and Alden ducked under the branches of some nearby shade trees, hoping to draw their attackers off. They charged back toward the town square and the well, the way they had come, keeping to the cover of the trees as much as possible. Unfortunately, there were not many trees to hide under.

Andy's heart raced. *Those things are gonna attack any minute!*

They reached the well only to find a group of men with long arms and beak-shaped noses waiting for them—the group was armed with all manner of weapons.

One look and the boys kept sprinting. But there was no place to hide! Stabbing stitches knifed Andy's side. Alden clutched his stomach, and Andy knew his friend experienced equal pain. Andy tried to gulp in air but breath would not come fast enough. Just when he felt he could run no farther, the Forest of Giants came into view. *No!*

The vulture-men closed in. *Yes!*

Without stopping, Andy charged into the forest. Alden hesitated only a moment.

CHAPTER THIRTEEN

King Abaddon

The pursuers gave up the chase as soon as the boys plunged into the forest. But taunts followed: "Ha! You won't last long in there!" "Our job is done, that's for sure!"

Andy and Alden stumbled behind a thick tree trunk and collapsed, chests heaving.

"You know why they let us go, don't you?" Alden panted.

Andy nodded, unable to speak. His stomach tied itself in a knot.

The edges of the forest were light with the morning sun. Even though no fog could penetrate the thick foliage, the dense canopy made it dark and the boys couldn't see far. As their eyes adjusted, they scanned the area. An eerie stillness blanketed the thick growth. Only a brave chirp or the hum of a flying insect disturbed the solitude. Andy swallowed.

Okay, I'm afraid. I can let it grip me, or…

Andy cleared his throat, held Methuselah up, and motioned for his compatriot to follow.

"Are you sure?" Alden squeaked.

"No, but we can't go back that way."

Alden let out a whimper.

The forest smelled musty, like wet towels after they've been sitting in a heap for several days (not that Andy would know anything about that). Dry, fallen leaves crunched under their feet as they stumbled through the dense undergrowth.

Something skittered where Andy was about to step and he jumped. He grabbed for Alden. When nothing leapt at him they continued on, slowly, cautiously. Every stray noise sent chilled fingers up and down Andy's back.

Methuselah's light only penetrated a short distance. Andy hunched over and kept scanning, desperately wishing he had X-ray vision or at least night vision goggles.

A dangling vine brushed the side of Alden's head and forced out a yelp. "Shhh."

They passed several hulking tree trunks laced together by thick vines that wove a tapestry through the wood. Stumpy ferns that rose to Andy's waist fought for purchase between bushes that had grown above his head.

At one point they found themselves surrounded by a particularly thick outgrowth that prevented their passage. Andy raised Methuselah. He was about to strike when Alden cautioned, "No! Don't!" The Cartesian pointed and took hurried steps away from the growth as it began to move.

Andy followed on his heels as a thick, variegated green coil unfolded itself and a diamond-headed snake flicked its tongue at them. The instant its belly reached the floor the boys yipped and took off. They ran around trees, ducked under vines, and hurdled rotted branches. A mammoth fallen tree trunk lying in the path finally brought them up short.

"Hey, I just realized something," Andy panted.

"What's that?"

"The plants haven't tried to attack us. I thought you said people believe they'll eat you."

"Yeah, that's the story. Or a giant'll grab you."

"Hello!" Andy yelled. "We're here! Come and get us!"

"Shhh! Stop that!"

Alden hunched over, ears perked, while Andy held Methuselah up, waiting, daring. Several minutes passed but nothing happened.

Alden's stomach gave a loud rumble. "Sorry," he whispered as Andy glanced at him.

"I think the rumors are wrong. This is just a huge forest of mammoth trees. Nothing more."

"I don't know…the rumors have to be based on something."

"No idea, but I think we're good. Now come on, we need to find food," declared Andy. "Are any of these plants safe to eat?"

"They don't look familiar. They're a lot bigger than anything I've ever seen—and more brightly colored, too."

They stumbled into a huge blackberry bush with leaves the size of Frisbees and berries as big as softballs.

"Wow!" the two breathed in unison.

Andy retracted Methuselah's blade and tucked the hilt safely in the pouch. He reached up to pick a huge berry.

"I don't know if the berries are safe to eat."

"Well, I'm starving!" Andy reached up, tugged a blackberry loose from the branch, and took a bite. It was delicious—juicy and sweet with a hint of tartness. The juices cascaded over his face and down his front. He took another bite and another.

Alden's stomach gave a loud rumble and he reached up and started wrestling a second berry loose. As Andy took another bite, one of the bush's tentacles wrapped around Alden's foot.

"Alden! The bush is alive!"

The words had barely escaped Andy's mouth when the plant grabbed Andy's arms and began dragging him. Squirming, kicking, and screaming, the boys fought against their bonds.

After a few yards, the blackberry bush tossed the boys at another thorn-covered plant, which in turn tossed them at a pricker bush. The handoffs continued for what seemed like an eternity. Sometimes they were thrown at a tree or shrub without spikes, but most times the barbs of the vegetation dug deep into their skin. Within minutes, nearly every inch of their bodies was scratched or bleeding.

Just when Andy thought he could stand it no longer, a tree whose leaves looked like poison ivy threw them into a clearing where three giants played cards at a huge wooden picnic table. One giant looked up from his hand of cards and smiled.

"Hey Hank, looks like our breakfast just dropped in."

"Yeah, Zank, looks like nice tasty morsels. Berry flavored. But there's not much meat on 'em," he chuckled with a dumb-sounding laugh. He reached down and scratched his butt through ragged leggings.

"Hey Tank, take our breakfast to Blank to prepare," ordered Zank. At this, the largest of the giants stood, upsetting his stool. He lumbered over to Andy and Alden and picked them up by the scruff of their necks. The boys grabbed at the tops of their tunics, trying desperately to raise their necks above the strangling fabric as they gasped for breath.

Tank lugged them kicking toward an enormous wood structure, through an open door, and into a large kitchen where a giantess labored over an immense hearth. She wore a white apron over a yellow and green plaid dress. Her white bonnet looked like a large muffin perched atop her round head. The fire was roaring. Blank looked up and frowned. "Breakfast is already set, Tank. I'll cook 'em up for lunch later. Hang them over there for now."

Tank dutifully obeyed, suspending Andy and Alden by the backs of their tunics on hooks near an open window before heading back to his card game. The boys continued struggling for air as the fabric cut into their necks. Blank finished her preparations, rang a loud bell, and moved her provisions outside to the picnic table. As soon as Blank disappeared, Andy gasped, "Put…your arms…up…and drop."

The two landed on the floor with a thud. The pouch around Andy's neck swung and smacked him in the head as he landed. "Oh," he moaned, rubbing the point of impact as he drank in great gulps of air.

"That was close," croaked Alden, gently scratching his arm where the poison ivy had hugged him. Andy started to scratch as well.

They watched several more giants emerge from the cabins—old grandpa giants walking with canes and baby giants sucking on their fingers, teenage giants talking back to the adults and middle age giants looking dumpy and slow. Alden counted 64 in all.

"Come on. Let's get out of here while they're eating," whispered Andy. The door to the kitchen stood directly in line with the gathering. They inched toward freedom.

Alden spied a pot of porridge simmering on the hearth and his stomach gave a loud grumble. "Psst! Andy." He pointed.

While it was about the worst thing either of them had ever tasted— *Wallpaper paste?* Andy wondered—it filled their hungry bellies. Several minutes later, Andy peered out the doorway to make sure all the giants were still eating. The coast was clear. They darted out the door and around to the side of the cabin. They waited in nervous anticipation for the sound of giant footsteps in pursuit, but none came.

Even though their bodies ached from the beating they had received by the vegetation, Alden gave Andy a thumbs-up and a big smile. Both boys were bleeding from various wounds and itching from poison ivy. Their necks burned where their tunics had cut into their skin.

"If we don't pick any fruit, I think we'll be okay," Andy whispered as the giants' carryings-on grew distant.

They crept along in the dim light, but nothing grabbed for them. The thick undergrowth was disorienting. After wandering for quite some time, neither knew which way they were going. To Andy it felt as though they walked in circles.

Their teeth chattered from the unrelenting dampness on bare skin, and they hugged themselves to try and retain even the smallest warmth. Then their stomachs started complaining once more. With the darkness, they couldn't tell what time it was.

"Now I understand why the legend says anyone who enters the Forest of Giants is never seen or heard from again," said Alden, taking off a sandal and shaking stones out. "I wish we knew which way to go to get out."

Andy opened his pouch and pulled out Methuselah. Quick as lightning, the blade extended from the hilt. Andy held it up straight, but the blade instantly tipped to the side. He corrected it, straightening its position, but again it tipped to the side.

"That's weird," Alden remarked.

"This sword does all sorts of things regular ones don't. Maybe it's trying to point us out of the forest," Andy hoped. "What have we got to lose? Come on."

Andy held Methuselah in front of him with both hands, like a water dowser he had seen on a TV documentary. They followed wherever the tip of the sword directed, eventually stumbling upon a clearing with a quaint little cottage. Staying well hidden, they crouched in the undergrowth and peered out to see if anyone came or went. The house had a small, well-maintained garden with abundant tomatoes, cucumbers, beans, peas, vegetables of all varieties.

After waiting several minutes, a hunched old lady came out the back door with a wicker basket over her arm and a pair of shears in her hand. She wore a freshly pressed bright blue apron over a crisp yellow dress. Her gray hair was neatly done up in a bun, and silver-rimmed glasses perched halfway down her nose. She headed to the garden and snipped some tomatoes and beans, putting them into her basket. Then she added a few peas to the mix and pulled a few weeds. But instead of returning to the house, she walked straight toward where the boys hid, stopping just feet in front of them. "You'll have to do better than that to hide from Anta Emm," she declared. "Come inside. Let me get you both fixed up and cook you a proper meal. Goodness, you'll catch cold if you don't get some proper clothes on."

Andy and Alden stared at each other. *That name sounds familiar. Where have I heard it before?* They slowly emerged from the underbrush and looked about nervously, half expecting to be ambushed by some unseen menace. Andy held Methuselah protectively, just in case.

"You can put that sword away, sonny. Won't be needing it here." The lady turned and walked back toward the house.

Andy continued to clutch Methuselah and look around suspiciously as they followed.

They walked in the back door of the tiny cottage and were greeted by the smell of freshly baked chocolate chip cookies.

"I was told to be expecting you," Anta explained, putting her basket on the kitchen counter.

The cottage seemed unusually spacious inside. It was neatly decorated with keepsakes and family pictures, the walls were freshly painted, and everything smelled clean. After all they had been through, this might have seemed like a welcome retreat, but Andy darted his gaze about, making note of another exit down the hall. Alden seemed to be thinking the same thing.

"Let me get my bandages," the woman declared, making the pair jump. She disappeared into a room.

Andy rubbed the back of his neck and Alden scratched his shoulders as they waited.

The woman took to cleaning their wounds in silence. She washed every scrape, applied cream to the poison ivy so it stopped itching, and bandaged anything that was bleeding.

When she had finished, Anta announced, "I have chicken and dumplings prepared. I understand that's your favorite dish, Andy."

Alden glanced quickly at Andy who gasped, "How?"

Anta chuckled and raised her pointer finger. "But before we eat, you need some clothes." She rooted around in a closet and found two tunics and clean leggings. She held them up. "These should do."

She left them to change. The clothes fit perfectly.

They sat down at a table loaded with fresh watermelon, sliced tomatoes, freshly baked biscuits, chicken and dumplings, cinnamon rolls, and more of their favorites. At first Andy and Alden picked at the food, unsure whether they should trust it. But in the end, hunger overcame their hesitation and they wolfed down huge helpings of everything.

When at last they finished gorging, Andy pushed back from the table and declared, "That was delicious!"

"You're welcome, boys." A smile filled the old woman's face.

"May I ask, what did you mean when you said you had been told to expect us?" Andy queried.

Anta smiled. "Years ago, when I felt the prompting to leave my comfortable life in the city of Oops and move into the Forest of Giants, people called me crazy. But I knew that's what I was supposed to do."

Andy interrupted absentmindedly, "That's it! I remember Mermin talking about you! That's where I've heard your name before."

Anta Emm grinned and continued. "Since I've been here, even though it seems like the last place anyone would want to live, I have had great prosperity. I've never understood why. But then, a few nights ago, I had another prompting, that a pair of boys would be coming. I didn't argue or doubt, just prepared for your visit the best I could. And here you are!"

Tension eased from Andy's shoulders. "When you said you had a prompting, what happened exactly?"

"Oh, I received a message in a pulsing sphere."

Alden raised a brow.

"Was it purple, and did it start with a trumpet blast?" laughed Andy.

"As a matter of fact, yes. How did you know?"

"I've gotten two of those now."

The three of them chatted for a long while, swapping stories and laughing until their sides ached. Andy and Alden helped clear the table and put away the leftovers while Anta washed the dishes. When the work was done, she ushered them down a cheery hallway to a bedroom that smelled clean and fresh. There were two twin beds lining opposite walls of the modestly furnished room, and a vase of freshly cut wildflowers stood on the nightstand before an open window. They washed up in the adjacent bathroom—the soft, warm towels smelled like sunshine. Andy was the first in bed and Alden followed shortly thereafter. The sheets soothed his injured skin. They opted to leave the door to the hall ajar…just in case.

Dreams came quickly.

Warm sunshine streaming through the window woke Andy the next morning. It felt good. Alden still slept. He glanced over to see the door to the hall cracked open, exactly as they had left it the night before, and he smiled.

After dressing quietly, Andy tiptoed out the door. Partway down the hall his nose detected blueberry muffins being baked, and he tracked the tantalizing smell into the kitchen. Next to the table, he found two new backpacks standing at attention, filled to the top with clothes and food.

"I knew you'd be needing them," Anta said as she entered the kitchen behind him.

"Thank you!"

Once Alden rose, they ate breakfast, packed up their gear, and said their goodbyes. After being without provisions, the weight of their backpacks felt comforting.

"I'm not sure where you're going, boys, but be careful. If you need anything, just let me know."

"We will, Anta. Thank you for everything."

When they were several minutes away, Andy pulled out Methuselah. The blade extended and guided them as it had yesterday. Andy hoped it would lead them out of the Forest of Giants.

They had awakened to warm sunshine at Anta's cottage, but the weather changed as they walked. The forest grew darker and they could hear thunder rumbling through the leaves overhead. Rain began to fall. For the first time, Andy and Alden were glad they had the thick canopy to keep most of the moisture away.

Hearty food coupled with the night's rest had renewed Andy's hopes. He was in a good mood and started to whistle. But a loud roar sounding through the trees put a quick kibosh on his merriment. It wasn't thunder. They froze and waited. The roar came again. Methuselah pointed them toward the source.

"No, Methuselah," Andy corrected. "We need to get out of here." He willed Methuselah to retract its blade, but it ignored him. So he started walking away from the sound. Still, Methuselah remained steadfast, refusing to move in any other direction.

"I can't believe this! We're being dictated to by this sword."

"Actually, I think it's trying to show us something."

"You want to get near whatever that is?"

"No, but so far it's given us good directions."

They followed Methuselah as quietly as they could. The roars grew louder. As they got closer, it became clear that they were overhearing an argument, even though neither of them understood the language. Several heated voices yelled and the roaring continued. Methuselah stopped and they took cover behind the nearest trees.

Peering through the foliage, they spied a beast, the likes of which they had never seen, standing in the clearing several feet in front of them. It was a monstrous red dragon with seven heads, ten horns, four enormous wings, and a gigantic tail that mowed down everything in its way no matter how big. A huge swath of trees and vegetation had been leveled in its wake. A liquid that looked like water spurted from three of its mouths, but when the clear liquid landed on its target, it sizzled and bubbled. A bright green mist spilled out of two other mouths, and fire out of two more.

Alden looked at Andy, his eyes wide. "What is that thing?"

Andy could not immediately tell which mouths spewed what, but the green mist looked familiar from his exploration of the castle and the dungeon door. When a whiff of the stench hit their noses a minute later, Andy knew without a doubt it was the same.

The dragon was furious, arguing with several oversized vulture-men. Not far from the gathering, Andy saw the fog-removing invention Mermin had given them!

The arguing continued in the unfamiliar tongue.

Andy gulped. *Please don't make me battle this dragon*, he pleaded.

They stood watching for several minutes until Methuselah guided them away at last. They left as quickly and quietly as possible.

Andy had a sinking feeling this was not the last time he would be seeing the creature, and a chill ran down his spine.

CHAPTER FOURTEEN

A Raging River

B y lunchtime, Methuselah had led them to the edge of the Forest of Giants. They stopped and ate some of the delicious food Anta had packed. Rain continued to fall, more heavily than it had earlier.

While walking in the rain was inevitable, the boys didn't look forward to getting drenched. After lunch, they rummaged through their backpacks and found Anta had remembered rain ponchos. Slipping them on over their packs, Andy started to laugh. Alden looked like an overgrown mutant turtle in his evergreen-colored getup topped off by his bushy, neon-green hair. Alden also broke out laughing once Andy had secured his own poncho.

They put their hoods up and ventured into the rain and dense fog, Methuselah leading the way.

Their feet became instantly soaked as they trudged through huge puddles. Having left the cover of the forest behind, it was difficult to stay hidden, but they quickly found the Great Wall that surrounded the land of Oomaldee and followed it. Andy hoped that between the downpour and the fog no one would see them.

They fell into silence as they walked. Every once in a while Andy would turn and say something to Alden, but his companion seemed deep in thought so Andy gave it up and trudged on in silence beside him.

A few hours passed before they could start to make out the Victory watchtower in the distance through the rain and fog. Even though they had ponchos, the boys were soaked to the skin as heavy rain continued to fall with no sign of letting up.

As the scant daylight began to fade, Alden suggested, "We need to find a dry place out of sight and camp for the night." Andy made no protest.

The flat, open plain they had been walking through this afternoon did not provide much shelter, but a short way off they spotted the outline of a large willow tree, its flowing branches tossing violently in the wind and rain.

"What do you think? Can we climb up there?" Andy questioned.

"Let's check it out."

The tree's massive branches were so thick, they reminded Andy of drainage pipes he had seen near his home. Clearly, the tree had been standing here for many, many years. Andy and Alden reached the willow and circled its base looking for footing to climb up. Halfway around, Andy found boards secured to the trunk that formed a ladder. He hesitated.

I hope no one else is taking refuge in this tree tonight.

He began his ascent. It wasn't the easiest climb, what with a flapping poncho that tried to insert itself between his sandal and each slippery wood slat as well as a bulky backpack weighing him down, but he made it. He stopped twenty feet up, standing on the lowest branch of the enormous tree.

"Come on up," he called down. "There's a little dry place up here."

Alden followed. Andy had found an area of dense branches and leaves that afforded some protection from the pelting rain. Upon further investigation, and to his surprise, he found another set of stairs leading higher up the trunk.

"Alden, look!"

Andy continued climbing another fifteen feet and found a round opening hollowed out in the trunk. It looked just big enough for them to squeeze through if they removed their backpacks.

Andy stuck his head into the hole and illuminated it with Methuselah's blade. Empty. He removed his poncho and backpack, hung them from one of the steps, and squeezed through the opening. He stuck his head back out and pulled his belongings inside. Alden followed.

The space was cozy with both of them plus their packs inside. More importantly, it was dry. There was nothing special about the space, no decorations or comforts, but in this weather it was more than enough. It seemed someone or something had taken great care to carve out this sanctuary while not harming the tree. Whoever it was deserved much thanks.

With scant room to move, Andy and Alden took turns opening their backpacks to pull out long-sleeved shirts, food, and other provisions. After adding an additional layer of warmth, they munched in silence as Alden's mood from earlier continued to dampen any conversation. Andy took quick glances at his friend.

At length Alden ran a hand through his neon-green locks and took a deep breath. He began, "I owe you an apology."

Andy stopped chewing and glanced up to see the muscles in Alden's face taught. "I haven't been very nice to you. It's just that…I just want people to—" Alden rubbed a hand on his leg. "Remember when you first got here? I told you I was 'just a servant.' You didn't agree." Andy nodded and Alden began moving a hand up and down his arm.

"I entered the Tower Chase competition, and I guess I saw it as an opportunity to earn some respect." He cleared his throat. "I couldn't believe it when Optimistic and I won." A smile edged its way onto his face. "When they presented me with my first prize medal, I shut them up. Every single one. No one heckled. It was awesome."

Alden reveled in the memory for a minute before continuing. "But then at the closing ceremony, when the governor brought you up on stage, the crowd cheered more for you than…and then when it seemed like everyone congratulated you and not…

"Then you talked about how you and your dad went camping together…and I wish my dad was still alive. Look, I'm sorry. It's not your fault. You saved my life. You're right, I'm jealous of…" Alden stared at the floor, his shoulders hunched. "I shouldn't have treated you like I did."

"I never feel like what I do is good enough, especially for my dad." Andy exhaled loudly. The admission drew Alden's gaze upward. "I'm always in trouble with him and Mom, even though I try to do what I think they want me to. Somehow I screw things up and they're always mad at me. For what it's worth, Dad and I only went on that one camping trip. I guess that's why I remember it so well. He's always so busy with his business he never seems to have time for me."

The two sat in silence, neither sure how to respond to the other's confession.

"Maybe we're both looking for people to respect us," Andy speculated a minute later.

Alden nodded. "I think it's what the King calls dignity."

"Well, I know he thinks a lot of you…and so do I, so you don't have to prove anything to me."

Silence again punctuated the night until Alden offered, "I've never had a friend like you."

"Yeah, me neither." Smiles mounted their faces.

Their reflections brought a calm despite the raging elements, and Andy noticed what had been uncomfortable silence took on a companionable air. He took a deep breath and let it out slowly as the songs of pelting rain and fierce winds sang the boys to sleep.

Andy's dreams started singing harmony to the tumult as he found himself walking in rocky, mountainous terrain. Brambles and thorn bushes, which could barely survive in the dry, desert conditions, jutted out from crevasses. It was dusk and he heard the baying of wolves in the distance.

As he passed by a rock outcropping, he heard the noise of shouting in a language he didn't understand. Someone or something was yelling at him. He turned slowly. Before him, the red dragon he had seen earlier reared up on its hind legs, blasting fire at him from two of its seven heads. Its wings fanned the flames hotter.

Andy jumped out of the way, barely avoiding the blasts. He drew Methuselah's blade, infuriating the beast further. The dragon flew at him. It was faster than he expected. Just as he was about to be overcome, Andy woke up sweating and trembling.

Darkness reigned and rain continued punishing the tree. He heard Alden's regular breathing and sighed. Sleep took its time coming after that.

Andy and Alden awoke to foggy sunshine and the sound of birds singing. What a different world morning brought! Andy didn't mention his dream to Alden. They ate breakfast, packed up their gear, and headed out of their hideaway. As they started climbing down, they paused to survey their surroundings. Through the dense branches and fog, they could see and hear a nearby river running in torrents, its banks overflowing. The uproar of the storm had masked its presence.

"That must be the Red River," Alden speculated.

They stepped down onto the ground and their sandals immediately sank into the gooey mud. It oozed through their leggings, between their toes, and sucked at their feet, laboring each step.

"At least it's not quicksand!" Andy commented.

Alden grinned.

With the river as swollen as it was, they walked up and down the bank hoping to find some low point to cross, but nothing even remotely like a solution presented itself.

"Now what?" asked Alden after several minutes.

Andy sat down on a thick tree trunk that had been uprooted and swept downstream overnight and was now lodged firmly in the bank. He set down his backpack and pulled the gold key from his pouch.

"When we were trapped in that house, this key opened the door."

"But there's no door."

"Yes, but based upon what it did to the stone statues, this key opens more than doors. Maybe it will show us a way across the river. What have we got to lose?"

Andy addressed the key: "Please, show us the way." No sooner had he spoken than a creature popped its head out of the raging water.

"Glaucin, cousin of Mermin twice removed, at your service."

The boys shifted back in unison. A merman! He was handsome, bare-chested from the waist up with aqua fish scales covering the lower half of his body. He had a robust tail that changed colors like a rainbow in the light. His hair and beard looked to be made of seaweed.

Alden shot a disbelieving glance at Andy.

"Where's your trident?" Andy queried

"New technology. I upgraded last year to a disc implanted under the skin in my right hand." Glaucin turned his hand toward the boys. "I don't miss having to carry that clumsy thing. Kept dropping it."

Andy cleared his throat, trying to bring the conversation back to the current situation. "We need to cross this river, Glaucin. Can you help us?"

"I can, but first you must answer a riddle. If you answer correctly, I will carry you across. If you answer incorrectly, I cannot help you."

"Why do we need to answer a riddle?" Andy asked, puzzled at the delay.

"I am the keeper of this river. The riddle separates those who are worthy from those who are not. If you are worthy, you will answer correctly."

"But we are on a quest for the King!" objected Alden.

"Then you should have no worries about answering the riddle. Are you ready?"

"If you're really Mermin's cousin—" began Andy.

"Twice removed," interrupted Glaucin, extending the index finger on his left hand.

"Fine. If you're really Mermin's cousin *twice removed*, why won't you just help us?"

"I am helping you in ways you cannot yet see."

"I don't believe you. All I know is that you're delaying us from our goal," Andy snapped.

"Ah, a testy one! Nonetheless, it matters not whether you believe me. You have no choice."

"So, you're saying if we don't answer your riddle correctly, we'll have to walk all the way to where the Red River begins, way up into the mountains, in order to get around it?" clarified Andy, his temper rising. "That would add several days to our trip!"

"That is correct."

"Fine! Ask your stupid riddle," Andy sulked.

"Very well. The riddle is this:

"If you break me, I keep working.

If you touch me, I may be moved.
If you lose me, nothing will matter.
What am I?"

"Can you say that again so I can get all of it?" requested Alden, joining Andy on the log.

Glaucin repeated the riddle.

"We have no time for this!" shouted Andy, waving his arms.

"You make time for what is important to you," countered Glaucin. "Nothing is more important to you than crossing this river as quickly as possible. With the rains, that is more difficult than usual, and I am your only option."

It killed Andy to admit that what Glaucin said was true. He detested having to settle down and figure out a riddle when they needed to be making progress toward the red dragon. *What a waste of time!*

Alden continued thinking. Andy paced. Glaucin waited in the rushing torrent, doing flips and dives to pass the time.

Several minutes passed with no ideas from Alden. Andy was losing what little patience he had.

Suddenly, Andy's inneru interrupted his thoughts. "You do realize you're being a butthead."

Ugh. You! Not now.

"Au contraire, yes now. Why are you so frustrated?"

He's wasting time. He should take us across!

"Why?"

A memory of Mom flashed in Andy's mind. At the time, she had been correcting him for being impatient and had informed him that she did not respond when he was being demanding. Andy kicked a stone.

"What a lovely day!" shouted Glaucin over the roar of the current as he came up and did another flip above the water. "I was out for a dive in the Sea of Mystery this morning, hunting for sand dollars, when I was asked to come. I figured it was such a beautiful day, why not help. By the way, I didn't write the riddle, but I think you have to agree that it's a pretty good one!"

This guy is driving me crazy, and this stupid riddle is taking way too long to solve!

"Tut, tut, tut," Andy's inneru interrupted. "Do you remember the definition of patience?"

No. Who cares?

"Let me see, it's in here somewhere." The inneru rummaged through several files in Andy's brain. "You could really stand to get a housekeeper in here, Andy." It sneezed, then continued searching. "Not exactly frequently used files," it muttered under its breath. "Okay, almost there. Let's see—J, K…N, O… Ah, here we are. P. Okay, patience, patience. Yes, this is it."

His inneru stopped and sneezed again. "How 'bout that. It was on your spelling test a year ago. Okay, the definition of patience: 'Adjusting your expectations to fit a situation as it is, not as you wish it to be.' Looks like someone hasn't learned patience yet. Just sayin'."

You're not helping! Andy raged, his pitch rising.

He kicked a pebble and continued pacing, then exhaled loudly as the phrase "adjusting your expectations" began to make sense. *We'd be really stuck if Glaucin wasn't here.*

Andy walked over to where Alden had been thinking. "Come up with anything?"

"Well, first I thought about things like a stick or something like that, because you can break a stick and it's still a stick, and you could say it keeps working. You can touch it and it moves. But if you lose a stick, it doesn't make it so that nothing matters anymore."

Andy started thinking aloud. "It has to be something that you don't touch with your hands, like an idea or something like that. That's the only thing that makes sense."

"What about love?" Alden pondered a few minutes later, then reversed himself with, "No, 'cause you don't break love."

"But you *can* have a broken heart," Andy countered.

> *If you break me, I keep working.*
> *If you touch me, I may be moved.*
> *If you lose me, nothing will matter.*
> *What am I?*

"That works! Alden, I think the answer is heart!"

They waited for Glaucin to surface again. When he finally did, Andy announced their response.

"Is that your final answer?"

"Yes," Andy confirmed. "It's the only thing that makes sense…and I can relate." He thought of the times he'd been disappointed when his parents were too busy to come watch him in a school play. He thought about having to go trick-or-treating with neighbors because his parents had meetings.

"You okay?" asked Alden.

"Yeah…just remembering."

"You are correct!" Glaucin exclaimed. "Now, grab your things and I'll take you to the other side."

Andy and Alden did as they were told and laid down on Glaucin's back. They put their arms around his thick neck. In no time they were standing on the opposite shore, dry except for their feet, which had been doused by spray.

Glaucin did another flip and then paused in front of them.

"Thanks, Glaucin," the boys said in unison.

Glaucin nodded and headed back downstream.

"I should have asked who sent him," Andy realized a second too late.

CHAPTER FIFTEEN

The Battle

G laucin had dropped them at the intersection of the Red, Blood, and Slither Rivers, and the boys now followed the Slither's banks toward Dragontail watchtower. Since crossing the raging current, they had entered a mountainous region with tall pine trees covering much of the terrain.

Through the boughs and patchy fog, they spotted large vultures circling and stayed under cover. The thick foliage had kept the ground dry from the torrential rains of the days before. Andy loved the pine smell and breathed deeply. As they walked, their feet began to dry and their spirits rose. Wolves howled in the distance.

"Those are herewolves you're hearing," announced Alden.

Andy remembered Mermin telling him about herewolves and seeing carvings of them.

They stopped briefly to eat lunch and then continued on. They hoped to reach Dragontail watchtower before sundown. As the afternoon shadows grew longer, they could just make out the Great Wall through the thickening fog.

"This is good," reasoned Andy. "The fog is getting thicker. We should be able to make it through without being seen."

Andy remembered the instructions the King and Mermin had given them. They were to look for a secret door that, from this direction, should be to the right of where the river flowed under the tower. It was the entrance to a tunnel that ran through the Great Wall.

We're almost to the red dragons! Andy realized and quickened his pace.

An hour or so later, with the sun just setting and its final rays beginning to fade, they reached the pines at the base of their goal. They crouched down and began searching for the stone that would open the tunnel.

"I don't see anything," Andy whispered a couple minutes later.

"Maybe it's closer to the river," suggested Alden.

A minute later they detected the crunch of dry pine needles underfoot. Alden motioned and the two hurried back into the pines where they ducked behind two hefty trunks.

A watchman doing his evening rounds ambled into view. He stopped not more than ten feet away. His freakishly long arms and crooked, beak-like nose betrayed the crowd he hung around. He stood there for what seemed an eternity, scanning all about. Finally he moved on.

"That was close!" Alden whispered.

"Too close. Did you see that guy?"

"Yeah, he's one of Abaddon's goons!"

They resumed their search for the secret door. Alden crawled over to where the wall met the river and peered into the tunnel. He felt around. "Andy," he whispered.

When Andy reached him, Alden said, "Check this out. There's nothing behind these front stones."

"What do you mean?" Andy clutched the face of the wall with his right hand and reached into the dark. "You're right. It's like a façade."

Alden nodded. "With the darkness in that tunnel, you'd never see the optical illusion unless you looked closely." A smile bloomed on his face.

"Good job, my friend." Andy patted Alden's shoulder.

"Thanks." The meaning was not lost on the Cartesian.

One at a time, the boys swung behind the false front. Alden nearly fell in the river when his backpack shifted unexpectedly. Andy grabbed his arm and pulled him to safety. They stood on a small piece of dry ground with the river rushing to their left.

"Excellent!" whispered Alden. "Let's find the secret door."

The roar of the river to their left concealed the sounds of their search as they pressed each stone nearest the floor. At length, Andy's foot sunk down slightly and the sound of stone dragging across stone filled the air. The boys grimaced, hoping the guard did not hear and come to investigate.

"You did it!" Alden whispered, shaking his fists.

They stepped inside the tunnel and found another stone that closed the door behind them. Only the angry sounds of the river's rain-fueled rage penetrated the quiet of their sanctuary. Andy pulled Methuselah out and illuminated the space.

They stood in a narrow, stone-lined corridor. Clearly, it had been retrofitted after the Great Wall was built. Large wooden support beams set every ten feet secured the weight of the wall where it had been cut to accommodate the tunnel. To the right was a sign that read CAMP—20 YARDS AHEAD. A handful of torches rested against the wall nearby. Alden rummaged for a match in his backpack and lit it. Curious at what they might find, the pair then headed further into the tunnel, which sloped downward.

The boys soon found a room hollowed out of the ground, like an animal's burrow only larger. They could no longer hear the sound of the river.

"We must be on the other side of the wall," Andy deduced.

Thick cobwebs hung everywhere. Alden burned these away with the torch, sending several eight-legged inhabitants scurrying. A pile of logs sat neatly stacked against the far wall, and next to that was a hole in the ground, a bucket attached to a rope nearby.

"It's a well," surmised Alden.

In no time they had a fire blazing, a real treat after going without for so many days. Andy was amazed that smoke didn't build up inside, but Alden explained the simple ventilation system he saw in the walls that allowed smoke to escape while hiding it from the view of anyone outside. He'd seen the design somewhere else.

The boys pulled food out of their packs and began devouring dinner. When they were done, Alden scrounged in the bottom of his pack and pulled out one more package, then removed the cover. "I found these after we left Anta's, but I didn't know what they were. Do you have any idea?"

Alden handed one to Andy. The round, white ball was squishy. After inspecting it closely, he took a bite and beamed. "They're marshmallows! How did Anta know?"

"What are marshmallows?"

"Only one of my favorite campfire treats!"

Andy pulled Methuselah out and extended the blade. He put one of the marshmallows on the end and held it over the fire. Alden bent forward.

"Hey, see if she gave us chocolate bars and graham crackers, too."

"What are those?" Alden had no idea what he was looking for, but a second later he pulled out a small tin box and opened it.

"Yes!" Andy celebrated, pumping his fist.

Andy showed Alden how to assemble a s'more and then helped him roast his own marshmallow.

Several s'mores later, Andy cleaned off Methuselah's blade and it retracted back into the hilt.

"Old-world craftsmanship meets twenty-first-century treats!" Andy laughed.

The boys laid out their bedrolls near the warm fire, and the sound of their steady breathing soon filled the air.

As on the previous night, the dragon he had seen in the Forest of Giants visited Andy's dreams. He again dreamed he was walking in rocky, mountainous terrain with brambles and thorn bushes jutting out from crevasses. This time, however, it was daytime and he was hunting. He held Methuselah out in front of him, ready to strike at the first sign of food.

He rounded a boulder and there in the path ahead crouched the red dragon eating a fresh kill. Andy froze. Unfortunately, his movement alerted the beast to his presence. It looked up, then squared its shoulders and flapped its wings. A split second later, it reared up on its hind legs and leaped at him, blasting fire from two of its heads. Just before the inferno hit him, Andy yelled and woke up sweating and trembling. He was still in the cave with Alden, next to the fire. Alden rolled over, made a few noises, and continued sleeping. It took Andy a long time to get back to sleep.

The grumbling of Andy's stomach woke him the next morning. After a quick breakfast, they packed up their gear and headed into a passageway on the far side of the room, hoping it would lead them into the foothills of the Zwellow Mountains as the King and Mermin had promised.

An ancient door greeted them at the end of the tunnel. Only after much grunting and groaning did they finally manage to push it open and find the source of their struggle: it had been hidden behind a mound of old brush and heavy tree limbs through which they had now tunneled.

"No wonder!" Andy exclaimed. "No one was ever going to find it there."

Alden nodded as he bent over, panting.

Recovering their breath, they looked around before emerging. Off to the left they heard a calmer Slither River babbling to itself. Nothing but fluffy white clouds filled the sky.

"There's no fog!" Andy realized.

"Yeah, we can see for miles!"

Unfortunately, the scene was depressing. Ahead lay a vast display of desolate wasteland, jagged rock formations jutting skyward every so often. What were once tall evergreens now lay broken, their skeletons dismembered and strewn about the rocky soil. The burned and blackened mountains off in the distance lay despondent, like a bum on the street needing encouragement.

"What is this place?" asked Andy.

"It's the land of Hadession, Abaddon's land."

Andy's throat tightened.

The shadow of a large bird skimmed the ground not far away. They ducked into the brush and waited for it to move on.

"That was close!" whispered Alden, clearly afraid his voice might carry in the dry, barren conditions.

They stepped out and hastily covered everything back up, then dashed for the first monstrous rock formation. No sooner had they reached its safety than a flock of shadows swooped by. They made a run for the next formation before the next patrol reached them.

By mid-morning, rumbling and roaring sounds wafted over the countryside as they continued dashing between tall sentries.

"I think those are dragons," Alden speculated as they ate a quick lunch sometime later. The muscles in his jaw tensed from more than just munching moonberries and goat jerky.

Andy surveyed the horizon and his stomach twisted as he remembered his dreams.

By late afternoon they reached the point where the Slither River became nothing more than a trickle—they had reached the Dragon's Lair.

For such a mighty river, its beginnings are unimpressive.

The land became more mountainous and the scenery reminded Andy of his nightmares. He took a deep breath. *I hope my dreams didn't foreshadow something about to happen to us.*

The volume and frequency of dragon roars had increased significantly, and Andy felt as if he was being given a final exam on overcoming fear. "

Compared to that dragon with seven heads, normal dragons don't seem so scary, at least not from this distance," Andy tried to convince himself.

Alden raised an eyebrow but refrained from comment.

Keeping a lookout for circling vultures, Andy and Alden spotted a cave and made a beeline for it when the coast was clear. They ducked into the mouth and halted, listening above the sound of their heavy breathing.

"Andy…" Alden whispered.

Rustling emanated from behind them.

Andy put his pointer finger to his lips then slowly set his backpack down and reached for the pouch, pulling out Methuselah. The shiny blade extended.

"Stay here and keep watch," Andy instructed.

"Are you sure?" Alden squeaked.

Andy nodded, turned, and crept into the cave.

As his eyes adjusted, Andy could see a pair of glowing yellow cat-like eyes the size of softballs following him. A large shape crouched in the dimness. The smell of smoke bit his nostrils. *Oh boy….*

Andy whirled Methuselah's blade around in a figure-eight pattern, trying to intimidate whatever it was. The creature let out an ear-splitting roar, and fire burst from its mouth as it charged.

Andy pivoted and dashed toward the entrance. "Alden, take cover!"

As he reached the mouth of the cave, Andy took a quick look over his shoulder to find a dragon nearly upon him. He hesitated briefly, trying to find something to hide behind, but there was no cover. The monster was much faster than he expected, and the back of his neck screamed as flames licked it. He darted out of the cave, struggling to formulate a plan.

Please have the same anatomy as the dragons in Dragon Slayer, he pleaded. From his video game, Andy knew the scales covering the beast's chest should thin out at its loins, leaving the skin unprotected.

In a move he had executed only once while playing Dragon Slayer, Andy stopped, whirled around, and dove at the beast, forming a tight ball as he did. He somersaulted toward the dragon.

Not expecting such a move from its prey, the dragon ran over top of Andy. The instant its underbelly hovered directly above, Andy thrust Methuselah up into the soft flesh. The sword buried into the animal up to the hilt.

The yellow dragon skidded to a stop, let out a thunderous roar, and started to collapse. Andy rolled out from under the giant, barely avoiding being crushed as it met the ground. He raced back toward the mouth of the cave to take cover. The yellow dragon let out a final burst of smoke and closed its eyes, dead.

With such a disturbance, Andy fully expected the vultures to investigate. And he was right. No sooner had he ducked into the cave entrance than the silhouettes of a pack of vultures came into view.

Alden poked his head out from behind a rock inside the cave. "Way to go!"

"No time to celebrate, we have company."

The first vulture-man landed next to the dead dragon.

The boys grabbed their packs and headed farther into the cave, praying there were no more occupants. They stumbled around in the darkness, trying to find something to hide behind in case the vulture-men searched the cave. They finally found a boulder and crouched down. Alden's labored breathing told Andy his was not the only stomach in knots.

Scritch. Scratch. Scritch. The sounds started out faint but grew louder.

From the mouth of the cave, scuffling footsteps of a vulture-man approached. *We're trapped!*

The boys ducked down. *Please don't find us. Please don't find us.*

Whatever was making the scratching sound reached them and paused. A nose sniffed around wildly. A second later, the vulture-man's shuffling stopped on the other side of their boulder. It sensed the other creature and froze.

The animal charged the vulture-man and a violent scuffling broke out.

Yip! The creature ran toward the mouth of the cave with the vulture-man in hot pursuit. Andy could make out dark brown fur and a long, rough tail. *It's a giant rat!* Andy bit back his terror. The creature would have come midway up Andy's thigh! It carried something round in its mouth that Andy could not make out, but it left a trail of shiny liquid all the way out of the cave.

Andy and Alden didn't move. Against the backdrop of light entering the mouth of the cave, they watched the vulture-man look around. After a few minutes it finally exited. Hearing no further sounds, they crept closer to the cave entrance. Many vulture-men had gathered and were examining the dragon carcass. Thankfully, they were not strong enough to push it over, so they did not see Methuselah still lodged in the beast's stomach.

After a long time, the vulture-men dispersed and the boys exhaled loudly as they came out of hiding.

"How are we going to get Methuselah?" Alden wondered aloud.

"I'm not sure, but we have another problem. This is a *yellow* dragon. Merodach said this is where *red* dragons can be found. The Dragon's Lair must have all kinds of dragons. I didn't realize they all live together. Problem is, we don't know which caves have red dragons. We can't kill every dragon we come across until we find a red one."

"That's right!" came a deep, gruff voice from several feet away.

Andy and Alden started, heads swiveling toward the utterance.

From behind a nearby outcropping emerged a large, balding, unkempt man with only three fingers on his left hand.

CHAPTER SIXTEEN

Daisy

"I thought I might find you here," began Merodach. "Still keeping with the likes of Cartesians, huh? Nasty habit."

Ignoring the insult to his friend, Andy said, "You never said there were different kinds of dragons here."

"You never asked."

"Would you have told us if we had asked?"

"I would have told *you*," the dragon master replied, staring at Andy. Alden rolled his eyes.

"So, which caves do red dragons live in then?"

"You expect me to just tell you? What's in it for me?"

Andy thought for a second. "Well, since I killed this dragon, it's mine. I'll share some dragon steaks with you if you tell me."

Merodach scratched his generous girth. "Fine. But I expect them cooked medium rare. Not rare. Not medium. Medium rare. Understand?"

Andy nodded. "If we're going to do that, I need your help getting my sword out of the dragon's belly."

"Wait a minute. First you want information and now you want me to help you get your sword?"

"It's the only blade I have to cut up the dragon."

"Oh fine!" Merodach roared.

The burly man singlehandedly rolled the dragon on its side, exposing the hilt of Methuselah. He took a closer look and his demeanor immediately changed. "Where did you get this sword?"

"It was given to me," replied Andy, yanking the blade free.

"By who?"

"I can't really say."

"You *can't* say or you *won't* say?"

"I can't. I'm not really sure."

Merodach paused, strangely satisfied. "Fine. Now get me my dragon steaks, medium rare. And while you're at it, cook me an egg."

"Huh?"

"That's a mama dragon you killed. I can tell from her coloring. She's flushed. See that reddish color behind her horns. Only happens to female yellow dragons just after they've laid their eggs. You should find some eggs in a nest back further."

The boys shared a glance.

Merodach stretched out inside the cave, gave a couple grunts and a fart, and began snoring. The pair snickered.

"I can cut up the dragon," offered Alden. "I've seen my Mom cut up carcasses for dinner. It can't be much different, just bigger."

Before handing Methuselah to Alden, Andy walked over to where Merodach lay sleeping, held the sword up, and pretended to cut off Merodach's head for all the trouble he was causing. Alden smiled.

Andy handed the blade to Alden, grabbed the rope Alden had brought, and set about gathering wood, not a simple task in the desolate place. *How much wood do I even need to cook dragon steaks?* A chorus of roars too nearby sent him skittering over the rocks. He dove into the mouth of another cave to avoid a flock of patrolling vulture-men, then finally located a small copse of pine trees standing tall despite a crush of boulders that threatened on all sides. Scrambling down the hulking rocks, Andy found an abundance of dry, fallen limbs. Clearly no one came this way often.

Andy gathered a generous pile then took Alden's rope that he had slung over one shoulder and wrapped it around the bundle, leaving a tail to haul it up with. He secured it about his waist and picked his way back up the stone face. Sweat streamed from his brow and soaked his clothes by the time he had completed five trips. He knew the supply would last the night no matter how many steaks the dragon master ordered.

Andy finished collecting wood just as Alden cut the last of the dragon. Red flowed everywhere in front of the cave, but he beamed at the pile of steaks that stood chest height. Alden's face, hands, tunic, and sandals were covered.

"Won't the carcass attract visitors?" Andy asked.

Alden looked around. "Help me drag it over there." He pointed to a sheer cliff ten yards away.

With most of the meat removed, the skeleton proved bulky but moveable. Andy pulled on a horn while Alden pushed on the hip bones.

"We should make Merodach move it," Alden chided, trying to catch his breath.

"We're almost there."

Ten minutes later the beast's frame teetered on the precipice and Andy joined Alden for the grand shove off.

"Ready?" Andy placed his hands firmly on a shoulder blade.

"Ready."

It took only seconds for the skeleton to meet the ravine below. A bellow from another cave nearby paid homage to the life that had been taken.

Alden excused himself to change when they got back to the cave, and Andy started a fire. Once his friend returned, Andy headed farther into the cave to find the dragon's nest. He slipped and slid several times on the shiny trail of liquid that the giant rat had left. *It must have been an egg.* The goo smelled rotten and made his stomach twist. *I'm not sure I want to eat a dragon egg, even if it is cooked.*

Just as Merodach had promised, Andy found a nest with three eggs. Each was the size of a medicine ball. He stooped to pick one up but couldn't. *What are these things made of? It weighs a ton!*

Leaning against the irregular sphere, he braced his feet and pushed—the first egg consented to leave the nest. He carefully rolled it to the entrance of the cave, slipping and sliding on its fallen nest mate. He placed it at the edge of the now-roaring fire to cook. Alden laid the first steaks on thin flat rocks in the middle of the fire while Andy returned for the other two eggs.

At the first mouthwatering scents of cooking steaks and eggs, Merodach stirred, rubbed his eyes, and sat up. "Got my steak ready?"

"Sure," replied Alden.

Merodach frowned.

"You're gonna have to take it from a Cartesian if you want to eat," he added, smiling.

Merodach quickly devoured the steak and demanded seconds and thirds, then fourths.

"How much can this guy eat?" Alden whispered to Andy amidst the sounds of loud chewing. "The guy has no table manners!"

After the fifth steak, Merodach belched loudly and then farted what sounded like a long trumpet blast with a high-pitched squeal at the end.

The boys looked at each other and unsuccessfully tried to hide their snickers.

"Gotta make room for more!" Merodach boomed. He ate two more steaks before asking for one of the eggs, which he inhaled.

Wow! I've never seen anyone eat so much! Andy marveled.

After Merodach finally finished, Andy and Alden sat down to eat. The first bite of dragon tasted like—no, not like chicken—like a beef steak, but with a strange aftertaste that was beyond gamey. It almost tasted rotten.

The steak is tender and moist, but it's certainly not a taste I prefer, Andy decided.

"I think it's the fire they breathe out that makes the steaks taste the way they do," offered Alden, seeing Andy's reaction.

Andy nodded. Between bites, he asked, "So which caves do the red dragons live in?"

Merodach did not acknowledge Andy's question. After a long, uncomfortable silence, Andy opened his mouth to ask again, but Merodach cut him off, growling, "I heard ya the first time!"

Silence continued.

Either he's debating whether to answer or he's just trying to be as annoying as possible. Either way, he's succeeding at being annoying!

After several more minutes, Merodach finally replied, "Red dragons live in three caves by the Rising Sun."

"Rising Sun?"

"It's an outcropping that looks like the sun rising. You'll know it by the reddish rock. Only one like it in these parts. 'Bout a half mile from here, due east. You're too late though."

"Too late? What do you mean?"

"I heard a ruckus up there yesterday, so I went to investigate. When I got there I saw King Abaddon and his goons swarming around the caves. I investigated this morning when no one was around. The caves are empty. Musta gotten wind that you were lookin' fer red dragons. Killed 'em all and cleaned up their carcasses. Nothin' left."

"Why didn't you tell us that before!" Andy fumed.

"You didn't ask," Merodach replied, smiling and picking dragon meat from between his teeth with a dirty fingernail. "I didn't have to tell ya, ya know."

"I don't believe you!" protested Andy.

"Not askin' ya to. Just tellin' ya the way things is."

"Tomorrow morning Alden and I will go see for ourselves."

"Suit yourself."

The next morning Andy and Alden rose with the sun, packed up their gear, including a couple uncooked steaks from the night before, and set out for the Rising Sun, leaving Merodach snoring next to the rest of the steaks. They peered over the ledge where they'd dropped the dragon carcass.

"Stripped clean," Andy assessed, eyeing the bones that now jutted up at odd angles.

Alden nodded. "Glad we moved it."

The pair gazed upward. There were no vultures circling above at this hour of the morning, and within half an hour they located the reddish rock that their annoying companion had described.

The roars of waking dragons sounded close by as they walked. Ahead, the boys found the openings to three caves that were double the size of the yellow dragon's lair. They approached cautiously, Andy holding Methuselah out in front of him. As they entered the first cave, all was quiet. They saw what looked like blood stains on the ground. Claw marks and charred areas littered the walls. There had been quite a struggle. Aside from that, the place had been scrubbed clean. Andy's heart sank.

Sensing Andy's thoughts, Alden said, "Come on, let's check out the other caves."

The second cave proved as disappointing as the first—blood-stained ground, claw marks, and burns covering the walls.

They moved on to the third cave. While it looked the same as the first two, Andy sensed something different about this one. Perhaps it was his refusal to accept defeat when they were so close to their goal, but he found himself filled with hope and optimism. They crept into the cave with Methuselah giving light. Everything was silent except for the sound of flies buzzing about. The cave was deeper than that of the yellow dragon. The orange rocks at the entrance now gave way to medium gray stone the texture of dragon scales. The boys heard the drip of water and saw it running down the walls in spots. After investigating for several minutes, they sat down on a boulder that jutted up from the floor.

"I don't get it," Andy puzzled. "When we walked in, it felt to me as if something was different about this cave. But we didn't find any dragon scales."

"I'd like to know how King Abaddon figured out we were after a red dragon."

"That doesn't matter. What matters is that we have nothing to bring back. How is the curse ever going to be broken without a red dragon scale?"

They sat in silence as Andy tried to figure out what to do next. *We can't go back empty-handed. The King is counting on us.*

A few minutes later, Andy wiped sweat from his brow. He bent down to remove his pack and a blast of flame shot over him, barely missing his back. He dropped to the floor as another blast found its target. This one hit his legs, bringing instant, searing pain. Andy grabbed his thighs while ducking for cover.

Seconds later, flames shot out at Alden as he ran for cover, but he wasn't fast enough and a wall of fire found him. He let out a piercing scream and then fell to the floor, unmoving.

That thing's gonna burn him to a crisp!

Through the light of the flames, Andy made out the figure of an enormous gray dragon. Its head was the size of a large bear and its body as big as a small house. Two foot-long horns sprouted from the top of its head, which was crowned by a bony ridge, much like Andy had seen on Triceratops dinosaurs in picture books when he was little. The monster stared at him.

Andy managed to haul himself behind a large boulder. Flames lapped the floor on either side of the rock and found their way to his left hand. More pain. Andy smelled his flesh burning again. He could not run. He could not walk. He could barely think for the pain. And the monster approached Alden one terrifying step after another.

The sound of a woman clapping and cheering—"Go dragon, go! Go dragon, go!"—added to the chaos. Andy shook his head. *Is someone cheering for the dragon to kill us? Couldn't be. I must be hallucinating!*

With no time to think, Andy struggled up. The blistering pain was more intense than anything he had ever endured, and stars began swirling before his eyes. *I've got to save Alden!* He managed to peek out from behind the boulder and saw Methuselah on the ground a few feet away. Another blast of fire shot toward his boulder and Andy ducked behind the rock just in time.

The monster was nearly upon Alden's motionless form. Clenching his teeth and stifling a cry of excruciating pain, Andy forced himself to stand. He moved around the boulder and fell to the floor, grabbing Methuselah. Instantly the blade extended. The creature saw him and shot more flames in his direction.

He expected to feel more intense burning, but Methuselah deflected the flames to either side.

Whoa! Andy held the blade steady. *Thank you, whoever sent you!*

The creature hurled more fire, but Methuselah prevailed. This stalemate continued for several minutes until the dragon finally gave up, rubbing its neck as if it had a sore throat from all the fire it had breathed.

The beast turned and slumped away, going farther into the cave. Andy's legs and hand seared with pain. Still holding Methuselah, he moved over to Alden to see how badly he had been burned. Alden moaned but did not move. Angry burns and singed clothing covered his body.

What am I going to do? I can't go for help, and I can't lift him. Andy felt his chest tighten and his breath came in rasps. He met the floor as his legs gave way.

He wasn't sure if he'd passed out, but a sound from the back of the cave brought him to his senses. *No way! It sounds like the dragon's...but no, that's not possible...*

Andy scooted back as quietly as he could toward the creature. Its frame heaved. It was crying so hard that its tears fell to the floor and were starting to form a stream. He inched closer, trying to formulate a plan.

His left hand slipped through the tear stream. Instantly, the burning pain stopped. *Wait! What just happened?* Methuselah's dim light revealed the skin was no longer bloodied or charred from the burn. It looked good as new. Not even a discoloration remained to suggest anything had happened. Andy flexed his hand.

Not one to argue with success, he stuck one leg and then the other into the stream. The pain again ceased. He examined his skin. Where his legs had been severely burned, they now looked—new! *How awesome is this!*

Alden moaned again.

Andy stood. After discarding his shredded leggings, he walked over to his friend. With grunting and groaning, he managed to pick Alden up while the dragon continued sobbing. He struggled as he carried Alden back to the stream of tears and laid him in it. Seconds later, Alden regained consciousness.

"Wh-wh-what...?"

"It's okay, I'm here. You were badly burned by a dragon, but you're going to be fine."

Alden sat up, yawned, and stretched, seemingly as good as new. "I thought I was dreaming. All I remember is seeing a huge monster and then flames. And then my body was on fire! The pain was incredible!"

"The dragon over there burned you badly." Andy motioned to where the beast crouched.

Alden gave a start and moved to flee, but Andy put a hand on his shoulder. "It's okay, Methuselah protected us."

Hearing them talking, the dragon composed itself and turned back to face them.

"Uh-oh," Andy whispered. Expecting more flames, Andy's arm shot up, shielding them with the blade.

"*You won. I won't attack you any more. I can't even do that right.*"

Andy shook his head. "Did you hear something?"

"Yeah—but wait, no," replied Alden.

"Who said that?"

"*I did.*"

"Who?"

"*Me.*" The dragon lifted its head and looked at them. "*I speak to you in your thoughts.*"

The pair exchanged glances as their jaws fell.

"*I'm sorry I hurt you. When I saw you, I thought you were more bad men trying to kill me.*"

"Why would you think that?" asked Alden.

"*Two days ago, angry men came and—*" The dragon paused, nearly breaking down again. "*—killed my family. It was awful. I hid back in the cave. When the slaughter was over, they searched but didn't find me. They carried my family away and cleaned up the mess. Why would they do such a thing? What did we ever do to them?*"

"I'm so sorry. By the way, I'm Alden and this is Andy."

"*I'm Sabella, but my parents…*" The dragon paused and sniffled loudly. "*My parents called me Daisy, because daisies were my mom's favorite flower.*" A tear trickled down her cheek.

"I don't think you did anything to anyone. I think King Abaddon knew we were looking for the scale of a red dragon and tried to prevent us from getting one. He doesn't realize he missed you."

"*Why do you need a red dragon scale?*"

Andy looked at Alden, debating whether they should tell her about their mission.

"It's fine, Andy. She's not on their side."

"Okay…"

Alden explained everything to Daisy. When he finished, Daisy said, "*I want to help you. They killed my family, and they'll try to kill me as soon as they know I'm alive.*"

"Where can we find a red scale?" asked Andy.

Daisy shook her head. "*I doubt there are any left here. The men scoured the caves clean.*"

"We *have* to find one. Let's at least look to make sure," suggested Andy.

The trio split up and diligently searched all three caves for the next hour before reconvening.

"Nothing," Alden reported.

"*Nothing,*" Daisy agreed.

"Nothing." Andy shook his head. "I can't believe we're this close but can't find one. We've come so far and gone through so much! There *has* to be one here!"

Alden stared at the floor and Daisy remained silent.

"We can't go back without one!" Andy paused and took a deep breath. "I won't!"

"Andy, there's nothing here. We can't just make a scale out of thin air."

"Let's look again."

"But Andy—"

"Let's look again!"

After another thorough search of all three caves, the three met up once more.

"Nothing," said Alden.

"*Nothing*," echoed Daisy.

"Nothing," sighed Andy, kicking the dirt. "This totally stinks! I feel like such a failure. I promised the King I'd do my best and bring back a red dragon scale so the curse can finally be broken." He paused, thinking for several minutes. "What am I going to tell him?"

Alden shook his head slowly, shoulders slumped.

Several minutes later, Alden turned his thoughts to Daisy and asked, "Daisy, what are you going to do? You're all alone."

"*I don't know.*"

"Are there other red dragon colonies?"

"*I remember my mom and dad saying something about that a long time ago, but I don't know where they are.*"

"That's it!" exclaimed Andy. "We'll find another red dragon colony and get a scale that way!" But even as he said it, his stomach tensed. *I hope Abaddon didn't wipe out all the red dragons.*

"Well, until we know where there's another colony, Daisy can't stay here by herself. Should we see if Merodach might know?" Alden questioned.

"You trust Merodach?"

"Then we'll go back to the castle and ask Mermin. The King said he's studied dragons for a long time. Surely he'll know," Alden countered.

"Can you fly?" asked Andy.

"*Yes.*"

"Would you mind giving us a lift?"

"*Not at all. Grab your things.*"

CHAPTER SEVENTEEN

Dragon Riding

"Feels like I'm riding Optimistic!" Alden yelled over the noise of the air rushing past.

No sooner had they taken flight than the boys spotted a flock of vultures circling nearby. In that same moment, the menaces saw them and formed a tight pack to begin dive-bombing the dragon.

Daisy was tough. She banked and turned. Her riders grabbed for purchase on her scales and held on for dear life. She avoided most attacks and occasionally got a clear shot, swatting several pursuers with her tail for a homerun. Unfortunately, there were dozens of them, and they kept coming no matter what she did. "*I don't want to breathe fire. The flames might hit you at this speed!*"

The vultures flew at Andy and Alden, trying to unseat them. They nearly succeeded at one point, but Alden pivoted and ducked under Daisy's wing just in time to avoid a direct hit—right in front of Andy, who sat behind him. Somehow Alden managed to stay on. After righting himself, he yelled, "A little trick I found when riding Optimistic!"

Andy clutched the scales more tightly.

The boys knew exactly when they passed back into the land of Oomaldee. Fog blanketed the sky, making it difficult to see their adversaries coming. The conditions did not slow the birds, however—they seemed able to see Daisy through the haze and continued their unrelenting attacks.

Daisy began to tire. She had been flying for several hours now with no relief from the opposition. She flew lower, trying to shake their pursuers. As she did, Alden exclaimed, "I recognize the landscape! I've flown Optimistic over this territory many times!"

"We're almost to the castle, Daisy! Can you hang on for just a little longer?" Andy coaxed.

"*I'll do my best.*" Daisy's thought came sluggishly as the vultures launched yet another frontal assault.

"Where can we land that Daisy can hide from these attacks?" yelled Andy.

"I know the perfect place. I just hope it won't upset too many people."

A few minutes later, Alden directed Daisy down to the cavalry's training facility. He hopped off as soon as they hit the ground and ran for the stable doors. "Andy, help me slide these open. She can take cover in here."

Five more vultures took the opportunity to extend their talons in an attempt to gouge out her eyes. Daisy deftly incinerated the birds.

"Way to go!" Alden cheered.

The boys heaved the mighty doors open and Daisy waddled quickly into the large space, then collapsed in the soft sawdust covering the floor. Andy and Alden pulled the doors shut again.

"Are you okay, Daisy?" worried Alden.

"*I will be. Just give me some time to rest.*"

The training arena was empty. Alden fetched water, and after drinking her fill, Daisy immediately fell asleep. Alden looked her over. Remarkably, despite all of the attacks, the dragon had no wounds. Her scales had protected her. Andy and Alden were not so fortunate. They were sore from riding on those tough plates and had more than a few scratches to show for it.

"Let's go find Major Cahill and tell him about Daisy, so he doesn't get a shock when he walks in and sees her," suggested Alden. Before leaving, he turned and patted Daisy on the head. "Thank you, friend. Now sleep well."

As they exited the arena, Andy glanced back over his shoulder and smiled at the light gray smoke rings that wafted from Daisy's nostrils with each breath.

The boys headed toward the major's office, which was located on the other side of the stable area. "Something's wrong, Andy."

"I was thinking the same thing. It's too quiet," he whispered back, pulling Methuselah out and extending the blade.

They crept into the stables. The pegasi were in their quarters and quiet. Sneaking around the first row of stalls, Alden led the way toward Optimistic. They had nearly reached the door of her enclosure when they heard someone coming and ducked into the shadows. A large vulture-man lumbered by carrying an oversize bucket of feed in each hand. His muscles bulged under the weight.

As soon as he had passed, Alden whispered, "I've never seen that guy before!"

They ducked into Optimistic's stall. Both Andy and Alden held out a hand for her to sniff and accept them. She whinnied her approval and Alden gave her a hug.

"It's good to see you!" he whispered. "What's going on around here?"

Optimistic whinnied again and started pawing at the straw.

"It's okay, girl. We're going to figure out—"

Optimistic stomped and pawed at the straw again, tossing her head.

"What's wrong, girl?"

Andy looked down at her hoof. Under the topmost layer of straw, he saw a piece of paper. "Alden, move her back so I can get that."

Andy grabbed the paper. Someone had scribbled a short message: "Cavalry captured. Men turned into vultures by Abaddon."

"That's Major Cahill's writing! I recognize it. Andy, this is really bad. He must have had just enough time to sneak that note in here before they grabbed him. What about my mom and the others?" Alden bit his lip.

"Let's get inside the castle and see what's going on," encouraged Andy.

Alden bobbed his head.

"Are there any other entrances? These guys are probably watching the back and the front doors."

"Not that I know of."

The boys crept along the row of stalls until arriving at the foyer, where a horse whinnied and a voice yelled, "Whoa, slow up Alexander. We have company."

Alden and Andy scuttled back into the stable, waiting for vulture-men to come see what the disturbance was. Nothing happened. After several tense minutes, the stone knight hopped down from his horse and introduced himself. "I'm Sir Gawain and this is Alexander. Glad to see you're still with us. I'm at your service, sirs."

"Shhh, keep your voice down," cautioned Andy.

Alden's eyes grew wide.

"No worries, sir. No one can hear me. Only those in the company of the golden key," replied the stone warrior.

"What's up with your friend?"

"Alden, I'd like you to meet Sir Gawain. Sir Gawain, this is Alden."

Alden stepped forward. "Uh…hi?"

"We're in kind of a hurry," Andy pressed. "It looks like King Abaddon captured our cavalry and turned them into vultures."

"Is that why I've been seeing so many vulture-dudes walking around!"

"So, you saw it?"

"Well, I didn't see him turn anyone into a vulture, but I've noticed an awful lot more of those guys around here in the last week." He paused and then, with a hand cupped to one side of his mouth, confided, "I know this sounds bad, but personally, they give me the creeps."

Andy laughed. "I'm with you. Out of curiosity, how long have you stood here?"

"Oh, probably 450 years or so. Yeah, da Vinci sculpted me. The King was lucky to keep that kid focused long enough to finish me. He's got ADHD bad!"

"You do know that he died, don't you?"

"Oh, I'm sorry to hear that."

"So, you know lots about the castle then, right?"

"Well, sure. What specifically do you want to know?"

"Do you know if there's another way in besides the back or front doors?"

"Well, now that you mention it…yes, I recall that when da Vinci sculpted us, his workshop was inside the castle, in the basement. These stables had not yet been built. When he finished, we were too big to take up the stairs, so they dug another way out. They brought us around and in through the front door. I stood in the entry hall for many years, until they built these stables. Poor Alexander's hoofs were killing him, standing in this pose for so long on that hard floor!"

"Do you have any idea where that other door might be?" interrupted Alden.

But the knight was not finished recounting his story. "Oh, I remember the day when I got my first glimpse of daylight. It was absolutely amazing! The birds were singing—I think they were celebrating us. Good creatures, those birds. I always like to hear them sing."

"Um, excuse me, sir," Andy cleared his throat, trying to get Sir Gawain back on track.

"Oh, right. Sorry. Let me see. I remember being rolled sideways up a log ramp. Yeah, those men really had to strain. Scared Alexander a bit when they nearly lost hold and we started to slide backwards." Gawain turned and patted his horse. "It's quite a challenge to ride a horse at full speed while tilted at an angle. I don't recommend it. Oh, and I remember seeing a huge tree in front of us."

Andy thought for a second. *I don't remember seeing any large trees around the castle.*

Alden jumped excitedly. "I know where he's talking about! When my mom and I first came to the castle, there was a huge oak tree over there." He motioned in the direction of the northeast side of the castle. "It got sick and they had to cut it down. Nothing but a stump left now."

"Thanks for your help, Sir Gawain!" said Andy. "We need to see if we can get in that way."

"My pleasure. Is there anything else I can do for you?"

"Just stay here and keep listening for any clues that might tell us what Abaddon is planning. And let us know if you see anything else going on."

"Very well, sir." The knight bowed and his horse gave a whinny.

"Come on, Alden." Andy stuck his head out the training center doors. "Coast is clear. You lead the way."

They made a dash in the direction Alden had indicated. The thick fog helped hide them as they cut across the cobblestone terrace and rounded the side of the castle. They could no longer see the training center as they stopped next to the stone foundation. Andy hoped that meant no one could see them either. "I've never seen this side of the castle."

Alden quickly spotted what remained of the stump and they both started searching for an opening in the wall.

"This is just like trying to find the tunnel under Dragontail watchtower," whispered Alden.

"I'm guessing they did something similar here," Andy reasoned.

No sooner had he spoken than Alden's foot hit an odd-sized rock. He pressed down on the stone and they heard the sound of rock sliding across rock. A small opening appeared.

"Way to go, Alden!"

Andy pulled Methuselah out as they slipped through the opening and into a dark tunnel. The sword's light allowed them to find another stone that closed the door behind them.

"I wonder where this will take us," commented Andy, climbing down a short set of steps and starting down a curving tunnel.

The boys walked for a few minutes until the tunnel branched off.

"Which way?" asked Alden.

"Let's keep going forward. We can always come back and see where that leads if we need to."

A minute later they reached a wall.

"Looks like this is the end of the line," said Alden.

"Yep. And I think that's the stone that will open the door." Andy pointed at a rock protruding from the wall.

Before depressing it, the boys put their ears to the wall and listened for any sounds that might indicate people on the other side. They heard nothing.

"Okay, here goes." Andy pushed the stone.

The door slid open and they found themselves in the corridor right outside Alden and Marta's quarters. No one lurked about.

"Wow! I had no idea this door was here. I always thought it was just the wall at the end of the hall."

They felt around and found the stone to close the opening.

"My mom and the others—" Alden worried.

"I know." Andy's stomach clenched. "Let's search the castle. We'll start down here and work our way up floor by floor."

They tiptoed down the hallway, checking each room. No one was about. Approaching footsteps descending the stairs made them scurry into the shadows as they reached the end of the hall. They held their breath but scowled as Razen hurried past. Andy and Alden exchanged suspicious looks.

A minute later, the whine of the dungeon's heavy metal door echoed up the flight of stairs followed by a loud bellow before it slammed shut.

"What was that?" Andy whispered then swallowed hard.

Alden shook his head, jaw clenched.

They crept down the flight of stairs. Wisps of green vapor rose from beneath the door, refusing confinement. Andy put an arm over his nose and tried the handle. It was unlocked this time. He put his shoulder to the obstacle and slowly pushed it open. Alden followed on his heels. As the door shut, another loud bellow reached them. *That sounds too familiar. Please don't be who I think it is,* Andy worried.

"Come on," he whispered, trying to silence the fear that sneered at his attempts to ignore it.

The dungeon was dim and had only a few torchlights, but they dared not illuminate the way with Andy's blade. They inched down another set of stairs shrouded by the green vapor, their nerves on high alert. Andy's breathing grew labored.

At the landing, they turned left and quickened their pace, scattering the mist that hovered about their thighs. They hurried down a hallway lined with cell doors on both sides, until they reached a corner to the right. Life-size statues of Sir Kay and Sir Gawain stood to the left. The two figures were slashing at each other with drawn swords thanks to the gold key.

"Stop fighting and follow me!" Andy commanded after making sure the coast was clear. He looked back to say something to Alden, but his friend was no longer following. *Where'd he go?*

A roar from up ahead arrested his attention and his head shot back. The darkness fled from a blast of fire.

"Aaaaahhhhhhhhh!" A blood-curdling scream made the hair on the back of Andy's neck stand at attention.

I'll find Alden later.

Andy and company dashed around the corner, Methuselah leading the way.

CHAPTER EIGHTEEN

Fierce Competition

They burst into a large open area. The King was tied to a chair in the middle of the room, his head slumped down. Several vulture-men stood watching as a multi-headed dragon leaned over the King. It swished its tail violently, hitting a pair of vulture-men and catapulting them against the far wall. The bird-men dropped to the floor in a heap. The dragon ruffled its wings as more putrid green vapor spewed from two of its mouths.

Despite the terrifying sight, Andy rushed forward. The dragon turned and glared at the intruders. The vulture-men prepared to pounce.

The King raised his head, recognized Andy through bloodied eyes, and groaned, "No, Andy. Run…"

"Sorry sir, I can't do that. I've come to free you." The words sealed Andy's resolve and silenced his fears. He willed his arms to stop trembling.

With a mighty flick of its tail, the dragon cut the legs from under the chair that held the bound sovereign, toppling it over. The beast narrowly missed the King's head as it stepped toward Andy.

Laughing and clapping erupted in Andy's ears, as if this were some kind of sick sport. A man's reprimand followed.

"Imogenia, stop!"

"There's nothing you can do to help him, Father," the woman cackled. "He's going to die!"

The voices barely registered as the dragon lowered its heads and shot blasts of fire from three of its mouths. Methuselah easily deflected these, making the beast furious. Andy scanned multiple pairs of the dragon's eyes, moving his blade in a figure-eight pattern, then lunged at one of the heads. His blade hit the hard scales covering it and bounced off.

In a chorus of raspy voices, the dragon taunted, "You are mine, and so is your King. Surrender now or I will finish you both." Several of its mouths moved in unison as the words flowed out.

Andy crept between the King and the dragon, shielding the monarch behind his blade. As he did, he studied his foe, looking for a vulnerability to exploit. Nothing betrayed the menace.

One of the vulture-men took the opportunity to pounce on Andy from behind. As soon as it did, Sir Kay, who had been waiting for a signal from Andy, charged. He skewered the creature through the side with his lance and flung it across the room. The move proved a catalyst, for all the vulture-men now entered the fray.

Sir Gawain drew his sword and, from atop his horse, beheaded several of the enemy as they charged. Andy whirled around with Methuselah, hacking and jabbing at each vulture-man that approached. Sir Kay continued around the room, wounding more bird-men. Three vulture-men had grabbed Sir Gawain by the foot and were dragging him off his horse. Andy raced over and disabled two of them, allowing the knight to remount and continue the assault.

The battle raged for what seemed an eternity. No sooner had the three subdued most of the enemy than more materialized out of thin air. Weariness sapped Andy's strength as the battle lengthened. Just when his arms grew heavy and he felt like he could fight no longer, the dragon's roar sent shock waves through him. A burst of fire filled the room. Andy thrust Methuselah up to shield himself and the King just in time. Many vulture-men weren't so fortunate—they screeched just before being consumed by the searing flames.

Sir Gawain, who because he was stone had not been harmed by the flames, drew the beast's attention, and Andy raced toward the dragon from behind. He leapt and wrapped an arm around his foe's thick neck as he plunged Methuselah into a small gap between its shoulder blade and back. Andy held on for dear life as the creature writhed, driving the sword further in. Fire, venom, and putrid green vapor spewed out like a shaken soda can. Sir Kay and Sir Gawain dismounted and began whacking at the beast's flailing heads. The creature staggered under the onslaught, let out a thunderous roar, and vanished.

Andy crumbled to the floor, exhausted but still holding Methuselah. "Whoa! What just happened? Where'd he go?"

The knights shouted and cheered at their victory. "That was awesome!" Sir Gawain pumped his arms in triumph.

"Yeah, I was getting tired of staring at your ugly mug, fighting you for all those years," trumpeted Sir Kay.

"Ugly mug?" Sir Gawain countered. "Just look at yourself!"

"I challenge you to a duel, Sir Gawain!" snapped Sir Kay.

"A duel? Why, you scoundrel!" Sir Gawain raised his lance.

Andy sat up and shouted, "Take it back to where I found you, guys!"

Both knights bowed to Andy, remounted their horses, and rode out of the room, taunting each other.

Andy shook his head. "Knights…"

The King moaned. Andy gathered his strength and scrambled over fallen bodies to where the King lay on the floor, still tied to the chair.

"Sir, are you okay?"

The King gave no reply.

Andy looked up as Alden raced into the room.

"Where have you been?"

"Razen grabbed me from behind. He tied me up, gagged me, and stuffed me in a cell."

"How did you get free?"

"Razen just up and vanished a minute ago, and I finally got myself loose. I came here as fast as I could."

Andy knelt. "Help me untie him."

They set the legless chair upright and cut the sovereign's bonds. The King slumped to the side, unconscious.

"Let's get him up to his chambers. He's got some bad burns," Andy instructed.

"We've got to find Hans! Only he knows how to heal him."

Standing on either side, the boys pulled the King up between them and wrapped his arms over their shoulders as gently as possible.

Several minutes later, the three stood outside the King's chambers.

"Open the door," Andy panted after the exertion of carrying the sovereign up several flights of stairs.

Alden hesitated. "I've never been in there before."

"Me neither, but we need to put him in bed. Come on."

Alden turned the handle with his free hand and pushed the door open with his foot. The room was expansive, ornately decorated with rugs and tapestries that made it feel cozy. A bed with lavish silk covers and larger than Andy or Alden had ever seen stood straight ahead.

After considerable effort because they were trying to be as gentle as possible, the King lay on his bed.

Andy turned and as he did, he glimpsed something on the desk not far away. He halted.

"What is it?" Alden wondered.

Andy walked over to examine the object more closely and picked up a shiny purple crest. It had a spider on the top, followed by a wavy line, and then a knight on horseback at the bottom. It was identical to the crest on the dagger shealth he'd found in the trunk back home!

He held it up to show Alden. "Do you have any idea whose crest this is?"

"No. I've never seen it."

Andy examined it a minute longer before finally replacing it. "Stay here with him. I'm going to try to find Hans."

"No, I need to find my mom."

"Oh, right." In all the commotion, Andy had nearly forgotten their original mission. "Yeah, the King should be fine while we find them."

Alden nodded his agreement.

The eerily quiet castle echoed as they descended the stairs toward the dining hall. Halfway down, they heard the first sounds of activity. Muffled voices grew louder as they approached. Reaching the landing and rounding the corner, they sighed at the sight of the entire castle staff busily untying one another. No one sported beaks, feathers or wings, only weariness and dirt.

"That's a relief! Do you see my mom?" Alden scanned the mass of people.

Andy looked through the crowd but did not immediately see anyone he knew. Finally, he spotted Hans and Hannah sitting on the floor and helping Marta out of her bonds.

"Alden, she's over there!" Andy pointed.

"You're back! Thank goodness! I was worried sick," Marta sighed, giving Alden and Andy big hugs.

"What happened?" asked Alden.

"About a week ago the castle was overrun by vulture-men. We tried to fight them off, but in the end were overwhelmed by their numbers. I don't know what happened to the cavalry. They were no help at all. The vulture-men forced us all into this hall and tied us up."

"I can tell you what happened to the cavalry," defended Alden. "It appears Major Cahill and his troops have been turned into vulture-men."

"No!" shouted Hans and Hannah in unison.

"But how?" the healer demanded.

"We don't know. We found this note that the major left in Optimistic's stall." Andy pulled the paper from inside his tunic.

Marta scanned it. "That's terrible! What will happen to them now? Hans, can they be turned back?"

"I've never seen it happen, so I have no idea what the possibilities are. We can only hope for the best." Hans frowned. "Do you know where they are?"

"We didn't see them," replied Andy. "We only found this note."

"Why didn't they turn you into vulture-people?" Andy's question was met with frowns. "Sorry, I was just wondering."

"My guess is that their magic does not work in the castle under the spell that keeps the King alive. That's also why they couldn't drag us outside and turn us. No one can be forced outside the castle against their will," Hans informed.

"Thank goodness," replied Marta.

"Hans, the King's been hurt," Andy interrupted.

"Hurt? How?"

"He's badly burned. We took him up to his chambers."

"Has anyone seen Mermin?" asked Alden.

"You look for Mermin while I fill Hans in," Andy instructed, leading the healer toward the stairs.

"And I'm going to prepare some food for everyone. They didn't feed us much of anything," huffed Marta.

"I'll help," offered Hannah, following her.

Several minutes later, Andy stood next to Hans who examined the King. The healer grabbed a towel next to the washstand and wet it, then started cleaning the sovereign's wounds. "You're right, Andy. He has some very bad burns along with swelling in his face, arms, hands, and legs. The best thing to heal burns is dragon tears, but I'm all out at the moment." Hans shook his head as he continued to examine his patient. "If we can't start his burns healing quickly, they'll get infected."

The King moaned, only partially conscious.

"I know where we can get dragon tears!"

Hans glanced up with a curious look.

"I'll be right back!" Andy ran out the door. Moments later he was back holding two bottles. He handed them to Hans.

"But, where—? And so much?" The healer gave Andy an incredulous look.

"I have my sources." Andy flicked his brows.

"Thank you. I'll treat his wounds with this. Then we'll just have to wait and see how he responds. Why don't you go help the others."

As Andy headed back downstairs, he noticed that the castle sounded like itself again. The corridors rang with the noises of people talking and moving about. He returned to the dining hall, where he hoped to find Alden with

Mermin. Sure enough, as Andy rounded the corner, there stood the wizard, talking with Alden and rubbing his wrists.

"Hans is with the King," Andy reported.

"Vewy good. How is he?"

"He was treating the King's wounds when I left. He said he'd have to wait to see how he responds. He's in pretty bad shape."

Mermin frowned and slowly shook his head. "Alden has just filled me in on what happened. You did well to fend off Abaddon."

"Well, I can't take all the credit. I had the help of Sir Gawain and Sir Kay. If not for them, I don't think I would be here. It was weird how Abaddon just disappeared, though."

"Andy, what do you mean you had the help of Sir Gawain and Sir Kay?" asked Mermin, his brow furrowed.

"When I wear the gold key, it opens anything that's locked. And I found that it makes the statues in the castle come to life. It's like it unlocks them, too."

"Fascinating!" replied Mermin, scratching his head. "I wonder how this is accomplished?"

"I've no idea. All I know is that it works."

"Well, that's good because King Abaddon will weturn, I am sure of it."

"How do you know?"

"While the fight you just won was bad, fwom everything I've wead, Methuselah appears for far gweater battles than that."

Andy glanced at Alden and swallowed.

Mermin continued, "Abaddon has appeared in the past, causing havoc and harm, but he's never done this much damage or hurt so many. He's merciless. He has never been severely wounded though. I'm guessing he wetreated to wecover."

"I just wish I'd been there to help. Raaazzzzzen—" Alden snarled, drawing out the name slowly and shaking his head.

A vulture-man walked into the dining hall from the direction of the grand stairway. Seeing Mermin, Alden, and Andy clustered together, he waddled toward them. Andy instinctively reached for Methuselah and the blade extended. Seeing this, the vulture-man paused and held his hands up in surrender before motioning a request to lower the sword. Andy held his ground. Hands still held high, the vulture-man approached the group more slowly and began speaking.

"Pardon my appearance. I am Major Cahill. King Abaddon turned me and all my men. While we look bad, those who are truly committed to our King remain loyal."

Andy studied the man. "How can we know what you're saying is true?"

"Did you find a note in Optimistic's stall?"

"We did. But how do we know it was you who wrote it?"

"Do you have a piece of paper and something to write with?" Upon presenting the bird-man with the requested items, he waddled to a table and wrote, "Cavalry captured. Men turned into vultures by Abaddon."

Alden picked up the paper and examined it. "It *is* Major Cahill! It's his handwriting. I'd recognize it anywhere. I'm so sorry—"

"Thank you, Alden. Abaddon and his men were after us. I barely had time to scribble that so you'd know." He paused before continuing, "The reason I came is to see if anyone knows about a dragon that is in the arena. It's not hurting anything at the moment, but we'll need to do something before it does."

"Oh my!" responded Mermin.

Andy held up a hand, laughing. "Yes, that's Daisy. She's our friend. Long story. Let's just say she helped us—a lot." Andy grinned at Alden who nodded. "Hans is using her tears to treat the King. I'm guessing she's getting hungry. We need to find another red dragon colony for her. Abaddon killed her family and she wasn't going to survive if we left her behind. Can you help?"

"It would be my pleasure to help her," Mermin said, smiling. "Let me consult my notes."

"You do that, and Alden and I will go see what we can find for her to eat."

"Begging your pardons," interrupted the major, "but my men and I would be honored to escort her to her new home if you need us to."

"That would be great," Alden acknowledged. "And I'll fly along on Optimistic, so she knows someone."

"Then we have a plan. Now, to get her something to eat—" The words still lingered as a fuzzy brown blur raced between Andy's legs. "This is not the time for more chaos and destruction!" Andy snatched two salt shakers from one of the tables. "Come on, Alden!"

"We'll be back in a few!" The green-haired Cartesian bolted after Andy.

The boggart raced down the hall toward the kitchens with the pair on its tail. A burly servant stepping into the hall blocked its entrance. It bounced off the man's large foot, careening toward the open laundry door stood as an open invitation.

Screeches and yips proceeded from the laundry, but the servants quieted as they caught sight of the boys' set jaws and fierce expressions.

"Shut the door and block the gap beneath. Don't let it escape!" Andy commanded.

The dozen ladies moved swiftly.

"This. Ends. Now," Andy growled, watching for the creature to betray its whereabouts.

"It's over there!" A plump servant pointed wildly.

With salt shaker poised, Andy stalked toward the mammoth basin that dominated the center of the space. He motioned for Alden to approach from the opposite side.

Andy skirted two mounds of laundry that rose to his waist and avoided a washboard leaning against the side of the wooden reservoir. Alden ducked between lines of hanging clothes.

A bucket of clothespins erupted, peppering its contents as the pair reached striking distance. A cascade of scrub brushes immediately followed, but the hunters did not waver. Andy leapt forward and threw a handful of salt while Alden flung some from the opposite side.

Howl. Eek! Eek!

The creature cowered against the washtub. "Yeah, how do you like it when the tables are turned!" Andy taunted. To onlookers he declared, "I need a cage."

"How about this?" a petite laundress suggested, passing a wooden bucket.

Andy glared at the whimpering menace and felt no pity as Alden plunged it into darkness then sat on top.

"Is there something we can slide under it to keep it trapped?" Andy asked.

A smiling servant fetched a circular board. "It's the top."

Andy's face lit up. "Perfect. That should work."

Thumping emanated from Alden's seat by the time Andy brought the lid close. "On my count, lift the bucket up just a smidge. I'm gonna slide this under and we'll secure the sides."

A minute later cheers erupted as thumping and thuds emanated from the makeshift cage.

"Now what?" Alden asked.

"Come with me."

Alden shrugged as he fell in line behind the warden. Andy headed up the stairs—one flight, two flights, three. He took a right at the fourth floor and knocked on the Goldery door.

Alden tilted his head as a grin erupted. "What can they do?"

"Watch and learn."

Henry wiped his dripping brow as he opened the door. "Hey Andy, Alden! Come on in. We were just getting things back up and running."

The bucket shook in Andy's hand, drawing the attention of all three goldweavers.

"Whatcha got there?" Max asked.

"The little pest that's been creating chaos in the treasury."

Scowls seared the bucket.

"I believe I know how to rid us of this 'problem'."

"Oh?" The trio brightened.

"The last time I was here, you explained how your machine is able to harness the flow of energy that exists in one thing and turn it into something else, right?"

Max nodded with a blank expression, not understanding where Andy was going.

"I want to convert this boggart into something else."

The goldweavers ricocheted looks as laughter broke out. "Yes! That's possible. But we can't change it into something inanimate. There's a principle called the law of equivalent exchange. Energy and mass cannot be created or destroyed, only changed from one form to another. That, coupled with the law of natural providence, which says something can only be transmuted into something else with the same chemicals and components as the original material. That means we have to convert it into something else that's living."

Andy and Alden exchanged slack expressions.

"In English?" Andy requested as the bucket lurched.

"Right. Sorry. What it means is that whatever we do, we have to maintain the same amount of content, and at least a portion of it still needs to be living."

"Could we convert it into a tiny mosquito?" Alden suggested.

"What, and have it suck our blood in the night?" Andy shook his head.

"Then how about a gnat?" the Cartesian countered.

Max nodded. "Yes, as long as you did something with the mass that's left over." Then thinking aloud he added, "You could convert it into carbon and salt, I suppose. They're in a body." He rubbed his chin.

"Let's do it!" the boys cheered in unison.

Oscar held up a hand. "This hardly seems humane. I know that boggart has caused all kinds of trouble for us—"

"Too many times," Henry interjected, shaking his head.

"Tearing up the treasury, which we still haven't finished cleaning up," Max added.

"Making chaos of the King's laboratory!" Alden added.

"It's bitten me, made a bucket full of water fall on my head, and tied me up in my own bed!" Andy waved his free arm.

"Okay, just making sure we can live with ourselves if we do this," Oscar cautioned.

"It won't be harmed," Max reassured, raising his hands. "It'll just be smaller…and more manageable."

Andy exhaled. "You're right, Oscar. While it's annoyed us all, I wouldn't feel right if we harmed it, no matter what it's done."

Alden nodded.

"You're sure changing it won't hurt it?" Oscar double-checked.

"Positive," Max reassured.

"Okay, then let's see what happens," Henry agreed.

Andy handed the wriggling bucket to Max who laid it on its side, cover toward his machine. "Andy, why don't you stand next to me and remove the lid when I say."

The goldweaver changed a few settings on his machine as Andy moved into position. Max started the pedal in motion. "Ready?"

Andy nodded.

"Okay…now."

Andy slid the lid back and Max spritzed the fuzzy brown nuisance as it shot from its confines.

Two small piles—one white, the other black—materialized on the machine's plate.

"I thought you said there'd be a living part?" Alden questioned a second later, biting his lip.

Heads craned and pivoted.

"Found it!" Andy's face lit up and his pointer finger bounced around, following the gnat's progress.

Four more smiles erupted and Max declared, "I don't think it'll be causing any more trouble."

"Great thinking, Andy." Henry patted his shoulder.

"Yeah, great idea," Alden echoed, giving Andy a fist bump.

The boy genius's grin spread. "Now that our work here is done, we need to find Daisy something to eat. Come on, Alden."

Andy was busy helping others the rest of the day, enough to distract his thoughts from the bigger problem at hand. But when he finally got to bed that night, even though he was dead tired and despite his triumph over the boggart, his mind would not rest.

I failed, his thoughts tormented. *I didn't get a red dragon scale. The King was counting on me. I tried my best, but it wasn't enough. I hope Mermin can locate another red dragon colony. If Abaddon wiped them out—well, I don't know how we're going to break the curse.*

CHAPTER NINETEEN

The Voice

A ndy woke to fog-filtered sun shining on his face. His restless thoughts from the night before zoomed back to his consciousness, haunting him. After dressing, he slogged up to check on the King.

"Come in!" the sovereign boomed from the other side of the wooden door.

The King, dressed in a pin-striped night shirt, sat up in bed. His lap and legs were concealed under thick silky covers. Razen was finishing tasting his breakfast.

Andy's eyes grew wide. "Sir!" He raced forward, reaching for Methuselah.

The King motioned him to stop. "It's okay, Andy. Razen has filled me in on what happened after I passed out."

Yeah, I'll bet he did... Andy scowled at the taster. Razen returned the gesture then bowed to the King, turned, and left.

"Sir, Razen grabbed Alden down in the dungeon when we were trying to save you!"

"Yes, he told me. He said he could only protect one of you. You were too fast, Andy."

"He said he was protecting Alden?"

The King smiled and patted the covers. "Come sit and tell me all about your trip."

Andy hesitated, his mind whirling. He finally took three steps and let his weight fall on the bed.

"What's wrong?"

Andy took a deep breath. "I'm sorry, sir."

The sovereign's eyebrows knit together.

"I failed. I didn't get a red dragon scale."

The King's smile faded and his chest fell. "What happened?"

Andy began recounting the details of their trip, trying not to leave anything out. As he got to the part where he and Alden had seen vulture-men on the Great Wall, there came a loud, rapid knocking on the door.

"Enter," instructed the King.

Alden threw open the door and rushed in. "Sorry to interrupt, sir," he said, looking at the King. Without waiting for permission to speak, he rushed on, "Andy, I was in the dungeon helping clean things up when I found these on the floor."

He thrust out his hand. Several curved, shiny, red objects rested in his palm. "Do you know what these are?" A grin spread across his face.

Andy looked between the objects and Alden. "Are they scales from Abaddon? But how?" Then, looking at the King, he asked, "Is Abaddon a red dragon?"

"Yes, he is. Why?"

A smile blossomed across Andy's face. "But when—?" He thought back to the battle. "I remember plunging Methuselah into his back..." He thought harder. "Right before I stabbed him…" Realization dawned. "That's right! Just before I stabbed him, I slashed at his back."

"You must have cut these scales off," Alden deduced.

Andy gasped and jumped up, pumping his fists and yelling, "Yahoo!" drawing laughter from the pair of onlookers.

After a minute, the King interrupted, "Well, it looks like you succeeded after all." A grin punctuated his expression. "Now then, where were we."

Andy picked up the tale. As he related their brush with the vulture-people in the village of Oohhh, the King's eyes grew wide. Andy told him about being trapped and then finding they had been drugged.

"I hate to think what might have happened to you if it weren't for that gold key," the King interjected.

Another knock at the door interrupted. "Enter," the King commanded.

"Thought I'd see how the patient's doing," explained Hans, approaching to inspect.

"I brought you some chocolate chip cookies. Figured it might help you heal quicker," Marta added with a wink and a chuckle.

"Looks like you're doing fine, Your Majesty," Hans pronounced after a thorough examination.

"Can't keep a tough ogre like me down."

"Tough ogre?" replied Hans. "I didn't realize I'd been treating an ogre. Well, that certainly explains a few things." He laughed.

The group chatted for several minutes until Marta excused herself to go work on lunch. Hans followed a minute later.

As the door shut, Andy picked up his narrative. The King grew more alarmed when Andy got to the part about vulture-men patrolling the Great Wall. "Sir, Abaddon has gained control of the Wall, at least at that point—"

"—and at least part of the village of Oohhh," the King finished. He rubbed his chin. "What's he up to this time?"

Another knock sounded at the door.

"This is certainly a busy place today," quipped the King, smiling. "Enter."

Mermin came in, hoisting up his robe and pushing his glasses back up his nose. "Good morning, sir. Thought I'd see how you're doing."

The King asked Andy to continue with the rest of the story. Once he had finished, his thoughts returned to the voices he kept hearing. "Sir?"

"Yes, Andy."

"When I'm battling something or in deep trouble, I hear a man's voice yelling at some crazy lady. I keep forgetting to mention it, but I heard it again when I was fighting Abaddon. Every time I've heard her, she sounded excited that I was in trouble. This time she shouted, 'There's nothing you can do to help him, Father. He's going to die!' And then the man's voice yelled, 'Imogenia, stop!'"

The King's breath caught and he searched Andy's eyes. "Are you sure that's what you heard?"

"Nnnoooo!" shrieked a shrill voice, filling the King's chambers. "He couldn't have gotten a red dragon's scale! After everything I did." The voice lurched to a halt like a rider yanking a horse's reins.

The four looked at each other, mouths gaping.

"That's her! I'd recognize that voice anywhere!" Andy pointed at the ceiling.

"Who?" quaked Alden, eyeing the door.

The King stiffened. "How?"

"Sir?" Mermin looked puzzled.

"If I'm not mistaken, *that* was Imogenia." The King's voice sounded empty, as if in a daze.

"But she's…passed on." Mermin scratched his head.

"Passed on? As in—dead?" Andy clarified.

The King nodded, a vacant look eclipsing his face. "Imogenia was my sister."

"Sir?"

"It was because of what I did to her that I brought the curse upon the land. They've never spoken to me, but it seems my father and sister are somehow watching us even though they have departed."

No one said anything for several minutes.

Since when do dead people talk? She sure doesn't sound dead to me. What'd he do to her anyway?

The King broke the silence when he called out, "Father?"

Heads pivoted, scanning the ceiling.

"Father? Are you there?"

"I am here, son," a baritone voice answered.

Andy, Alden, and Mermin all stared at the King, eyes wide.

"Why didn't you tell me you're here?" the King inquired.

"You did not ask."

"It never occurred to me *to* ask. I've never thought about talking to someone who has departed."

"Open your mind."

"How long have you been here, Father? How are you doing? Is Mother with you? Imogenia?"

"We are well."

"Why are you here?"

"We are well."

"I don't understand. What do you mean, you're well? That's not what I asked."

"Open your mind, my son."

"Are you here to help break the curse?"

"We are well."

"Can you not say more?"

A silent minute passed before the King understood. "Ah, I see. You can't say. Well, can you at least tell me if you're the one who's been filling my dreams with things about Andy, like his favorite foods and such, and giving me visions of what he's doing?"

Andy glanced at the King. "Really?"

The sovereign shrugged and raised his eyebrows.

"Father?"

Silence.

"Mother?"

Silence.

The King sat thinking for another minute. He seemed to be debating something. Finally he called out, "Imogenia?"

A second later, the man's voice commanded, "No, Imogenia! I forbid you!"

"Fine!" came a curt reply. "Then I'm leaving!"

"Imogenia!" The male voice faded.

"It appears she's not very happy about your success, Andy," the King observed.

"So it would seem." *And here I thought* my *family was bad.*

"You've no idea how many times I've thought about what I'd say to her if I could—" The King shook his head. "After all this time…" His voice trailed off as he looked toward the window. He sat quietly for a minute, rubbing his brow.

"Sir," Mermin broke the silence.

"Yes?"

"You looked twoubled."

"I am. First, I find that Abaddon has penetrated our northern wall and the village of Oohhh. Then I discover Imogenia and my father have been watching me from the afterlife—and she's reveling in Andy's obstacles. That last outburst sounds like she may try to do more to thwart us." The King sighed. "When Methuselah appeared, I knew something catastrophic was in the works. As I said before, that blade does not appear except to overcome significant evil. This is not good, not good at all."

Andy's stomach did a cartwheel, threatening to revolt.

The King cleared his throat. "You boys have certainly demonstrated diligence and responsibility. I'm very proud of you. I'm sure when the time comes and others learn about what you've done, you will command great respect. You've earned it."

Mermin nodded his agreement.

The King smiled then cautioned, "Please be sure not to tell anyone about any of this just yet. We have more ingredients to collect. The fog still lingers. The curse is not yet broken."

"Yes sir," the boys replied in unison.

"So, what's the next ingredient we need to collect?" asked Alden.

"I don't know," replied the King. "Perhaps we should consult the gold book. Hopefully it will tell us."

"I guess I'm not going home anytime soon then, am I?"

"We need to alert your family. They must be worried sick," the King announced.

"I could dwop them a note. Send it with the Appeawo Beam," Mermin suggested.

The King leaned in. "Andy, you said the sender of that message sphere claimed responsibility for bringing you."

Andy bobbed his head.

"I don't want to hold you against your will, Andy, although we could really use your help." The King glanced at his mage.

There's something big and bad going to happen. Andy swallowed. *They treat me differently here; they're nice and don't yell at me. And now Alden's my friend...* The decision came easily: "I'd like that."

"Yeah!" Alden cheered, giving Andy a fist bump and drawing a chuckle from the wizard.

"Thank you, Andy." A half smile broached the King's lips.

"Where should we keep these?" Alden held up a fistful of red dragon scales. "Would you mind if I keep one?"

"No, go ahead. But I better put the rest in the gold book for safekeeping." Andy started to stand but spotted the purple crest on the King's desk. "Can I ask you one more question, sir."

"Of course, what is it?"

"Where did you get that?" Andy pointed.

The King followed Andy's finger. "Bring it here, please."

Andy did so. The sovereign studied it, slowly running his finger over the pattern. His eyes betrayed sadness. "This used to be my family crest. When I dishonored my family, my father forbade me from using it anymore. After that, I designed the crest we currently use." He sighed. "Why do you ask?"

Andy hesitated, remembering the note had told him not to mention the trunk to anyone. *Surely it would be okay to tell them.* "Sir, the night before I came here, I was up in my attic during a thunderstorm. I'd seen the light come on and then mysteriously turn off. I thought it was strange, so I went to investigate. In the dark, I tripped over an old trunk that I'd never seen before. When I opened it, I saw what I think is a sheath for a dagger. It had this crest on it. I'm sure it was the same."

The King's eyes darted to Andy. His face took on a look of alarm and he opened his mouth to speak. But before he could utter a word, the thunderous roar of an angry woman filled the room: "Andrew Farrin Smithson! What in the world do you think you're doing?"

Instantly everything went black for Andy.

Andy's behind absorbed the shock as he splashed down on the flooded kitchen floor. Mom stood glaring at him, hands on her hips, a posture he knew could mean only one thing. Water flowed everywhere: it poured off the counter, down the cabinet front, and from between the cabinet doors. His pants slurped up the wet. He dropped the red dragon scales.

"What have you been doing, young man? I told you not to make a mess! Just look at this kitchen! Where did you get that blue T-shirt? What are those?" She pointed at the dragon scales. "And what is that thing hanging around your neck? What in the world have you been doing?"

"Mom!"

"I don't want to hear it, Andy!"

"No! This is terrible! How am I supposed to help break the curse if I'm here?" Then, staring at the ceiling, he shouted, "I'm sorry I said anything about the trunk. I need to go back! They need me! Send me back!" Andy protested, flailing his arms.

Mom gasped. "Fred. Fred! Please come here and talk to your son!"

On the scene in an instant, Dad shot Mom a look that held more than alarm at the mess, leaving Andy to wonder: *What are they not telling me?*

"If you enjoyed this book, would you **leave a review** on Amazon at http://amzn.to/**1PmmhkQ**" - L. R. W. Lee

Andy Smithson Trivia

Did you know L. R. W. Lee leverages symbolism extensively?

- The fog of the curse symbolizes blindness and oppression.
- The magic key unlocks doors and brings stone statues to life. Put another way, it symbolizes bringing forth, opening up, and revealing (that is, taking responsibility).
- Methuselah is not only a weapon and helper, but also represents justice as it divides good and evil. Consistent with life, justice requires diligence to uphold.
- Spheres have no beginning or end and represent the eternal. They also represent wholeness or dignity.
- Blue is the color of freedom, strength, and new beginnings. The color of the household of King Hercalon V is royal-blue for this reason.
- Purple is the color of royalty.
- The purple message spheres trumpet and then broadcast words from the King's father in the Afterlife.
- Because of its resistance to heat and acid, gold is a symbol of immutability, eternity, and perfection. The gold envelopes contain messages from the Ancient One who knows the end from the beginning and orchestrates events.

Did you know that in keeping with traditional fantasy narratives, L. R. W. Lee uses the numbers three, seven, and twelve for a reason?

- Three is considered the number of perfection.
- Seven means security, safety, and rest.
- Twelve is the number of completion or a whole and harmonious unit.

Did you know names are also important in this series?

- Andy means "brave" or "courageous."
- Alden means "helper."
- Hannah means "favor" or "grace."
- Imogenia means "blameless."
- Kaysan, the King, means "administrator."
- Hercalon is a derivation of Hercules.
- Mermin is a parody on Merlin.
- Methuselah was a priest whose origins were unknown. He appears suddenly in the historical biblical record and has therefore become equated with having no beginning.
- Stone of Athanasia—The term *athanasia* means "deathless" or "immortal."
- Glaucin the merman—A derivation of the name Glaucus in Greek mythology. He was a mortal who became immortal by eating a magical herb and turned into a prophetic god of the sea.

Have you noticed alchemy used throughout the series?

- Alchemy played a significant role in the development of modern science. Alchemists sought to transform base metals into gold or silver and/or develop an elixir of life that would confer youth and longevity and even immortality.
- In the series, the first instance of alchemy begins with the goldweavers, Max, Oscar, and Henry, spinning straw into gold to manufacture the wealth of the kingdom.
- The four elementals—air, earth, fire, and water—are seen on Methuselah's hilt.

Did you know the titles of the books manifest yet another layer of meaning? The titles reveal Imogenia's evolution.

- Beginning with *Blast of the Dragon's Fury*, Imogenia is furious at what has happened to her and she fuels her emotional hurt.
- Stay tuned to see what *Venom of the Serpent's Cunning*, book two in the Andy Smithson series, reveals.

The next book in the series is *Venom of the Serpent's Cunning (Andy Smithson Book Two).* Read the first chapters beginning on the next page.

Contact the Author:
http://www.lrwlee.com
http://www.twitter.com/lrwlee
http://www.facebook.com/lrwlee

Chapter 1 & 2 of Venom of the Serpent's Cunning,
Book Two in the Andy Smithson series

Longing

Andy woke himself hollering, "No! No!" He breathed hard, as if he had just finished crawling fifty laps around the track in gym class. His room was dark except for the light of the moon filtering between the slats of the wood blinds. He looked over at the digital alarm clock on the nightstand next to his bed: 2:07 a.m.

Andy wiped the sweat from his forehead on his undershirt before getting up and heading to the bathroom.

He turned on the faucet and splashed cold water on his face, trying to forget. Peering over the towel he held in both hands, he saw the reflection of an unremarkable eleven-year-old boy—brown hair, brown eyes, average nose, average chin (nope, no whiskers yet) illuminated by the orange glow of the night light. His pediatrician had called him "small for his age."

He tried to forget the dream, but the images kept flashing in his mind. Andy walked along a deserted dirt road. In the distance, through lighter-than-usual fog, he could just make out the silhouette of a house in the fading sunlight. As he approached, he saw its broken porch railing, smashed front window, and peeling paint. Several of the windows on the upper floor were also broken. Shards of glass lay on the ground below. He walked up onto the crumbling porch, nearly falling through a rotten board on his way to the front door with a NO TRESPASSING sign nailed across it.

The board and door mysteriously dissolved and Andy walked into a dust-covered room with broken furniture strewn about. It smelled of decay. He heard voices coming from upstairs and headed toward a staircase, its risers broken in places. He picked his way upwards, making the boards creak as he shifted his weight on each step. Reaching the landing, he turned right and inched down a hallway with peeling paint, illuminated only by the light filtering through the doorway at the end. The smell of decay grew stronger.

He stopped at the doorway but did not go in. Before him were two creatures in conversation. One was a dove with drops of blood on its pure white feathers. It spoke to a creature that kept changing forms. Beginning as a large bird, the creature flapped its enormous wings, and in a rush of thunder and wind became a weird-looking rhino with a jet black corkscrew horn. The beast pawed the ground and snorted, readying a charge, then just as quickly transformed into a being that looked like water in the form of a person. As the figure stood and wildly waved its arms, it morphed into a growling wolf with a smashed-in nose and huge paws. This in turn became a monstrous serpent that changed into a seven-headed red dragon with ten horns, four wings, and a thick tail. Every time the transforming creature took on the form of the seven-headed dragon, it would stand and roar, "I will rule the world and live forever!" The dove did not react, only continued mumbling something about a stone.

When the two creatures finally noticed Andy standing in the doorway, the changeling, now in the form of the huge bird, flew at Andy, beak open wide and talons poised to rip into his flesh. At this point Andy woke up yelling and sweating.

Andy shook his head. He had been having the same dream on and off for the last three weeks. Each time it had become more detailed and more frightening. Tonight had been the most disturbing yet. He recognized the seven-headed red dragon as Abaddon, whom he had fought and beaten. But the rest of the dream made no sense.

He exited the bathroom and walked slowly back down the hall to his bedroom. Passing his parents' door, he heard his dad thunder out a loud noise that sounded much like the hippo on the nature show Andy had watched that evening. He slid back between his covers and stared at the ceiling, afraid to fall asleep. Sleep must have finally overcome him, however, because he awoke with the clock now reading 8:38 a.m. He dressed and went downstairs for breakfast. His mom greeted him with a hug and kiss.

"How'd you sleep?"

"Okay." He wasn't about to tell her about his dream.

"I'm working from home today."

"Why?"

"I just thought it would be nice to spend the day with you and Maddy before your summer vacation is over. I thought we could go to the library and get ice cream later. We don't get these opportunities often."

Andy's mom and dad were CEOs of separate companies they each had founded and grown. The companies took a lot of their time and put them on edge. His dad believed neither he nor his older sister, Madison, appreciated all the privileges owning and growing the companies afforded them, and he reminded them of this fact regularly.

After Andy finished his cereal and toast, Mom suggested, "Why don't you go outside and play for a while. I'll get my work done and then the three of us can head out."

Not for the first time since his return home from Oomaldee, Andy stood before the ugly, three-foot-tall concrete garden gnome. Its full, white-painted beard and long, crooked nose were complemented by a bright red pointy hat, patched black pants, and a blue jacket that looked like it could fit two gnomes. It somehow reminded Andy of Mermin, the king of Oomaldee's kindly old wizard. His mom insisted it looked "So cute!" every time Dad hinted at moving it to a less conspicuous spot in the backyard.

Quickly, Andy scanned the patio, looked between nearby shade trees, and glanced around the long-neglected wooden playhouse, making sure no one watched. He pulled a gold key from the pouch hanging around his neck and begged, "Please wake up. Please?"

He stared intently into the gnome's bulging eyes, hoping to see the slightest movement. Not a blink. Not a dart. Not a twitch. Nothing. Not that way down deep he had expected it to move, or that he had wanted to awaken a garden gnome and have it think he was its friend. That would be weird! All the same...

Andy let out a long, slow sigh and hung his head.

No stone statues that come to life when the gold key is near, no fire-breathing dragons, no flying pegasi, no vulture-men or Abaddon to battle. *Well, that part I don't miss,* he thought. *But what I'd give to see the King, Mermin, Alden, Marta, and Hans again. And to taste Marta's awesome chocolate chip cookies!* He could almost smell the fresh-baked aroma that wafted down the stone-lined hallway outside the castle kitchens every time Marta made them.

Andy laughed. *I must be sick. I even miss the smell of cow farts.* He smiled, then reached down and rubbed his stomach. It felt like a tiny King Abaddon fought within him, blasting fire and poison at his insides. In fact, his stomach hadn't been feeling well for quite some time.

I wonder if I'll ever get to go back.

He remembered the night he had been abruptly sent home after telling the king about the old trunk he found in the attic. The note inside the trunk expressly told him not to mention it to anyone.

I'll never make that mistake again! If only whoever sent me home would forgive me and let me go back. If only…

Madison, older than Andy by two years, stuck her head out the back door and yelled loudly enough for the neighbors to hear, "Mom, Andy's trying to make that gnome come to life again! I just saw him."

Andy quickly stuffed the gold key back in its hiding place and turned to glare at her. "You have no idea what I was doing!"

"You had that same look as when I saw you trying to make the angel on the top of the Christmas tree and the knight above the fireplace come to life. You're pathetic, Andy."

She pulled her head back inside.

Through the screen door he overheard his mom say, "Maddy, dear, you know Dr. Frandangle said we need to encourage and support Andy. He's going through a difficult time."

"Dr. Frandangle's a quack!" Madison replied, slamming the door behind her.

Andy agreed. Dr. Frandangle, his "counselor," was a quack. A quack who had been introduced into his life a couple months after he'd returned from Oomaldee. Apparently, waving his arms at the ceiling and yelling that he needed to go back to break the curse had upset his parents more than a little. And insisting that he told the truth when they questioned him about his change of clothes and the pouch that hung from his neck only made the situation worse. That, combined with him no longer wanting to play his video games (who wants to fight a pretend dragon when you've battled one in real life?) and no longer arguing with his mom when she asked him to mow the lawn, take out the trash, or go to bed, put his parents on edge. Go figure.

He remembered his dad calling a family conference the night before his first appointment and doing his uncomfortable best to explain that he and Mom understood Andy's needs were greater than what they were equipped to handle. Dr. Frandangle was going to help them help Andy.

Gotta love Dad. Trying to "fix" me, Andy remembered thinking. And when his dad made it clear that no one outside their family was to know Andy was seeing a shrink, he remembered laughing to himself. *Can never be less than perfect in this family!*

Between Dr. Frandangle asking about any dreams he might be having or invisible friends, Andy began to wonder about this doctor's qualifications. He hated having to talk about his feelings with a stranger. In the end, the doctor had come back with a diagnosis of severe low self-esteem, suggesting that treating Andy "more gently" would help him build some self-confidence. The diagnosis had worked because his parents started paying more attention to him.

For the first time in he couldn't remember how many years, Dad had taken him and Madison trick-or-treating. Both—yes, both—his parents had actually come to hear him sing in the choir as part of the school Christmas pageant and had attended his spring play, *The Princess and the Pea*, even though he had the part of a servant and only spoke seven lines. But the best part by far was that all this attention made his sister, Miss Perfect, jealous. She resented the fact that Andy, in all his glorious imperfection, somehow got more of their parents' attention. It drove her crazy. He loved it!

Unfortunately, while his parents paid more attention to him, he could tell Dad still did not accept him for who he was and didn't approve of his grades, even though he'd (unsuccessfully) tried to bring them up.

Andy came inside. When she saw him, Mom said, "I'm not quite finished with what I need to do. Why don't you read a book or find something else to do for a little bit. I should be done shortly."

He headed up to the attic. As quietly as he could, he opened the door at the end of the hall and climbed the stairs, hoping Madison wouldn't hear and announce to the world that Andy was once more trespassing in forbidden territory.

Reaching the top step, he saw the old, weathered trunk. He had first found the oak pirate chest after tripping backwards and falling over it. From what Mermin told him, Andy knew it could only have come from Oomaldee. But he still hadn't figured out how it ended up in his attic. What he did know, though, was being near the trunk made him feel connected with Oomaldee even if he couldn't be there. He thought again about what Mermin said—that he often observed Andy's world for the King to get ideas to break the five-hundred-year curse that caused thick fog to blanket the land and prevented the King and himself from dying.

Mermin might be looking down on my house this minute. Andy half-smiled.

He lifted the heavy top of the trunk as he had so many times since his return and propped it at an angle that would prevent it from smashing his fingers. The unsigned note that he had disregarded, precipitating his sudden return, sat in the uppermost tray next to the black leather shealth with the King of Oomaldee's purple family crest. He remembered the King telling him the purple crest was no longer used; his father had forbidden it after he had dishonored his family. Whatever he had done to shame his family so much, the King had not confided in him, but Andy could relate.

He lifted the tray out and set it on the floor next to the trunk. Reaching in, he counted the scrolls again. One, two, three, four…fifteen. All the scrolls were still here, just as he'd found them when he looked in the trunk the first time after returning. Some had characters on the back, others didn't. He pulled one out that did and unrolled the parchment, again studying the detailed drawing of a triangle with a key, a sword, and a ball at its three corners. The key looked like the one he had been given from the invisible gold book in Mermin's library. From the detail of the sword's hilt, Andy could tell it was Methuselah. He had no idea what the ball was, however.

Why would drawings of the key and Methuselah be on an old scroll in this trunk? The question had puzzled him since he first discovered it. *And what is the ball? I've never seen a ball. What does this mean?* Writing appeared below the triangle, but he did not recognize the language. Early on, he had searched online to see if he could figure out the letters, but his searches turned up nothing. He had even written down some of the words and shown them to his school librarian, as well as to the librarian at the public library where his parents took them frequently. Neither recognized the characters.

He rolled the scroll up again and pulled out another. This one had no characters on the back, and like the other, it had lots of writing that he could not understand. Nevertheless, Andy studied the characters, memorizing their shapes. *Never know when I might find someone who knows what these letters mean.*

Rolling this parchment up, he replaced it and pulled a third scroll out of the trunk. This one had characters on the back like the first. It was his favorite, not because it was the largest, which it was, but because it was the fanciest of all the scrolls. It was the drawing of a family tree. There was a sketch of a man or woman next to each branch with what was probably their name written underneath. The tree was tall and the drawing detailed. It clearly went back a long time. It was also clear that the tree was incomplete since it stopped suddenly, as if the person who had been recording all the births and deaths had died. *But why? Whose family was this?*

He remembered the message sphere telling him his ancestors had come from Oomaldee and relived the anxiety he felt when that same message sphere declared he would become a great leader in the land if he did what the sender of the message told him—it predicted that even the King would follow him. After studying the scroll for several minutes, Andy rolled it up again and put it back in the truck with the others.

He lifted out the tray containing the scrolls and placed it on the floor next to the upper tray. Only one object remained in the trunk. He reached in and gingerly grasped the handle of a dagger between his thumb and forefinger as if it would bite him. It had a beautifully carved handle like Methuselah's, but its ten-inch blade was speckled with patches of rust. He had examined it many times, but dark flecks of an unidentified substance on the handle and blade made him feel creepy every time he saw it. After studying it yet again for several minutes, he returned it to the trunk, put the other two trays back in, and slowly closed the lid.

A trunk full of mysteries. If I ever get to go back to Oomaldee... He walked back downstairs to the kitchen to see if Mom was ready yet.

The rest of the day was uneventful. The three of them visited the library, and before returning home he and Madison had a heated argument about which flavor of ice cream was the best. After eating dinner and watching a couple TV shows, Mom announced that it was time for bed. Without argument, Andy headed upstairs.

Entering his room, he approached his desk that stood just inside the doorway, picked up a red marker, looked at the calendar hanging on the wall above it, and crossed off today's date. *Nine months, 23 days since I returned.* He sighed. *At least there's only three more weeks until summer vacation is finally over.* It wasn't that he loved school, for it seemed he was always getting in trouble with one teacher or another for being disrespectful. No, he longed for the start of school so he would be distracted for a large part of the day.

I sound like Madison. I must be sick, Andy thought as he got ready for bed.

CHAPTER TWO

Pony Express

The following afternoon, Andy lay on his bed reading *Stance, Balance and Poise: The Art of Sword Fighting*, one of the books he had gotten at the library. Mom had raised her eyebrows when she saw the book he wanted to check out. In the end, he had convinced her he was curious about how people fought way back when.

"It goes against my better judgment," she'd added. She knew Andy too well.

Looking at a picture of two knights facing off with swords drawn, Andy stood up and pulled Methuselah's hilt from the pouch hanging around his neck. Unlike in Oomaldee, the blade did not extend. Nonetheless, Andy tried to mimic the stance of one of the knights, putting his right foot out in front of his left. He read aloud, "Keep your feet shoulder-width apart as much as possible. Never cross your feet or bring them together as you move." He checked his stance. "Align your wrist with the hilt to grip the sword. When you strike a target, you want the strength of your wrist behind it instead of your thumb. Your thumb should be pointing left or right. If your thumb is pointing up, you are not holding the sword correctly."

Andy checked his grip. "Yep, got it."

Feeling nature's call, he put Methuselah back in the pouch around his neck and laid the book face down on his bed. He wandered down the hall. He was alone in the house; Dad was at work and Mom had taken Madison out shopping for school clothes. "You're growing too fast," she had complained while smiling at Madison over breakfast.

When he reached the bathroom, he caught a glimpse of the front yard through the wood blind. *What? Where did that come from?* He let out a loud gasp as he recognized a life-size statue of Sir Gawain charging full speed ahead on his horse, Alexander. It looked exactly like the statue he'd seen in the cavalry training center in Oomaldee. Unmoving, it listed at a precarious angle, its stone base sunken a foot or more into Dad's perfectly manicured lawn.

Andy bolted downstairs and out the front door to get a closer look. As soon as he left the porch, both Sir Gawain and Alexander started struggling to free themselves from the ground. By the time Andy reached them, Alexander had cleared the hole and pranced across the grass by the street, making divots in the lawn.

Dad's grass!

Out of the corner of his eye, Andy saw one of their neighbors stick her head out her window, staring at the spectacle.

"Glad to see you're doing fine!" boomed Sir Gawain as Andy reached him. "Whoa, Alexander!"

While Andy wanted desperately to come right out and ask what in the world they were doing here, he thought better of it and instead asked, "Can I help you?"

"*Au contraire*, sir. I have come to help you!"

Andy glanced over. Nosy neighbor talked on her cell phone, wildly gesturing at the spectacle. *Announcing the festivities to the entire street, I bet. Dad's going to flip!*

"What do you mean you've come to help me?"

"An envelope arrived for you at the castle yesterday." Sir Gawain pulled a gold envelope from a pouch hanging around his neck. "Do I need to put it in the mailbox? Mermin wasn't sure."

"No," replied Andy. "I'll take it, thanks."

As Sir Gawain reached down to hand Andy the envelope, a passing car startled Alexander. The stone horse reared up, scaring the unfortunate driver. The driver yelled and waved his hand, laying on the horn. Alexander took off galloping toward the backyard.

"Whoa, Alexander! Slow up!" called Sir Gawain to no effect. "Whoa!"

Andy ran after them. Alexander whinnied, his eyes huge and wild. He bolted toward a tree, nearly unseating Sir Gawain as he lunged under one of the low-hanging branches. The knight ducked just in time. Andy tried running around the other side of the house to cut him off and keep him in the backyard, but when he tried to block the stone horse's path, Alexander nearly trampled him. Out of breath, Andy stopped chasing and retreated to the safety of the deck. He watched the chaos as Alexander ran laps around the house.

Then he had an idea. As Alexander rounded the corner and charged into the backyard again, Andy pulled the gold key from his pouch and held it up. "Please make him stop."

As quickly as Alexander had taken off, he came to an abrupt halt. He stopped so suddenly, Sir Gawain nearly catapulted over his head. Alexander shook his mane and snorted, eyeing the key and breathing heavily. The knight let out a snort of his own and exclaimed, "Wow! Alexander's never done that before!"

"He's never been honked at by a car before!"

Andy scanned the lawn. *Dad's going to kill me!* There were deep divots scarring the whole backyard. It looked like someone had turned up ground to plant a garden. *The front can't look any better. I'm so dead!*

Sir Gawain guided Alexander to where Andy stood on the steps of the back deck as Andy dropped the gold key back in the pouch.

"Sorry about the mess," Sir Gawain apologized. "I hope I don't get you into too much trouble."

"Yeah, me too."

"We best get back," Sir Gawain said, finally handing the gold envelope to Andy.

"Before you go," Andy stopped him, "can you tell me how you got here?"

Alexander tossed his head about as Sir Gawain explained. "Well, like I said, this gold envelope arrived at the castle yesterday. It being addressed to you, the King asked Mermin to find a way to deliver it to you since you'd told him it was illegal to open other people's mail. Mermin knew the easiest way was to use the Appearo Beam, but he feared the letter was too small and might not travel well. Since I'm a statue, and he remembered what happened with your gold key, he decided to see if I could deliver it. And, well, here I am."

Andy's heart jumped. "Thank you, Sir Gawain! I've missed everyone so much." He paused and then asked, "How did Mermin know you'd come to life once you got here?"

"He didn't. He hoped the key would wake me up like it did in Oomaldee. He put this pouch with the letter in it around my neck just before he beamed me here. It's funny, Andy. Ever since the key woke me up, I can hear conversations and other sounds, I just can't move if the key's not nearby. Fascinating what people will say around me. I feel like a knight on the wall, listening in on people's conversations."

"I don't get it. I've tried waking up that gnome statue for months. Nothing's ever happened," Andy said, pointing at the ugly statue standing nearby.

"A gnome?" replied Sir Gawain, laughing.

"Yeah."

"Andy, that's no gnome. Gnomes would be insulted if they knew what you just said. My guess is, the key only works on objects from Oomaldee, where its magic comes from."

Andy thought about that until Sir Gawain interrupted, "Great seeing you again! I think you'll need to take the key inside so I can change back into a statue before I go back. Mermin said only non-living objects can transport with the Appearo Beam."

"Oh, right," he replied. "Thank you, Sir Gawain. Please tell everybody I miss them."

"I'll be sure to let everyone know."

Andy smiled. It had been so good seeing someone from the land he loved.

"I need to head to the front yard so Mermin can see me and take me back with the Appearo Beam. Sorry again for messing up your grass," he said, waving. "Give me a couple minutes to get back into position before you go inside, okay?"

Andy stayed on the deck for several minutes before heading in. When he did, he raced to look out the front window. Sir Gawain and Alexander had gotten back into the foot-deep hole and were again listing greatly on their stand. Alexander had resumed his pose, running full speed ahead, with Sir Gawain bracing for battle. They disappeared a minute later.

As soon as they departed, Andy saw movement in several windows down the street as spectators left their lookout posts.

Great, the whole neighborhood'll be talking. Andy groaned. *Dad's going to have a fit about his yard.*

He looked down at the gold envelope in his hand. The address read:

Andy Smithson, he whose longing shall be satisfied

Despite his sense of impending doom at what Dad would say, a smile broke out across his face. He ripped it open. A single piece of parchment read:

You have learned your lesson well,
On the past you should not dwell.
For with sorrow, you're replete,
Your misstep, ne'er to repeat.

Turn now your attention,
And give not in to apprehension.
For the urgent task at hand,
All your might it will demand.

Enemy without, a threat,
Bold incursion to regret.
Enemy within, a debt,
All things right you must set.

Andy could not contain himself. He jumped up and down, celebrating, "I'm going back! I'm going back!"

He danced around the downstairs, running laps from the living room through the family room, into the kitchen, and around the breakfast nook. He finally collapsed, happily falling into the couch as he passed through the family room for the umpteenth time. The smile would not leave his face—at least not until he remembered the mess and glanced into the backyard a few minutes later. *Yikes! I better see if I can fix any of that before Dad gets home!*

He spent the next hour doing his best to restore his dad's prize lawn. He ignored the nosy neighbors when they reappeared while he worked on the front yard. When he finished, he stood admiring his handiwork. *Well, it looks a lot better than it did. But Dad's still gonna notice.* Andy had managed to flatten areas where the sod had been disturbed, but the bare areas that Alexander's hooves had trounced repeatedly—there was no hope of fixing those, at least not to a standard his dad would approve. He went back inside and showered, and since no one had come home yet, he picked up his sword fighting book with greater purpose.

Not long after, Andy heard the first explosion. Mom and Madison were back and had seen the yard.

"Andrew Smithson," came the call from downstairs.

Well, she didn't use my middle name. That's got to be a good sign…I hope.

Andy found Mom looking out the front window, shaking her head.

"What happened, Andy?" She tried hard not to lose her temper. She took measured breaths and moved her hands up and down to calm herself.

"Well, a horse—" Andy began.

Madison stuck her face around the corner and gave him a smile that said, *Let's see you get out of this one.*

"Thank you, Madison. You may go," Mom said, having seen her with the eyes in the back of her head.

Madison scowled and headed upstairs.

"Mom, I'm telling the truth. This horse got loose in our yard. It ran around the house several times. I tried to stop it, but it almost ran me over."

"And where is this horse now?"

"How should I know?" As he said it, his conscience protested. He hesitated, opened his mouth to say more, then thought better and closed it again.

She remained quiet for several minutes, thinking hard.

Andy broke the silence, "After the horse left, I went out and pushed down the worst parts, but there are some spots that are bare. I couldn't fix those." Andy hoped his parents would not hear the neighbors' version of events anytime soon.

Mom let out a long, slow breath. After a few more minutes of silence, she finally looked at him and said, "Andy, I don't know what happened. From the looks of the lawn, it's clear a horse was somehow involved. Thank you for trying to fix what you could. Because there are no stables anywhere near here— I've no idea—" She shook her head, disbelieving, then added, "Your father's going to be furious."

Andy didn't respond.

"Please go find something to do until dinner."

Madison slammed the door of her bedroom as he reached the top of the stairs grinning.

A week later, the tornado of Dad's fury had blown itself out. Madison stood against the wall of the pantry in her PJs, one side of a cereal box resting on the top of her head, the bottom of the box snug to the wall. Mom drew a line and wrote, "Maddy, age 13."

"You're next, Andy," Mom said.

Andy stood as straight as he could and waited for her to mark his height on the wall. When she finished, she wrote, "Andy, age 11 + 2 mo."

"You're still the same height as you were two months ago," his sister teased. "The same height as me when I was nine!"

"That's enough, Maddy," Mom warned.

Yes, Andy had to endure Madison's birthday today. When Little Miss Perfect had asked to go to the museum with several of her friends to celebrate, his only thought had been, *You've got to be kidding.*

"That's a great idea, Maddy!" Dad had exclaimed. "An educational birthday celebration!"

So today he and a squawking, screeching gaggle of girls would be stuffed into a SUV to go to the natural history museum, one of the most boring places on the face of the planet. This particular hoard of girls happened to also find boys of his size and maturity great sport. Only the thought of returning to Oomaldee kept his spirits up. He had read the letter more times than he could count, and while its ominous tone concerned him, the promise of seeing everyone again more than made up for it.

"Better go get showered and dressed, Maddy. We need to leave in an hour," Mom said after breakfast.

Madison went upstairs. Andy followed.

Several minutes later, Madison let out a blood-curdling scream. Sitting on his bed, Andy smiled and laughed.

"Mom! There's…there's…there's a snake in my room!" his sister screeched.

Andy heard Mom and Dad's hurried footsteps on the stairs.

"Andy! Come here!" bellowed Dad a minute later.

"I came back from the bathroom. I didn't have my glasses on and, and, and—that was on my floor!" Madison stammered, pointing.

Andy entered the violent peach room, trying desperately to hide a smile that hadn't gone away for the last several days. Yes, he felt like his old self again.

Dad held up a twenty-inch inflatable toy snake and shook it as he entered. "Might you have any ideas what happened, Andy?"

He couldn't hold it in. Sneaky snickers escaped, giving him up to face punishment. He doubled over in laughter.

Mom and Dad attempted to stay straight-faced and serious, but Mom launched into a fit of giggles and then, shockingly, Dad couldn't keep it together either and snorted. His laughter soon turned to roaring and he, too, doubled over.

Madison watched, fuming.

"Ma-Mad-Maddy, we're not laughing at you," Mom managed to get out. "It's just that it's…it's been…" She doubled over again in a fit of laughter.

Dad finally composed himself, clearing his throat. "What your mother's trying to say is that it's been a long time since Andy's played a trick on anyone, let alone laugh like he is. It's just good to see." He smiled at Andy.

Andy stood there, not knowing what to say. Not only did he not get in trouble, but Dad laughed.

"Oh honey, come on. Lighten up. You have to admit, the joke was pretty funny," Mom said as Madison continued pouting.

"It wasn't funny," Madison insisted through gritted teeth.

An hour later, Andy found himself wedged between the door handle and bony Ashley in the backseat of his mom's new SUV. Sitting by the other door, Madison behaved like her usual annoying self. She kept whispering to Sarah, Ashley, Alexis, and Taylor, who would all snicker and glance over at him. Mom and Dad, comfortably seated in front, chose to ignore this.

The ride was long and boring. Andy tried to ignore the squawking and screeching inside the car as he endured the monotony of square houses and limestone buildings passing by on the outside. At long last, Dad pulled up in front of the stately natural history building. The girls, including Mom, got out.

"The men will go park the car," Dad announced, winking at Andy in the rearview mirror.

After finally finding a parking space, he and Dad got out and started the trek back to the building.

"Your mom says you've been in a better mood over the last week. Did you want to tell me anything about the lawn?"

Andy frowned and replied, "No." He looked down at the pavement as they walked.

"I expect you to behave yourself while we're here, son."

Andy chose not to respond.

Upon reaching the girls, Mom handed him a map of the exhibits.

"Ooh, I want to see the dinosaur fossils!" Madison shouted, examining her own copy.

"The wooly mammoth looks awesome!" added know-it-all Sarah. "Did you know that scientists say the last wooly mammoth went extinct four thousand years ago?"

"Why, no I didn't, Sarah. Thanks for sharing that," replied Mom, smiling.

Satisfied that her contribution had been appreciated, Sarah added, "Yeah, and I read that scientists think they may be able to clone one and bring it back."

"Well, that would be fascinating, wouldn't it?" replied Mom.

Andy rolled his eyes. *She's more annoying than Madison.*

"Can we see the volcano exhibit?" asked Alexis.

"I don't see why not," replied Mom.

"And I'd like to see the Animals of the Plains," chimed in Taylor.

Seeing a pyramid drawn on the map, Andy asked Dad, "It says here there's an exhibit, Snakes of Ancient Egypt. Can we see that?"

Dad smiled and said, "If we have time, son."

They spent the better part of three hours looking at stiff wooly mammoths, stuffed furry gophers, rigid rabbits, petrified penguins, and starched Tasmanian tigers (extinct in the twentieth century, the sign said). The girls oohed and aahed in an annoyingly high-pitched squeal at a baby dodo bird they all agreed was "so cute." Andy grew bored. *Enough furry, stuffed animals,* he thought. While Mom and Dad read a sign next to the stiff, glaring cave lion, and the gaggle of girls pointed at the various occupants of a Stone Age scene, Andy slipped away to look for the Egyptian exhibit. Using his map, he easily found it up on the third floor.

As Andy walked below the massive archway into the enormous room housing Snakes of Ancient Egypt, he noticed a larger-than-life model of a golden snake slithering up the wall, crawling upside down along the curve of the arch, down the other side, circling the perimeter of the entire room. A fancy sign read, "Apophis was an evil god in ancient Egyptian religion. So large was this golden snake that his body stretched for miles. Every day he attempted to swallow the sun, invoking the wrath of Ra, the sun god."

"Cool," Andy said in awe under his breath.

Nearby, Andy saw another sign labeled "Snake Facts." Curious, he read, "Snakes are cold-blooded and do not have the ability to keep their body temperature at a constant level. Unable to hear, snakes sense predators and prey by picking up vibrations through their jawbone. Snakes use a forked tongue to smell, which is why they keep it moving constantly. Snakes do not have eyelids. All snakes are carnivores, and most varieties have over 230 teeth, which are pointed backwards to grip prey."

"Good to know," he acknowledged aloud.

He walked past elaborately detailed stone sculptures of serpents the Egyptians worshiped, eventually coming to several spiral snake pedestal tables. While there were instructions about how to play Mehen, the Forbidden Game of the Snake, Andy didn't stop. An ancient golden statue of King Tut had caught his attention. He walked toward the far wall to check it out, but before getting there he saw a statue of a winged snake. He stopped briefly to read the sign: "Winged drakontes were believed to live under frankincense trees. They could have been a big problem for ancient Egyptians if not for the fact that the female killed the male during mating and the young, born live rather than via eggs, ate their way out of the womb, thus killing the mother."

"Uh, yuck, that's disgusting."

Arriving at the statue of King Tut, Andy felt dwarfed by its size. He leaned forward to examine the headdress more closely and noticed a giant cobra poised to strike carved in gold above the king's forehead. While he had seen pictures of King Tut in this same headdress before, he had never paid attention to the cobra on it. A sign nearby read, "The uraeus was seen as a royal symbol. Historians believe the goddess Isis created the first uraeus and considered it the instrument by which she gained the throne of Egypt for Osiris."

"Awesome!" whispered Andy.

A larger model of the uraeus stood nearby, inviting closer study. Positioning himself squarely in front of the poised cobra, Andy stared into its round, quarter-size eyes. Remembering that snakes do not have eyelids and therefore cannot blink, he jumped when the serpent in front of him suddenly did just that.

Buy Venom of the Serpent's Cunning (Andy Smithson Book Two)

Dedication

*To my wise and skilled mentors who have helped
me grow as an author.*

Acknowledgments

Thanks to my husband for his support and encouragement, without which my writing journey would lack much of the meaning it holds.

Thanks, too, to D. Robert Pease, my cover designer. His gift of taking a concept and bringing it to life continually amazes me.

Thanks also to my editor, Amy Nemecek. I can see how my craft has improved since I began working with her and for that I am eternally grateful.

I want to also recognize two author groups I'm privileged to be a part of—Dragon Writer's Collective and Emblazoners. I've learned and grown from working with the amazing authors in both. Thank you!

Thanks also to Kimia Wood, a self-described twenty-something, who shared her detailed, specific and in-depth thinking about this book. Because of her willingness to engage in a significant dialogue, she helped create the end result you have enjoyed. Many, many thanks!

35840463R00113

Made in the USA
Middletown, DE
17 October 2016